Wedding Bell
Blues

Also by Ruth Moose

Doing It at the Dixie Dew

Wedding Bell
Blues

*A Dixie Dew
Mystery*

Ruth Moose

Minotaur Books

A Thomas Dunne Book
New York

This is a work of fiction. All of the characters, organizations, and events portrayed in this novel are either products of the author's imagination or are used fictitiously.

A THOMAS DUNNE BOOK FOR MINOTAUR BOOKS.
An imprint of St. Martin's Publishing Group.

WEDDING BELL BLUES. Copyright © 2016 by Ruth Moose. All rights reserved.
Printed in the United States of America. For information, address
St. Martin's Press, 175 Fifth Avenue, New York, N.Y. 10010.

www.thomasdunnebooks.com
www.minotaurbooks.com

Library of Congress Cataloging-in-Publication Data

Names: Moose, Ruth, author.
Title: Wedding bell blues : a Dixie Dew mystery / Ruth Moose.
Description: First Edition | New York : Minotaur Books, 2016. | "A Thomas
    Dunne Book."
Identifiers: LCCN 2016003506| ISBN 9781250067418 (hardback) |
    ISBN 9781466875722 (e-book)
Subjects: LCSH: Women—Southern States—Fiction. | Bed and breakfast
    accommodations—Fiction. | Murder—Investigation—Fiction. | GSAFD:
    Mystery fiction.
Classification: LCC PS3563.O69 W43 2016 | DDC 813/.54—dc23
LC record available at http://lccn.loc.gov/2016003506

Our books may be purchased in bulk for promotional, educational, or business use.
Please contact your local bookseller or the Macmillan Corporate and
Premium Sales Department at 1-800-221-7945, extension 5442, or by e-mail at
MacmillanSpecialMarkets@macmillan.com.

First Edition: August 2016

10 9 8 7 6 5 4 3 2 1

For the late, great Talmadge Moose, with much love.
You were absolutely right!

Acknowledgments

A great big thank-you to all who read and loved *Doing It at the Dixie Dew*. Double thanks to those who e-mailed, attended book clubs and discussion groups, came to readings, contacted me via my website, or stopped me in the PTA Thrift store to ask, "What's happening in Littleboro now? How's Crazy Reba? Will Beth and Scott get married?"

I could only tell them to stay tuned. I especially thank the Read and Go Group of 50 who read *Dixie Dew* and came to spend the day in Pittsboro, aka Littleboro. I have to thank Jane Dunlap, who actually named the town Littleboro when I was totally at my wit's end. And Toni Goodyear, who gave me the Southern joke. Vicky Thomas at Country Hair, for all the hairdresser humor. Thank you to Anna Lees and Betty

Lou Cobb, who let Nadine, their very precocious turtle, come to lunch. (She's a very light eater! But not much on conversation.) Peter Mock, Matt, Keebee, and all the gang at McIntyre's Books in Fearrington Village, North Carolina. (Hey, Louise Penny, remember your gala here? Hugs and high fives back!) Other writer friends who listened to me kicking and screaming over rewrites: Molly Weston, who gave me the best life advice in two words: "Grow up." I hope I have. More thanks for Cathy Kidd, and she knows why.

The biggest thanks of all to Jennifer Letwack, who is a dream of an editor, sharp and careful, all knowing, all seeing, but helpful and kind to the tip of her toes.

Wedding Bell
Blues

Chapter One

When I heard Crazy Reba's voice on the phone I knew immediately something was wrong. Really wrong. My first thought was where in the world did Reba ever get a cell phone? The homeless and street sleepers like Reba weren't flush with extra cash (if any) each month. Maybe somebody had given her one of those phones where you buy the minutes up front. A phone for her own protection. Some kind person, the thought of which made me feel bad since I had not been the one to think of it. Any other place I might have thought of a cell phone for safety. Protection for all kinds of things. But Littleboro? Not *my* Littleboro. Except these days it wasn't safe to be alone and on the loose . . . even in Littleboro.

"Miss Beth," Reba said. "You gotta come." Then she started crying.

"What?" I said. "What's wrong? Where are you?"

Reba must have seen a loose cell phone somewhere and simply taken it. Somebody's dresser. She was in and out of a lot of houses in Littleboro, mostly at will. Or maybe it was from one of the stores downtown. The library? Somebody somewhere simply laid their cell phone down for a minute, turned their back and Reba must have said to herself, "Hotdadaluck, found my cell phone."

"Miss Beth," Reba said again. "You gotta come." Then she cried louder.

"Where are you?" I handed the Dixie Dew latest reservations printout to Ida Plum, who, hearing my end of the conversation, raised one eyebrow and shook her head no. She was saying don't. Don't you go getting involved in this. Remember how you almost got yourself killed poking your nose where it doesn't belong. Ida Plum's motto was "Curiosity killed the cat and it could kill you."

"He's dead," Reba said. "You gotta come."

"Who?" I hoped Reba wouldn't drop the phone and walk off, get distracted by something or someone, forget she even had a cell phone

"God." Reba snuffled. "God is dead."

"Whoa," I said. "Repeat that." I didn't think I heard what I'd heard.

Ida Plum leaned closer to my shoulder, listened, then shook her head side to side and walked away. As if all this was too crazy for her and what was the world coming to?

"Calm down," I said. This had to be the same God that Reba was marrying. The one the whole town had been co-erced into helping plan a wedding for that nobody in their right mind believed would ever happen. Who would marry Reba? And did marrying God mean she was going into a convent? Where *was* the nearest convent? And Lord knows they sure wouldn't take Reba. Five minutes into an interview and they'd know this flower child gone to seed was not a can-didate for nunhood. For a month Reba had been talking about being a June bride. Pure imagination, but with Reba you didn't argue. You didn't want to upset her. It was best to just go along. The whole town went along with her like a petted child. It was easier to indulge Reba—she had so few needs—than argue or go around her.

"You gotta come *now*," Reba said.

"Where? Where are you?" I grabbed my purse, fished out my car keys. "Hang on," I said. "Tell me real slow. Where are you?"

"The green one. Down the road from the green one."

Did she mean Motel 3? Out by the Interstate? Or the four-lane road us locals refer to as "the Interstate"? Green? The motel that was now Al and Andy's? Al was Allison, Andy was Andrea. It used to be Mr. and Mrs. Pinkston's, a real mom-and-pop operation. Now it was half under renovation. A room or two open for business, the rest of the units still in skeleton shape with stark two-by-fours standing, old bits of drywall hanging from walls being pushed down, no doors. Piles and small mountains of rubble to be leveled and prob-ably fill dirt brought in, added on top. What a mess. Last time

I noticed, a bulldozer was running back and forth on the scene. All the units but two were open to the air. Had Reba been in one of the finished units?

"I'm coming," I told her. "Try to calm down."

"You gonna call anybody?" Ida Plum asked. She stood between me and the back door.

"If you mean who I think you mean, of course not. Would you? Let me check this out first."

Ida Plum was my right hand at the Dixie Dew Bed-and-Breakfast. My wise woman, level thinker, practical friend who tried her dead level best to keep me on track. Keep me safe.

"I don't want Ossie DelGardo and his buddies laughing their heads off down at the barber shop at my latest misstep," I continued. "I'm not opening that door." I'd be the joke of the week, maybe joke of the month or year here in Littleboro if this turned out to be some nightmare Reba had while she was sleeping in the woods and I'd had the nerve to disturb Littleboro's finest, our trained professional police chief, over nothing, some wild-goose chase taking his "valuable" time. I would not subject myself to his amusement.

After all, this could be nothing. With Crazy Reba you never knew what was real and what she imagined.

Reba could have found a stray dog and named it God. Who knew? Reba was the kind to remember that old childhood thing about "god" being "dog" spelled backwards and think dogs were meant to be named "god." Who knew how someone like Reba thought? Of course, she had been walking around for a couple months sporting a diamond big enough to choke a horse saying God gave it to her. Except we all knew a rock that big was pure glass Reba must have picked up at some yard sale or the Dollar Store. Or got it out of one of those gum machines.

I walked past Ida Plum to the driveway, cranked Lady Bug, my yellow Volkswagen beetle, pulled onto Main Street and drove through a downtown Littleboro that was empty as a movie set. Only one car at the car wash on a Saturday morning.

I drove past Juanita's Kut and Kurl, which she had recently changed the name to Kurl Up and Dye. I was sure Ossie Del-Gardo, her most recent "intended," had something to do with the name change. It sounded like an Ossie idea to me.

I drove past the Betts Brothers' Fine Flowers for Fine Folks. They did all the funerals in Littleboro, North Carolina. We didn't have all that many dinner parties to decorate, so the enterprising Ronnie and Robert Betts had put a little gift shop area in what used to be the dining room of the big white house they inherited from their great-aunt Flonnie. They went to floral conventions and stocked up on greeting cards, knickknacks and just plain stuff, all of which you could do without, but sometimes ended up with to mark an occasion. Their yellow cat, Bella, sat on the front porch, washing herself.

A hand-lettered YARD SALE sign was propped on the front lawn of a blue-and-white corner house that time and weather had washed down to gray. A few cars were strung along Main Street, but it was early still.

Fridays and Saturdays were yard sale days. Tag sales were held in the better neighborhoods where people hired Tom Jenkins and company to clean out, arrange and tag everything from a spinet piano to wheelbarrows and hedge trimmers. Jenkins did estate sales. Yard sales were a couple notches below and what you found came from an attic, storeroom or some closet. I liked both kinds.

I didn't have to drive far on the Interstate before I saw a huge white moving-van-type truck in the pull-off picnic area. A woman was bent over a man sprawled across the picnic table.

I parked, opened my car door and heard Reba crying as if her heart would break. She cradled the man's head to her cheek and patted his face. "God won't wake up," she said. "Wake up. Wake up, honey."

If this was the God she was marrying, then he was real all right. For anybody who had ever doubted his existence, here he was. In the flesh. Right beside the Interstate. And he had a red beard. His scrawny stick arms were covered with tattoos. Not the God I had somehow pictured all my life, the one with the booming voice like thunder and lightning that would strike and sizzle me to bacon when I did something wrong. So fearful was I that it made me almost a Goody Two-Shoes, a real Miss Prissy.

This God was not even Jesus, whose picture I had seen in the church of my childhood. The Jesus of the dark skin, beard and blue eyes. I'd been startled then to see the blue eyes. Who knew Jesus had blue eyes? And what color were the eyes of God who was always watching? I remembered asking my grandmother, Margaret Alice, if God was watching when I went to the bathroom. Saw me naked in the tub. She had just rolled her eyes, kissed me on the forehead and given me a sample of something sweet and warm from the oven.

This God's eyes, whatever color they were, were rolled back in his head.

"He won't wake up." Reba's face was wet, her nose all red and runny. She kept wiping it with the back of her hand.

"Oh Reba, honey," I said. "Let me check."

She moved aside and I felt for a pulse underneath his copper bracelet, which jangled a little in the silence. He even had hairy hands. On his little finger I saw Reba's diamond(?) engagement ring. He had taken it back? What a rat. I pulled it off and handed it to Reba, then felt for his pulse.

Nothing. I felt at his throat. Nothing.

"Do you know CPR?" I asked Reba. This might have seemed a stupid question, but with Reba you never knew. What she did know could sometimes surprise you. She didn't answer, but stood up and started turning in circles.

I climbed on top of God, unbuttoned his flannel plaid shirt that had a huge green stain on the front. I pushed on his chest, which was hairy as a bear. Where in the world had Reba found this guy?

I pried open God's mouth and saw he didn't believe in dentists. Brown, ragged teeth. I took a deep breath, bent down and forced myself to kiss those tobacco-colored lips that were getting whiter and whiter. His breath was awful to say the least. Sour. Garlic and whiskey and cigarettes. Oh, Lord.

Nothing.

I buttoned up his shirt. Crookedly. Two buttons were missing. I stepped back and then I hugged Reba. "I think we better call 911."

They would get Eikenberry Funeral Home. Eikenberry,

Littleboro's legendary undertaker, would love this one, I thought. I could see him, curly black mustache and all, rubbing his hands together. Business. Eikenberry's first thought, and probably his last thought before he went to sleep at night, was business. People in Littleboro said if you ran into him at some social function, he looked you up and down, like he was taking your measurements for what size coffin to order. Maybe it was just a nervous tic, but he did have the habit of moving his head up and down as he talked to you.

As I dialed 911 and gave particulars and directions, I pulled Reba around to the other side of the picnic table so her back was to God and hugged her close. Sometime this spring Reba had stopped wearing her orange-colored blanket and gotten some pullover cotton tops and cammo cargo pants with pockets. Reba loved lots of pockets. If you met her at M.&G.'s Grocery she'd have to unzip, unsnap and show you every one. And you'd have to stand there, ooh and ahh, before she'd let you go.

She smelled like some kind of aftershave. Men's cologne, something brown and spicy. No roses and lavender for Reba. But where had she spritzed herself so generously and so recently? Whose aftershave had she helped herself to? Did God wear Old Spice?

I heard the sirens in seconds, knew the blue and red lights on the MedAlert vehicle were flashing as it screamed toward the Interstate. Barring no dogs crossing Main Street, it would probably take only minutes to arrive. And fast behind that green-and-white truck would be Ossie DelGardo, chief of Littleboro police.

There was no love lost between me and Ossie DelGardo

because there had never been any to begin with. I felt like he came to Littleboro, New Jersey accent and all, brought big-city crime with him and infected Littleboro with it. Not long after I moved back, there were two murders in two weeks and somehow he always acted like I had something to do with them. We weren't archenemies, just on opposite sides of every-thing each of us stood for.

No sooner had the MedAlert shot in, spewing gravel in all directions, and the attendants had jumped out, grabbed a stretcher and run toward the picnic table than Ossie and Bruce Bechner screeched up, spewing more gravel and flash-ing more lights. I shaded Reba's eyes.

Ossie and his sidekick, Bruce Bechner, sprang out and Bruce ran to the body on the table while Ossie, in white cow-boy hat and shiny snakeskin boots, strode up, hands on his hips with a tight little, what looked to me like a snarl on his lips.

"You." He pointed a finger at me sharp as his voice. "Stop making my job work." He took off his cowboy hat and fanned himself with it. This was his new look, one he'd started wear-ing the same time as the boots and his engagement picture had appeared in the paper. I wondered if this was Juanita's idea and if he'd get married in cowboy hat and boots. Some-how I had trouble seeing Ossie as the good guy, the hero in the white hat.

I stepped back as he took Reba by the shoulders and gently sat her down at the picnic table. "Now, miss," he said. "Let's see what's going on here."

Reba leaned her head into his chest and cried while he pat-ted her on the back. "He was a better man," she choked out. "A better man."

"Now, now." Ossie pulled a handkerchief from his pocket and wiped her face.

This was a side of Ossie I'd never dreamed existed, and I wanted to stage-whisper to Reba, "Don't trust him. Don't say a word. It's a trap."

Meanwhile, the MedAlert guys and one gal had put an oxygen mask on the man who lay flat on his back on the picnic table. They whipped out all sorts of machines that made clicking and whizzing sounds. I couldn't see what they were doing except they seemed fast and efficient. Two of them held a stretcher at the ready. I saw them load the man into the truck, machines and all.

One of them had an iPad and was inputting information. Reba had snatched Ossie's handkerchief and was wailing into it, so the EMTs turned to me. They asked me for the dead man's name.

"I don't know," I said. I could not say I heard his name was God, or that's what he went by.

"Address?"

I wasn't about to say "Heaven," so I said, "I have no idea. You can get the information from the police later."

They slammed shut the double doors and roared away.

Reba and Ossie sat side by side at the picnic table. I heard Reba saying God was dead and she killed him. Ossie had produced a tiny tape recorder from somewhere and was getting it all on the record, trying to get more information from her. In between her crying and snuffles I only heard bits of words here and there. "Wine" and "June bride" and "best man" and "no wedding" and it was "late, too late," and she wanted sweet tea but he had fried chicken, KFC. None of her answers seemed to make sense but she kept insisting to Ossie she'd killed him.

Meanwhile I just stood there not knowing what to do. I started to go sit beside Reba, but I knew to Ossie that would look like I was interfering with a "trained law enforcement professional," an expression to which I wanted to snort a big "Ha."

Cars whizzed by on the Interstate. A few slowed, but nobody stopped. A lumber truck groaned and wheezed up the hill, loaded to the rails with tree bodies so freshly cut I smelled the dripping sap as it passed. There goes progress, I thought, or destruction, as tree body after tree body from the Uwharries, a little bitty mountain range back of Littleboro, went bleeding past. I felt like crying every time I saw a loaded log truck.

Bruce was in the patrol car talking to somebody or pulling up something on the computer from the license plate on God's big white truck. I'd seen Bruce walk around behind it. Now he shut the patrol car door, walked over and got in the truck, cranked it up, gunned the motor, then let it idle and waited. But waited for what?

"Don't," I said when I saw Ossie help Reba up, put his arm around her and start leading her toward the patrol car. "Don't you dare."

He stopped, and still with his arm holding Reba, stared me down. His dark little eyes told me not to come a step closer. "This is police business, I thank you, missy."

"But she hasn't done anything. The body doesn't have a mark on it. She doesn't know what she's saying."

"Back off," he said and held the car door for Reba. "Go

bake your muffins. Isn't that what you do, little girl?" Little
girl? I wanted to slap him. The nerve, making fun of me
trying to make a living making homemade pastries for my
B and B guests, trying to help my friend. Oh, the nerve.

I always felt like Ossie looked down on Southerners, as
though the minute we opened our mouths it sounded like we
didn't have enough sense to get in out of the rain. Me in par-
ticular. At least he was being nice to Reba. For that I was
grateful. If only it could continue.

Ossie escorted Reba to the backseat of the patrol car,
helped her in and closed the door. The metal *click* of the door
lock was a shock to my heart.

Ossie started the car and pulled away.

Reba lifted up her head long enough to wave bye to me
and smile. I wanted to run after that car, beat on the door
with my fists and say, "You let her out. She's innocent as a
child." Reba was like a child who just loved to ride, anywhere
with anybody. For years she had hung around the Interstate
and hitched rides with anybody who stopped. She had a fond-
ness for truck drivers. It's a wonder she hadn't been killed.
Maybe she'd just been lucky so far.

But where was Ossie taking her? Not to jail, surely not. If
I knew Reba, she was like a captured wild bird who would
beat its wings against a cage until it fell down dead.

As soon as Ossie pulled away, Bruce followed in the big
white truck. That's when I saw the tall black lettering on the
side. G.O.D. GENERAL OVERNIGHT DELIVERY.

God.

That's why Reba thought she was marrying God. I didn't

know whether to laugh or cry. She hadn't been making all this up. God was in the big white truck.

As I started toward Lady Bug, I saw something flat in the gravel under the picnic table. Reba's cell phone. I must have dropped it after I dialed 911. Beside it lay a key. I picked both up. The key was an old-fashioned metal room key stamped "Motel 3." How long had it been here? Where had it come from? One of Reba's pockets?

Ossie was long gone. The MedAlert team, too. The back of God's big white truck wasn't even in sight anymore. All that was left was me, the cell phone and that key.

I got in my car and headed up the road. In my rearview mirror I saw the empty roadside pull-over, a bare picnic table, the woods behind it and an emptiness. Even the air seemed still, like none of this had really happened.

I pressed hard on the gas pedal and roared up the road like the Devil himself was on my tail. If God was dead, then that must have left the Devil in charge.

Chapter Two

Of course I drove straight to Motel 3 and put that key in the door of one of the finished rooms. If there was any way I could get Reba out of this mess, maybe I'd find something here. Door number 1. It was like I could hear some offstage announcer saying, "If you choose door number one, there could be a new car or a trip to Cancun or ten thousand dollars. Or death. Which will it be?"

What I saw were two queen-sized beds—one slightly rumpled (Reba's site of sin?), the other pristine under a fluffy-looking white coverlet with blue stitching. It offered the remains of what looked like last night's supper.

I picked up a half-finished bottle of champagne. Dom Pérignon. God had good taste. Somehow I couldn't see Reba buying it, though she had always said grape juice was her "medicine" and drank Welch's straight from the bottle, not even chilled. Two champagne glasses stood on the bedside table along with an open bottle of Scotch and a half-finished bucket of Kentucky Fried Chicken on the bed.

I looked in some of the cardboard tubs of sides. A couple of potato wedges, half a serving of coleslaw, one lonely ear of corn on the cob, some garlic bread and half a Tupperware bowl of green beans. Since when did KFC put carryout in Tupperware? KFC and champagne? Only Reba.

I put lids on the takeout, which stirred up a roach underneath the garlic bread. He twitched his antennae as if to say, I got first dibs here. Go get your own. I left him to it. One of the least lovable of God's creatures.

I opened the closet door to see a white suit, some sort of western-type jacket with silver beading, sequins and fringe like a rock star or an Elvis impersonator might wear. On the closet floor, looking back at me, was a large pair of spectator shoes in blue and white. I picked one up. Size twelve.

On the closet rod hung Reba's wedding dress, the one we'd put together at The Calico Cottage. Somewhere in a piled-up storage room, Birdie Snowden, who had owned and run The Calico Cottage as long as I could remember, had unrolled a bolt of Chantilly lace so old it had yellowed on the edges. But when she held it up, Reba had clapped her hands and said, "June Bride, June Bride," then stood still while Miss Birdie draped it over her. "I'm a June bride," Reba said with a beatific smile. I'd always wondered what a beatific smile was and now I saw it. For a moment, Reba glowed. She looked serene and even a bit lovely.

"I'll fold it in half, cut and bind a hole big enough to go over her head," Miss Birdie said, "then seam up the sides, let it fall to her ankles, hem it and presto, change-o, Reba, you got a wedding dress."

Reba turned around, stood on tiptoes, twirled, let us see the back. It was like helping a child play dress up.

When we laughed, she laughed. It was all such fun. We weren't laughing *at* Reba, but *with* her. This crazy, silly business of weddings, which made me tear up and remember I'd never had one. Mama Alice would have loved to see me in her back garden, under the rose trellis in my mother's wedding dress and veil, serving her super-duper wedding cake that all her friends would ooh and ah over. But it never happened. Mama Alice probably planned my wedding a dozen times in her head, made up the reception menu, dreamed of the wedding cake she'd make. She never said a word, never made me feel guilty I didn't go that route.

When Ida Plum heard about all the wedding dress preparations the rest of us were doing, she donated a long white satin slip from her underwear drawer and it fit Reba like it had been waiting for her. Hmm, I thought, when was the last occasion Ida Plum had to wear a long slip under a formal dress? Did she have more of a social life than she wanted me to know? Ida Plum also bought some netting and made a veil and twined plastic ivy around the top. "We can weave in some fresh white roses on the big day," Ida Plum said, then out the side of her mouth, "if such a day ever comes to pass."

So we had the something old (Chantilly lace) and something borrowed (Ida Plum's slip). We still needed something new and something blue.

Malinda, my best friend in high school and again now that we were both back in Littleboro, brought over a lace-trimmed blue garter. "Never worn," she said, and handed it to Reba, who tried to put it on her head like a headband until she had us all in stitches. "No, no," Ida Plum said. "Leg. You put it on your thigh." Ida Plum pulled up her skirt to show Reba, who blushed but wouldn't model it. Instead Reba tucked it in one of her many pockets, zipped it shut and patted that pocket like it held a secret.

Malinda went to UNC on a Morehead Scholarship when women became eligible for the program. Everybody thought she was headed for med school and assumed she was in it for a while. Years passed and the next thing anybody knew Malinda was back in town with a crisp white coat, a pharmacy degree, a job at Gaddy's Drug Store and a baby in tow. If anybody knew her story, they didn't tell and nobody asked questions. In Littleboro we are polite, especially when it comes to people's past and private lives. If a person wants us to know something, they'll tell us in their own good time. Meanwhile we go about our daily lives, live and let live. It keeps the peace and harmony.

Not one of us ever expected this wedding to come off, but it was fun to play along with Reba, to see happiness surrounding her. That was last week. Reba had been so full of hope, not like this afternoon, shredded and hysterical. I thought how quickly life can grab you by the throat and dash you down.

Now I picked up the white flip-flops somebody around town had given Reba or she had picked up from somewhere. Who knew? Who cared? We had decorated them with big white bows. I put them back on the closet floor.

On the back of the closet door hung a thick burgundy robe embroidered with the logo and name of some resort in Scottsdale, Arizona. God did get around, I guess. Standing on the dresser was a row of orange prescription bottles and Reba's bridal bouquet, its plastic white roses and resurrection lilies tied with dangling blue satin ribbon, stuck in a glass of water.

Next to the bouquet was a man's leather billfold, so worn its corners curled. I pried it open to find some credit cards and a driver's license. Staring back at me was a photo of Butch Winston Rigsbee, age sixty-three, Akron, Ohio. This guy had dark hair and brown eyes and a killer of a gleaming smile that nearly blinded me. Looked like he had all his teeth or some darn expensive dental work. There was no resemblance to the guy on which I'd tried to perform CPR, the one Reba was calling God.

I flipped to other photos in the billfold. In one, Butch was sitting with his arm around a big gray cat. Standing behind him was a tall blond woman who looked like she either Roller Derbied or was a *SmackDown* wrestler. The look on her face was one my grandmother would say was enough to curdle sweet milk. She didn't look like the kind of woman anybody would ever want to meet in the dark . . . or the daylight. Not a woman anybody would want to get on the wrong side of. Behind that photo was the same woman with two girls, daughters maybe, who looked to be about twelve and fourteen. Both wore the same sort of pouts and they weren't pretty. They were just about as tough-looking as their mama. The money compartment was empty, not even a dollar bill. Reba, I wanted to say, if Butch was your fiancé, he wasn't taking you on much of a honeymoon, not even to South of the Border for the day.

I read the label on one of the prescription bottles, something for blood pressure. Several labels sounded like painkillers. None of the labels had a drugstore name nor were addressed to this Butch Rigsbee, which was odd. Had they been pilfered from somebody's medicine cabinet? I picked up one I recognized was for diabetes. I knew because Mama Alice, my grandmother, had taken it at one time. Another bottle was some highly advertised weight-loss formula, then there was a rolled packet, a generous supply of blue Viagra pills. Hmm. I had to chuckle. If Butch had really been the omnipotent God I knew, he wouldn't need those!

I opened a dresser drawer that was empty except for a supersized box of condoms. Optimist, I thought, and closed the drawer. Suddenly I felt guilty. Snooping into people's lives. Why had I really come here? What was I really doing? Ida Plum always said I had too much curiosity for my own good, that I liked to meddle.

But I wasn't meddling here. I was truly trying to find something that would both connect Reba to all this and prove she had not killed the guy on the picnic table. But who was this Butch Rigsbee? How did she get herself into such a situation? And what were the rest of us doing playing along with her about a wedding? Had we gotten her into a lot of trouble when we should have tried to divert her? Somebody could have given her a gift card to Walmart and she probably would have forgotten the whole wedding thing. But no, we had been having too much fun, apparently at her expense. All of us ought to be ashamed.

Then the cell phone in my pocket vibrated against my hip.
I'd forgotten it was there. I'd automatically shoved it in my
pocket when I picked it up from under the picnic table. I
flipped it open and squeaked out a startled "Hello," only to
have an angry voice nearly rupture my eardrum. "I know
where you are and what the hell you're doing with my thieving, no good, two-timing lizard of a husband. I'm going to
cut his tail off and it won't grow back."

I gulped. "I'm not—"

"Whoever you are, Miss Hussy, I'm going to find you and
when I do, I'll kill you. And don't think you're going to keep
a cent of what you find. It's mine. Mine." She had a rusty
chainsaw of a voice that made my ear hurt. She clicked off.
I could almost feel the heat of her anger in my hand as I stood
holding that little piece of electronic accusations and feeling
like the walls around me weren't there, that this woman on
the phone, this wife person, could see me and I was in danger.

My next thought was I'd better head straight for home, the
Dixie Dew B and B, where Ida Plum manned the range and
could wield a mean iron skillet or two, and Scott maybe had
popped in from his latest remodeling job. I knew my doors
had locks on them and it was a bright, well-lighted place just
down the street from the police station, a place quite conve-
niently within hearing distance of bloodcurdling screams. If
I ever got to the point of needing to scream something bloodcurdling I'd probably just open my mouth and saliva would
drip out.

There was a polite little tap on the door and without
waiting for me to get to it, the door cracked partway open.

Motel 3 was so cheap it didn't even have chain locks on the doors.

"No," I screamed. I pushed my whole body against that door and whoever was on the other side pushed back. Pushed heavier and harder. "Help, somebody," I yelled. "Help!"

Chapter Three

I felt the pressure from the other side of the door ease off a little, but I didn't trust whoever was out there. They could be gathering up steam for one giant push, so I grabbed the first things I could get my hands on: Reba's wedding dress, which I yanked off the hanger and held in front of me, and a flip-flop. Nobody would shoot a bride, would they? Or if they did, I'd make a mighty sweet- and innocent-looking corpse.

Someone tapped on the door again. Light little polite taps, not killer taps. Still, how could you know? Could be a sneaky killer trying to get me to open the door and slide in fast, grab me by the throat and that would be the end of me. Could have a weapon, a quiet weapon. Who knew I was here? Ida Plum knew I was going to find Reba at the picnic area by the Interstate, but that was all. Nobody would think to look for me at Motel 3. Nobody knew about the key I'd found.

Were Reba and Butch involved with something illegal? Drugs? I hadn't found any but then I didn't know what illegal drugs looked like. All the pills in the pill bottles looked to me like ads I'd seen in newspapers and magazines. I hadn't seen any white powder, if that's what the bad stuff looked like. The only white powder I knew was laundry detergent and baking soda and powdered sugar.

Money laundering? I couldn't ever get my hands on enough money to even try to think how somebody would launder it. I didn't know any big-city crime stuff. I didn't even watch TV. I could be in something over my head in a million different ways. Oh, Lord. An innocent person did not go poking around in strange motel rooms in the middle of the day. Ida Plum would say (over my dead body) that I set myself up for it.

I grabbed the other flip-flop and backed away from the door. Then someone called, "May I come in?" The voice sounded a little familiar.

"No," I said, just to be safe. "No, you may not." Since when did killers use correct English?

"Is this Reba's room?"

It was Pastor Pittman from the First Presbyterian Church. I recognized his voice.

I opened the door. "It's Beth," I said. "There's not going to be a wedding."

"I know," he said. "There never was going to be one."

He came in, looked around, took a seat on the end of the slightly rumpled bed and eyed the remains of the picnic on the other bed. I'd always heard you should feed preachers chicken. My grandmother Margaret Alice did. But then she liked to feed everybody chicken in some shape or form. Should I offer him some chicken? The bucket was still almost full. But who was I to go offering somebody the remains of Reba's supper? My thoughts were as jumbled as Reba's.

"Reba called me to meet her here," he said. "I was going to see if we couldn't put an end to this whole charade. Though I have to say it's kept the entire town entertained these last several weeks."

"I'm not snooping," I said, still holding the wedding dress and the flip-flops.

He grinned. "Nobody ever said you were." He looked around as if he expected Reba to come from the closet or bathroom.

"She's not here," I said. "Long story."

"I got an hour." Pittman looked at his watch, sighed and leaned forward, head in his hands. "Is this a confession? You haven't killed anybody lately have you?"

"No, I certainly have not." That made me mad. I bristled. "I never killed anybody in my life. No matter what you heard." He knew since I came back to Littleboro I had been associated with two murders, one in the Dixie Dew, the other in the Catholic church, but he also knew I had nothing to do with either. Gossip, stories and tall tales in this town took on lives of their own.

He laughed, put both his hands up. "Okay, what's going on? Where's Reba?"

"She may be in jail." I really did not want to start explaining Reba's God and the truck and all to a preacher. It all seemed unbelievable, even to me who had been accused of having an overactive imagination by the sages in this town.

He sat up. "I've married people in jail before. Not the best of circumstances, but one makes do. One is called on to serve in so many situations." He wove his fingers together into a sort of church, like I had done as a child. You lace your fingers together, thumbs up, say "Here's the church, here's the steeple." You fold them back and say, "Open the doors and see the people." I wondered if he'd ever heard the rhyme, if he had done that as a child and it had become a habit as a preacher?

"She kept saying she killed him."

"Killed who?" Pastor Pittman looked toward the window and sighed, as if what I was going to say was just another bit to add to the town folklore. Ida Plum had said First Presbyterian Church had been losing members. What was once a congregation of nearly two hundred was now down to seventy-eight or so. Pittman must have had time on his hands, plus been a bit bored in a town like Littleboro watching the same ecumenical calendar roll around year after year.

"God," I said. "Reba said she killed God."

"You and I both know Reba has a lot of imagination, which I would never discourage. Makes for good storytelling. And we have all enjoyed Reba's little fabrications over the years, especially during these last few weeks."

"He's real," I said.

"Of course he is." Pittman looked down at his hands folded in his lap like two white nesting doves. "I've never doubted for a minute." He glanced at the ceiling, hesitated a bit. "Oh, well, since we're both being honest, maybe at times I have doubted . . . now and then. A little. On occasion. I'm only human." He sighed again, this time very deeply.

"I was getting some things to take to Reba in jail," I said. Except what was there to take? I hadn't seen any underwear or cosmetics. Not even a hairbrush.

On this pretext, I went in the bathroom, where there was a hairbrush and the biggest bottle of Old Spice shaving lotion I'd ever seen. And a bottle of vitamins. Another of sleeping pills. My Lord, there's half a pharmacy here, I thought. I took the hairbrush and wrapped the wedding dress and flip-flops around it.

I lifted Reba's wedding veil from the lamp shade and put it on my head. Didn't want it to get mussed. Ida Plum would kill me. Even if Reba wasn't going to use it, maybe sometime, somebody would, and Ida Plum didn't believe in wasting anything. Now I did have some things to take Reba, after all, since that had been my excuse and a darn good one. Pastor Pittman had bought it, or seemed to. But what about Butch's stuff? I guess it was all evidence and Ossie would haul it in.

I stood in front of the dresser, reached quietly behind me and slipped Butch's wallet into the roll of things to take Reba. I don't know why I took it. Maybe I thought there might be some evidence incriminating Reba, but now it made me a thief for sure. In for a penny, my grandmother would say, in for a pound.

Pastor Pittman stood at the door and pulled at his shirt

collar as if he were ready to leave. "Let's go talk in my car. I'd feel more comfortable."

I didn't say I would, too, but I was relieved. Here I was in Reba's den of sin with a prominent pastor from Littleboro. Oh, the gossip mills would lick their lips on this bit of news. How did I get myself into these things?

I followed Pastor Pittman out, pulled the door closed and looked down at the key in the lock. Should I take it, too? On second thought, I left it.

If this was a crime scene my fingerprints were all over everything. If, and that was a big fat if, Reba had indeed killed somebody, then I'd be in trouble for being here. Wouldn't Ossie love this? His number two suspect. He'd probably lock me in with Reba and throw away the key. Did jails have keys these days? Wouldn't they have electronic locks? Not in Littleboro. I bet the cell in the basement of the courthouse had some rusty old lock going back to the Civil War, or the "recent unpleasantness," as we sometimes spoke of it when we were reminded. Ossie DelGardo was just the type to let somebody, especially me, rot in jail. I could imagine him rubbing his hands in absolute glee at finding my fingerprints here. Plus now he had an eyewitness, Pastor Pittman. Who could be more reliable than a Presbyterian minister?

Then I thought, has Pittman touched anything? Not even a chicken wing. And I was the one who had opened the door. But he did sit on the beautiful puffy white coverlet and his body image might glow in the dark if the police used one of those ultraviolet lights. Just thinking of all the possibilities made me feel better. I wasn't in this alone and somehow I'd get Reba out of Ossie's clutches. Maybe. All I knew was that the whole thing was not going to be easy. So far it wasn't even believable. God and Reba and Pastor Pittman. Butch Rigsbee and the guy on the picnic table. What was the connection? And somewhere a woman who sounded crazier than Reba was threatening to kill me.

+—|—+

Chapter Four

Pastor Pittman opened the passenger door of his car, a silver BMW, and I slid in. Leather seats. "Oh my goodness," I said. I was impressed. Lady Bug's upholstery had long been worn down to the foam rubber and I used big blue bath towels for seat covers. Pittman caressed his steering wheel, which also had a leather cover.

"I've got a parishioner who owns the dealership in Southern Pines. He gives me a good deal, says I'm good advertising. Of course I don't know that's true. Parking it at Motel 3 is probably not quite what he had in mind."

Pittman laughed, reached up and straightened the little gold cross hanging from his rearview mirror. I saw an oval St. Christopher medal dangling right behind it.

He grinned. "I try to cover a lot of bases," he said when he noticed me staring at the mirror ornaments.

I leaned back, let out a breath. Here I was outside a seedy motel in a fancy car with a preacher. Anybody from Littleboro driving by was sure to notice. We Littleborians don't miss much, not when one of our own is out of place, or somewhere they're not supposed to be or doing something they shouldn't be doing. All this was not good for my reputation, which wasn't all that sterling to start with. There are those people who live in Littleboro who remember me from my first Easter bonnet and white patent leather Mary Janes to the time I ate the communion bread before the blessing. Or the time, dressed as Little Bo Peep in the first-grade play, I threw up onstage. Those were just bits in the local folklore. There was worse later.

Memories, especially embarrassing ones, lingered long in Littleboro. Too long. Maybe that's why when I was eighteen, the minute I graduated Littleboro High School, I couldn't wait to leave for art school in Rhode Island. Lord, was I lucky to land there among my own kind. And one of the things I was dealing with since I came crawling back home on my weary knees was baggage—that was the current term. I carried a lot of baggage and it wasn't exactly plaid and polka-dotted and pretty.

Then I thought another thought. Pastor Pittman's reputation was more at stake here than mine. Motel, parked with a woman in his car. His parishioners didn't do motels, at least not in broad daylight.

"You first," he said.

"No, you." My hands were still shaking from the scare of

having to bargain with some stranger, who turned out to be Pittman, trying to barge in the motel door.

"My explanation is simple," he said. "She'd asked me to pick her up here and take her to the gazebo at Lemon Lake for a 'rehearsal.' She'd heard the word in all the wedding talk. Then she called this morning hysterical about something. I couldn't understand what it was all about. Since I was planning to come, I just came earlier."

"She wasn't upset about the wedding stuff," I said. "That was supposed to be tomorrow."

"You believed she was really getting married?" he asked.

"Of course not, but what did it hurt to play along with her?"

I wasn't sure I believed his story. Pittman was a darn good-looking man with a prissy blond Barbie of a wife who Ida Plum said probably only let him have sex on Sunday mornings so he could get charged up for loving that pulpit and speaking to the "Frozen Chosen" while she sat in the first pew with a smug Cheshire cat smile. Barbie Pittman was skinny as a stick and wore her butter-blond hair in a tight twist of an upsweep. I felt like a brunette, ponytailed Raggedy Ann around her. But Reba? Even though she'd cleaned up lately, gotten a cute new haircut (and Juanita had even put in highlights so you didn't notice all the gray), the idea of hanky-panky with Reba was too far-fetched even for a nonromantic like me.

"And?" I waited.

"And I planned to listen to her hysteria, talk her out of this most recent craziness, buy her some ice cream, maybe even one of those banana splits at the S & T Soda Shoppe. That would keep her eating half the day and so full of sugar and

chocolate and nuts and whipped cream she'd forget the whole
June bride business and go back to her tree." He turned to
me. "Anything wrong with that? What's your story?"

"I guess it's more involved." So I told him about it in detail: Reba's phone call, the white truck, God, my attempt at
CPR, the man on the picnic table, the MedAlert.

"Wow," he said, which startled me and made me wonder
if he thought I was making the whole thing up, that some of
Reba's imagination was catching, like measles. Then I guess
I expected him to pat my hand, pull out a Bible from somewhere and read me some verses. Maybe the 23rd Psalm I'd
memorized at some point. I thought about the part of pre-
paring a table in the presence of "mine enemies." Ossie could
be considered "mine enemy" of sorts. Something.

"That's some story. Good to know you can do CPR," he
said. "And where's Reba now?"

"Jail. I guess. Ossie took her off in the squad car and Bruce
drove the truck behind him." I fingered the roll of Reba's
clothing in my lap. "I thought I might find some of her things
in the motel, take them to her." I didn't say what was obvi-
ous. Reba didn't need her bridal gown in her jail cell. Maybe
it would even be cruel to remind her, for her to see it. Maybe
I should just drive over to Walmart and buy her some new
underwear, a robe, slippers. I should have taken that burgundy robe I found in the room. It wasn't too late. I could just
pop out and go get it. The key was still in the door.

That sounded logical, reasonable and believable.

Pastor Pittman sighed. "The poor woman. Who knows her
pain?"

I'd never thought of Reba having pain, being in pain before. She was rarely upset about anything or anybody. She seemed so happy, talking to the birds, singing to herself around town, borrowing anybody's bathtub (and bath salts if she couldn't get her hands on bubble bath—Reba loved a good bubble bath and you had to clean the bubbles she left in your tub; she'd been known to empty a whole bottle in with her), sleeping under her tree. I saw her, and maybe the whole town did, too, as an oversized child. Sweet and innocent. Now she might be hurting. And scared out of her wits thinking she'd killed somebody. I tried to shake the image of that fellow (whoever he was) out of my mind. That awful sour taste when I did the CPR. I wiped my hand across my mouth. Yuk. Was there any mouthwash in Reba's motel bathroom?

"Just a minute," I said, and hopped out, leaving the car door open and the bundle for Reba on the seat. But just as I had my hand on the motel-room doorknob, somebody clasped me on the shoulder. "Oh, no you don't. You can't go in there."

I turned around to see Al, or Allison Petty as I'd known her in high school, close behind me with a vacuum cleaner, bucket and mop. And a roll of yellow tape. "Bruce just brought this over. Didn't you see the car? He was in and out like light-ning. I was going to clean the room, but he stopped me just in time."

Damn, I thought. Maybe her cleaning would have wiped and washed away all my fingerprints and Reba's sin. Evi-dence if she had indeed killed the *real* Butch Rigsbee aka God.

"I just wanted to get a robe to take to Reba," I said.

"No, not on your life. Ossie'd kill me if I let anybody in that room. He'd seen that white 'God' truck parked here yesterday, the one at the pull-off he just hauled off to the police station." She unrolled the yellow crime scene tape across the door. "This isn't going to do my business any good." So she'd heard the story already, at least part of it.

"Okay," I said, and fully expected her to ask me how I knew there was a robe in that room, but I would be willing to bet she saw me drive in, knew every minute I was in there. From her view from the little office on the corner I bet she didn't miss much. And Pastor Pittman? She saw him, too. And she'd probably told Ossie. Oh boy, when the gossip mill got this going, it would really build into a giant tale. More folklore for the lengthy Littleboro legends, some of which were hundreds of years old, going back to the founding of the town on some king's grant that bestowed favors on those few who came over and fought for him during the Revolution. This little bitty patch of dirt.

Allison turned and waved to Pastor Pittman sitting in his car. He'd tried to duck down and hadn't quite made it. What is *he* hiding? I thought. My Lord, this town has secrets within secrets.

I bet the business of Reba being hauled in by Ossie, the body of Mr. Whoever-He-Was loaded into the MedAlert ambulance on the Interstate and maybe even me seen there with Pastor Pittman at Motel 3 was all over town by now. This was one tale I'd never live down.

I reached in Pittman's car for the things to take Reba. I waved goodbye to him and got in Lady Bug.

Maybe I could get back to the Dixie Dew before the gossip reached Ida Plum and whatever guest might be lingering in my dining room. Give them half a chance and they'd write up a report for the Bed and Breakfast Association, but what could they say? I knew my food was good, my beds were clean and soft and my house was warm, welcoming. The town I couldn't do anything about. The busybodies, the gossips who liked nothing better than a good scandal to chew over, they went back to Noah's Ark, those who escaped the flood. I'm sure some of them were there, riding on the roof of that ark. They must have hopped down at the first hint of dry land, called it Littleboro and passed on their legends for generations.

I drove faster than the speed limit. Ossie and Bruce would be too busy to worry about speeding tickets today. And Reba? Had she really killed this guy? And where was the man she had called God . . . her so-called intended? I knew the fellow on the picnic table did not in any way look like the photo in the wallet, and those clothes hanging in the closet were big enough for two of him. Maybe Reba and this guy she called a "better man" had killed the real Butch Rigsbee? Then she tried to kill this man? I couldn't see Reba killing anyone. Not even the proverbial fly.

I hadn't seen blood from any gunshot or knife wound on the man on the picnic table. Somehow I couldn't see Reba doing anything like that. Strangled? I hadn't looked for marks on his throat, but I couldn't see Reba doing that, either. She could have smothered him with a pillow, but I remembered all the pillows were still in place on the beds. And if she'd done any of that, how could she have gotten the body to this pull-off beside the Interstate? Reba didn't even drive. So he must have driven the truck, maybe had a heart attack and pulled over, then trying to get air, gotten out and somehow pulled himself over to the picnic table. That's when Reba

grabbed his cell phone and called me. Reba might have more
common sense than any of us gave her credit for.

All I knew for now was I'd seen a strange man that I
thought was a dead man on the picnic table, and Reba had
called me and Ossie had hauled Reba away in his police car.

Lots of questions. No answers. And I was threatened on
the phone by some big bruiser of a woman who wanted to
kill both her thieving, rotten, lying husband and me who had
never laid eyes on him until I saw his photo in the wallet.
Hussy? I'd never been called a hussy in my life. I looked at
all the rubble around me. This crazy woman could be lurk-
ing in the woods behind Motel 3, eyeing me in her gun's sites,
if she was the shooter type. Somehow the picture I had of this
woman looked like the strangler type. She could grab me, put
those iron hands around my throat, give a mighty squeeze,
I'd croak dead, then she'd walk off and never look back. She
also looked like someone who could hot-wire a bulldozer if
she had to, toss my body in the rubble of concrete, drywall
and bricks, push more rubble over it and nobody would ever
find me. Just that thought nearly scared me to death.

I couldn't get out of the place fast enough. So I locked my
car door for good measure and lead-footed the gas pedal all
the way home.

Chapter Five

Of course by the time I got to the Dixie Dew, word had already overtaken me.

Ida Plum met me at the kitchen door, dish towel in hand. "We heard Reba has killed a man and you were seen hugging up Pastor Pittman at Motel 3."

"No, no, no," I said. "That's not the way it was."

Scott stood at the kitchen island, poring over catalogs, flyers and envelopes. He often picked up his mail from his box at the post office, then came by the Dixie Dew for a quick cup of coffee and whatever else was baking or had been baked recently. As he sorted his mail sometimes I got a quick brush of a kiss, which made Ida Plum shake her head and say, "You two. I don't know about you two."

Now Scott just grinned, said, "You can take off that veil unless you're going for vows of chastity, which I sincerely hope is not the case." He aimed a pat at my blue-jeaned butt as I walked by.

"Missed," I said and poked my tongue at him.

"Cute," he said. "You think you're so cute."

"Ha, ha," I said and reached up to snatch off the bridal veil netting. I'd forgotten it was on my head. And there I had been in Pastor Pittman's car wearing it, then with Allison at the door of room number 1. Nobody had said a word until Scott teased about a nun's veil. "Oh, my God."

Ida Plum took the wisp of a veil from me and started fluffing it. "I'm not making another one."

"You won't have to," I said, and told them about Ossie hauling Reba off in the squad car after the MedAlert folks loaded Mr. Nobody from the picnic table. I didn't mention the business about God (or GOD) or CPR or the motel room picnic.

"So she *did* kill somebody?" Ida Plum asked. "My Lord, what a mess."

"She kept saying she did. She was hysterical and Ossie got it all on tape," I said.

"You get yourself into more situations. Ossie's going to love hauling you in. He'd like nothing better than to put you in the cell with Reba and throw away the key," Scott said.

He slid the envelopes inside his catalogs and flyers before I could get a good look to see which was what. What I could see looked like envelopes for bills or checks, and an oversized manila one like those that come with stock reports or from lawyers. Could the big one contain divorce papers? I didn't know if Scott was still married or if he had ever been. Ida Plum said she *thought* she'd heard Scott had married Cedora Harris, who became Sunnye Deye, a famous songbird, and the voice behind commercials singing about soaps and detergents, Depends, lately some foreign cars. But who knew for sure? Those envelopes looked like they meant serious business, but what kind of business?

"Thought you were tied up with building booths at the fairgrounds for the Green Bean festival," I said to Scott, ignoring his comment and hoping to move on to address the work he'd promised to do at the Dixie Dew. He seemed to suddenly have a lot of jobs in places other than the Dixie Dew, and I desperately wanted a gazebo built in the backyard in time for Ossie and Juanita's wedding, which was less than a week away. Ossie was an outsider and not one of my favorite people in the world, not even close. But Juanita was one of us, and in Littleboro, we make big allowances for our own.

I'd seen gazebo doodles Scott had made on paper napkins, but nothing actually taking shape in my long-neglected backyard. You couldn't call it a garden now. I yearned for the days when Mama Alice had iris that bloomed so big and tall they fell over in glorious purple-and-white fainting blossoms. Even those iris had long ago died out. Iris are hardy for years, generations even, but not these. Not in *my* "garden." This spring I'd had some azalea blooms, half attempts that afterwards hung like dirty rags on the bushes. Awful, awful and I didn't have time nor money to make the yard picture-perfect beautiful. A fresh, sparkling-white gazebo would be a centerpiece. Maybe the rest wouldn't get noticed so much.

"I was just passing by when my cell phone nearly jumped

off my truck seat," Scott said. "Somebody"—he paused and glanced over at Ida Plum—"seemed to be having an emergency."

"Upstairs bath," Ida Plum said. "That leak under the sink. You don't have it fixed." She turned her attention to me. "Gonna rot that floor out and the tub and all the bathroom stuff will come down through the ceiling onto our heads." She put one hand atop her head as if the falling of porcelain seemed imminent.

"It's not that bad," Scott said. "But I think you better call an RP."

"What's an RP?"

"Real plumber." He tapped the end of my nose with his forefinger. "Don't wait too much longer. Leaks don't fix themselves." He headed out the door, but looked back, said, "And keep that funny little freckled nose out of Ossie's business."

I heard Scott laughing as he went down the back steps and I knew he was probably right about Ossie wanting to haul me in with Reba. And that I ought to call a real plumber. Real plumbers meant big bucks, of which I had scant. Sometimes I thought this house was held together only with wallpaper paste and paint, plus the McKenzie good name. At least it had a sparkling new roof and gutters. I love roofs and gutters and the feeling of both being new and solid over my head. I'd like them even better if they were paid in full. But I was getting there, month by month.

Ida Plum took off her apron, one of Mama Alice's aprons that was so old, so washed and worn, the pattern had faded to an all-over gray. I bet it was one Mama Alice had made of feed sacks. She used to get those at the Feed and Seed, said there was nothing like good, solid cotton and you couldn't buy better dish towels and aprons than those made from the sacks.

Ida Plum put the apron on the back of a chair at the kitchen table and said, "Sit. I want to hear all the gory details."

I sat, but wasn't about to go into the details. I was trying too hard to get them out of my head, the taste of that CPR stuff out of my memory. It wasn't easy.

"A cup of tea is what I need." I started to get up.

"Sit, sit," she said again. "I don't want you messing up my kitchen."

She got up and flipped the switch on the electric kettle.

"*Your* kitchen?" I started to argue. That little jab went right to the quick. I was guilty of getting myself involved in situations that took my time and attention off running the Dixie Dew, not to mention my flagging little tearoom, The Pink Pineapple.

"Seems I spend more time in it lately than you do," Ida Plum said. "Running this business would go to nothing if somebody around here didn't mind it." She got china cups from the dining room, not the usual coffee mugs from the kitchen. Cups meant a special occasion. Serious talk. Truth maybe. Lingering. No sip, swallow and run, as I tended to do with coffee.

"I checked in your guests and gave them beautiful explanations about how their lovely hostess and innkeeper had momentarily—and I emphasized the momentarily—stepped out for an errand or two and would be back soon to greet them warmly." Ida Plum set a cup and saucer in front of me. "I did not tell them you had gone to rescue a crazy person who had killed somebody and was arrested and then gone poking around a motel where you didn't belong, not to mention with a preacher in tow."

"Whew," I said. "Thank you."

I told her about finding the motel key and Pastor Pittman surprising me while I was looking around the motel room. I told Ida Plum I thought Reba might be in more of a mess than I originally suspected when I went flying out after she called. I didn't have it all sorted out. I wasn't ready for a scolding—or the truth.

I was in trouble, Crazy Reba trouble. An angry woman on the phone had threatened my life. What had been wedding plans (of a sort) had gone astray in the worst possible way. Murder? Things were not adding up. Whoever Reba said she killed was not the man in the driver's license picture. No way. But was the man on the picnic table her "intended"? All she'd ever said was she was marrying God and we had smiled and nodded, said to ourselves, Sure you are, honey. Sure you are. We'd played along. Such imagination. Reba was one of a kind, but she was our own. Rethinking all this now, I knew for certain the men's clothes hanging in the motel closet didn't look one bit to me like they fit that scrawny, plucked chicken of a body I'd done CPR on. The taste of his nonexistent oral hygiene was still in my mouth. Yug.

The Pilot, the newspaper of the Sandhills in North Carolina, was published in nearby Southern Pines. I subscribed to it by mail, but I suddenly remembered it was online. They were up-to-date, upscale, mod. I usually waited to read the hard copy when it came by mail, but sometimes, just for kicks, I'd scan the online version. I knew *The Littleboro Messenger* (locals called it *The Mess*) would never go online. It was too far back in the dark ages. Sometimes I even imagined them scribbling away on parchment using quills.

At the computer in my pantry/office, I searched to see if there was anything about a mystery man, a body rescued from a picnic table beside the Interstate near Littleboro.

There was: a tiny item at the bottom on the first page. No photo, thank goodness, just a description of the man, scraggly red beard and all, except it didn't say scraggly, just gave his height and weight and that he was in "critical condition" and next of kin was being sought.

Then another thought hit me. If this mystery guy was still alive, where was God? aka Butch Rigsbee? Maybe Reba had really killed him. If so, where was the body?

I yelled for Ida Plum to come read over my shoulder to see if she saw what I was seeing. He was alive. We read together that Ossie DelGardo was asking for anyone with a missing family member or with further information to contact him in Littleboro.

Well, I would certainly do that. Right away. I didn't have much information, but maybe just enough to get Reba off the hook right now.

"Keep the kettle on," I called to Ida Plum as I went out the door. "I'll be right back. Or . . . if I'm not back by lunchtime, call anybody who can get me out of Ossie DelGardo's stainless-steel clutches." I shook my shoulders at the very thought of being grabbed, arrested or held by the likes of Ossie.

Chapter Six

I was upset, relieved in a way, that the mystery fellow was still alive, so I metaphorically pulled up my big girl panties and marched downtown to the Littleboro police station. I stormed straight past Wanda Purncell at the reception desk and into Ossie DelGardo's office.

Ossie swung his legs off his desk and his boots hit the floor with a *blam, kerthump*. He even wore his big white cowboy hat in this office! Bad, bad, Mama Alice would have said. You take off your hat when you come in the house. That was manners. Where had the man been raised? Now he leaned over and with the blade of his hand wiped any boot prints off his desktop. He raised a finger like he was signaling me to give him a minute. What I planned to give him was a piece of my mind.

"I'm not Reba," I almost shouted. That was not what I meant to say but it was the first thing that came out. What I meant was that I had not been messing around with Butch Rigsbee and had no idea why Reba had said she killed the "better man." Only in Reba's eyes and mind could anyone refer to that scrawny man on the picnic table as better.

"Whoever said you were?" He laughed and rolled his eyes, then smirked a smile at the corners of his mouth as though sometimes he'd gotten the two of us confused and weren't we somehow, somewhere a bit related? Two crazies in the same town. Too much.

"And I'm being threatened."

"Calm down, missy," he said, coming around from behind his desk.

I hated being called "missy" and double hated it when Ossie DelGardo did it. So I stood there and steamed. I felt heat rising off me.

"Suppose you take this comfy little chair right here and tell me all about it."

He pulled out a straight chair and patted the back of it. Not for a minute was I going to sit down in his office. I was going to say my piece and high step it out of there.

"The man Reba has been seeing. The one she called God, who she said she killed. He does not look like the photo in the wallet, and his wife is threatening me."

"Whoa." Ossie held up his hand like a stop sign; all he needed was a whistle. "Hold on. I don't know what you're talking about."

"Reba. You got Reba in jail for a crime she didn't commit and some crazy woman is threatening me and nobody knows where her husband is. Butch Rigsbee, the driver of the 'God' truck. He could be murdered for all we know."

"And how do you know all this?" He stood toe-to-toe with me, his big cowboy boots touching my scruffy size seven sneakers. One move and he could crush all my toes to bitty bones and jelly.

I stepped back. I would have to confess I had the wallet. I'd trapped myself.

"I just know," I stammered. "I was in the motel room where Reba had been with him."

"Him who?"

"The man she thought she killed."

Ossie started laughing. "Of all the tales I've heard about you since I've been in this town, you tell the wildest. Was this a threesome?" Now he laughed louder.

"I have the wallet." I felt like stamping my foot. He didn't believe a word I said.

"What wallet? Whose wallet?" He laughed more, slapped his sides laughing. "Now you're into stealing? Well, missy, you bring me that wallet and we'll take it from there."

He turned back to his desk, opened the drawer and picked up a pen, clicked it on and off. Ignored me. He closed his desk drawer but not before I saw a scrunch of red satin and lace. A thong? Juanita's? Then I noticed three framed photos of the engaged Juanita lined up on the windowsill. Big photos with gold filigree frames. No wonder he wasn't interested in any crime or criminals in Littleboro. One of the huge photos showed Juanita sprawled on her back, legs outstretched, arms wide open in a come-here-you-big-hunky-man sort of pose. She reclined in her red heart-shaped bed. The other photo was a close-up of Juanita hugging a white Pekingese dog. The third photo was Juanita, a much younger Juanita in a bathing suit at the beach. A pinup pose if I ever saw one.

"Meanwhile," I said my hand on the doorknob, "you let Reba go this minute."

"Miss Reba is fine where she is. In fact, I heard her over there singing her heart out."

I stomped out so fast I stirred a hot breeze as I whooshed past Wanda Purncell's desk. I knocked off a vase that had a big, fat red rose in it and didn't stop to pick it up or apologize. Wanda just said, "Oh," and put her hands to her face. I kept going.

Chapter Seven

When I got outside I heard Reba's clear, fresh voice singing "Amazing Grace." The jail was in the basement of the courthouse across the street. I thought yes, how sweet the sound of Reba singing. I expected to hear her crying. It wasn't all that many hours ago she was crying and crying hysterically.

I entered through the basement door and demanded to see Reba. The skinny deputy at the desk, who didn't look a day older than eighteen, didn't even ask for my ID. It was Danny, the bag boy from M.&G.'s, in a police uniform. Must have been his first day on the job because I'd seen him bagging groceries just last week. Maybe he'd been hired on temporarily to keep an eye on the prisoner now that there was one. The last prisoner had been Miss Tempie's handyman. That was over a year ago and they'd transferred him fast to the Wake County jail where they had full-time guards and windows that didn't open.

"Sure thing, Miss Beth," he said. "Keep her quiet for a while, don't think I can stand much more of that singing."

I looked through the bars and there she sat on the edge of her jailhouse bunk making a cat's cradle.

"Look," Reba said, holding up the dirty strings she must have pulled from her jail blanket and had woven around the fingers of both hands. "Isn't it pretty?"

I swallowed. "Beautiful," I said. "Can I bring you anything?"

"Beans." She grinned. "Some green beans from KFC. Extra crispy."

"Oh, Reba," I said, "Ossie's bringing you supper and I think you already had enough beans for today."

"Not me." She dropped her cat's cradle and came to the bars, held on to them just like you see in movies.

"The better man. But he wasn't," she whispered. Then she lifted her head toward the ceiling and started singing, "Itsy bitsy spider climbed up the water spout . . ." while making the climbing motions with her fingers.

I'd bring her some towels, a washcloth and shampoo next time I came. I squeezed her fingers, noticed her nails were in better shape than my own and waved goodbye. Somebody at Juanita's had evidently done a gratis manicure for the June bride. The bride who wasn't to be. She didn't seem upset at all.

I bet Ossie wasn't buying any of this as anything but typical Littleboro craziness. Just some unfortunate somebody

lying on a picnic table out by the Interstate. And an aban-
doned room at Motel 3 that he'd asked Bruce, who handed
the job off to Allison, to tape off as a crime scene until he got
around to investigating it. Let Reba cool it off in jail. A confession from her wasn't worth a hill of beans, as Mama Alice
would say.

I was the only one upset. I was the only one in danger.
Unless it was Butch Rigsbee. And where the hell was he?
Rigsbee's wife must have seen me go into the room at Motel
3, asked Allison my name and so forth. Maybe she had waited
for me at the Dixie Dew with some awful plan in mind. Kid-
napping? Taking me out somewhere in the boondocks and
doing me in? And why wasn't she trying to find her husband?
I was only in this thing because Reba got me involved. And I
was in it up to my neck.

Chapter Eight

The wallet was the ticket to all this confusion.

I stormed back to the Dixie Dew. On Lady Bug's front seat, I riffled through the bundle I had planned to take Reba but forgot, I was so intent on confronting Ossie. Maybe it was better that I had forgotten. She didn't need her bridal dress and flip-flops and even seeing them would only remind her of God and the better man and Ossie hauling her in and that would start her crying again.

The wallet wasn't there. I unrolled Reba's dress, laid the flip-flops on the seat, shook out the dress and no wallet. Well, dammit. I knew I had put the thing in there when I left the motel room to go sit in Pastor Pittman's car but it wasn't there. I felt around on the seat, under the seat. Nothing. No wallet.

Mama Alice used to say I would lose my head if it wasn't fastened onto me.

I folded everything back together, laid it on the seat and got out.

Maybe the wallet had fallen out in the Motel 3 parking lot, never even made it to my car.

Ten minutes later Lady Bug and I pulled in the empty parking lot at Motel 3, a depressing sight if there ever was one. What had once been ten units that stayed freshly painted and respectable as a mom-and-pop motel could be, now had only two rooms ready to rent. Since the Motel 3 franchise had bought it last year and torn down a good portion of it, the remaining buildings stood surrounded by scaffolding and construction waste. Even in daylight it looked like the set for some down-and-out drama production, a dark murder mystery. The piles of rubble pushed behind the buildings provided a perfect backdrop of chaos. A big yellow bulldozer sat atop the rubble.

I looked around the parking lot, which was littered with cigarette butts, checked very carefully the area where Pastor Pittman's car had been parked, and then around the door of the room where Reba and her "intended" had their tête-à-tête, their last supper. Yellow crime scene tape still blocked it off.

I rang the doorbell outside the end unit marked OFFICE. Background sounds of Dr. Phil's TV pop-psychology advice show drifted out. "And just when was the last time you had contact with your last lover?" I heard him ask amid the wailing sobs of a woman. The door unlocked and Allison stuck out a hand holding a lit cigar. One of those smaller, more dainty ones aimed at women smokers.

"Beth?" She opened the door wider. "What are you doing back here?" She motioned for me to come in. Before I could answer, she clicked off Dr. Phil from the oversized flat-screen TV, then went behind the desk and picked up her coffee cup. "I only got one room available now. Looks like Ossie is trying to put me out of business."

Allison and her best friend Andrea had been the Littleboro High School bad, bad girls. Rumor was that the two of them had written their phone numbers on all the men's restroom walls all over town. I wondered if the numbers had faded or the two kept the paint fresh and kept Motel 3 in business. If so, it sure didn't look from the outside that business was booming.

"Don't talk to me about 'Mr. Ossie,' as Reba calls him," I said.

Inside was a different story. A new-looking leather sofa took up half the room. There were matching glass coffee and end tables, and a huge hanging copper light fixture. The biggest flat-screen television I'd ever seen covered one wall. In the corner stood a whole modified kitchen unit with refrigerator and a microwave oven, one of those fancy espresso and latte maker units. I knew because I'd priced one of the coffee thingies for the Dixie Dew: $450 just for the coffeemaker. Everything looked top quality. Very nice indeed. Who would have expected such fine, expensive furnishings inside this run-down remains of a motel?

"I lost something when I was here and wondered if you found it," I said.

"Oh, okay. I was kidding about the room earlier. Didn't think you'd come to rent it, seeing as how you got a big house full of rooms over at your Dixie Dew."

Was that meant as a dig? Did she know how desperate my bed-and-breakfast business was these days?

She reached behind her to shut the door to a bedroom, but not before I saw the rumpled sheets of a king-sized bed and what looked like somebody still in it. Was this where she and Andy lived? Did all this make sense? Fix up the living quarters first, spend your franchise loan fast and furious on "the best," then deal with trying to get the business going and make some money. I'd done the opposite. I'd fixed up the dining room, guest bedrooms, and the outside of the house. The rest would have to be done later. The plaster ceiling in my bedroom had gaps big as the map of Texas, and the living room . . . I couldn't even think where to start on it.

"Haven't touched that room," Allison said, her right hand on her heart and her left arm raised as if she was swearing she was telling the whole truth and nothing but the truth. "Haven't found anything you'd be interested in either."

"A man's wallet?" I asked.

"Describe it." She looked at the ceiling.

"Black leather, old, curled at the corners. Had photos in it. Driver's license. That sort of thing."

Allison reached in a drawer of the desk and pulled out a black wallet, held it over her head.

"That's it," I said, and reached for it.

She held it out at arm's length behind her. "Doesn't look like anything that would belong to you. Why do you want it?"

"I want to take it to Reba. I think it belonged to her friend, Butch Rigsbee."

I lied, crossed my fingers behind my back. So what if I did not intend to take it to Reba? But now I would have proof that the guy flat out on the picnic table was not the Butch Rigsbee in the wallet's photo.

"He who? Butch? He's one of our regulars. Has been for a couple years. Stays here on his route to Florida and back. Funny guy. Good-time guy. We've talked of putting in a bar and naming it after him. Always flashing a roll, and Lord, what a roll." She flapped the wallet back and forth over her head. "There was not one bill in it when I found it. Empty as this town." Then she started flipping through the photo flaps in the wallet. "But if you say you're taking it to Reba, then you better be taking it to her. I don't want to get mixed up in any-thing not on the up-and-up. I have a reputation to protect."

I almost said "Ha," but checked myself.

Allison rolled her eyes, laughed a little. "Butch had this thing going with Reba. She thought he was going to marry her. We like to have laughed our heads off. Then she took up with our handyman who wasn't all that handy, but was the only one of us who knew how to crank and run a bulldozer."

"So where is this Butch now?" Maybe he was who I saw in Allison's bed before she closed the door.

"On his regular Florida run I guess. He was here Friday night." She lit a new cigar, waved out the match and tossed it in an ashtray already overrun with spent matches and butts. "His truck's gone. Gone when I got up this morning."

"The white truck was out by the Interstate and Bruce drove

it into town." I gave her that information but I think surely she already knew all this. Had Bruce not explained anything when he asked her to seal off the room? I guess he didn't have to. Police business with our "trained professionals" had to remain confidential.

"Oh"—Allison blew a smoke ring toward the TV—"then I guess he must be still around here somewhere." She came from behind the desk, looked out the back and used a remote to close some very expensive window treatments. "That's what I told the woman who came looking for him. She saw you come out of the room, then get in the car with Pastor Pittman. She was so mad she could have spit tenpenny nails."

I reached for the wallet.

"Nothing doing." Allison held it tight.

I waited.

"I thought Butch might be in trouble with all the Reba marriage and stuff, but this woman only wanted the money he was carrying. She threatened me about stealing all the money. Me! Little ole me! Money was all that woman had on her mind."

"What money?" I asked.

Allison gave me a hard look. "Honey, if you don't know dirty business when it's right in your face, then you don't know anything in this world."

With that she threw the wallet at me. Whiz-bang. I grabbed it as it hit the door behind me, fell to the floor. I picked it up and made a fast exit, didn't even say thank you.

Well, I thought as I stood outside. So much for manners. I turned the wallet over in my hand. Oops. The wallet Allison had thrown at me wasn't Butch Rigsbee's wallet. This wallet was smaller, newer and must have been buried somewhere. It stunk like a landfill or the bottom of a dumpster. Phew. And it was totally empty. Not even a photo, just the blank plastic holders with not a face among them.

"Wait," I said but she had slammed shut the door.

I tried the knob. It didn't turn. Had she locked it? Locked me out? Damn. I knocked very nicely. "Allison?" I called.

She didn't come to the door and I heard the TV turned up full blast. She didn't *intend* to come to the door. I stood there holding the wrong wallet. One that wouldn't do me the least bit of good or prove a thing to Ossie.

As I turned Lady Bug around in the parking lot I noticed a red truck, spattered with paint and rust, parked behind the office unit. Randy's red truck? Randy, who sometimes worked with Scott on construction projects and music gigs. Is that who was in Allison's bed?

I had not seen Randy with Scott lately. Had they parted ways? He'd seemed a nice guy, sort of Scott's right-hand man, but come to think of it, Scott had not mentioned him lately. Randy was also one of Scott's musician friends. Had they done any gigs together recently? Scott was going to play keyboards for Mayor Moss's trashion show fund-raiser on Sunday afternoon.

Things and people in Littleboro surprised you sometimes. Just when you thought you had somebody and something all figured out, they took a left turn. I thought I remembered Scott saying Randy was married, but that didn't necessarily mean he was happily married. Was anybody ever happily married? I shifted gears and headed home to the Dixie Dew.

Chapter Nine

Ida Plum took one look at me, and instead of her usual cluck-ing and fussing made me cream of tomato soup and a grilled cheese sandwich, told me she had sheets to hang on the line and then she was going to iron awhile. She was the only per-son in the world I knew who actually *liked* to iron. I liked to hear the *thump, whump* of the ironer that did mainly our bed linens. Regular clothes ironing had to be done the regular way. Board and steam, hand guiding the iron. Mama Alice taught me how to iron, starting with handkerchiefs, her aprons, pillowcases and dish towels. Dish towels! Who even used handkerchiefs anymore? She said it was one sure way to kill germs and most people didn't know that.

Then she graduated me to blouses, skirts and dresses.

When I got to art school I met girls in the dorm who'd never plugged in an iron. I had to teach them to press creases in their jeans when they "dressed up" for dates. Otherwise all of us wore our jeans like a second layer of skin, just not washed as often. The more paint caked your clothes, the more impressive. A pallet of paint colors were like merit badges showing how serious an artist you were, how hardworking.

"You look done in," Ida Plum said over a heaped laundry basket of wet sheets. "You need a nap."

She'd read my mind, which was a frequent occurrence.

"Not even thinking about a nap," I said. "Got food to do for the mayor's big trashion thing. And paperwork in my office."

I thought ironing would be much more pleasant with its certain soothing rhythm and the wonderful smell of clean—soap and water and sunshine—than what I had to do.

I had lied about the paperwork. I did not plan to go to the little Dixie Dew office that used to be Mama Alice's pantry and bury myself under the stack of forms and bills and just plain stuff. I had other plans.

I finished the last of my iced tea (June is the time I mostly switch to the iced stuff, but sometimes, at stressed as well as quiet moments, only the hot kind will do), put my dishes in the dishwasher and sneaked out the front door.

Chapter Ten

If the wallet wasn't at Motel 3 and not in Lady Bug where was it? Somewhere, it had to be somewhere. I must have dropped it, but where? Where had I been with this stuff for Reba before I put it in Lady Bug?

Of course. Pastor Pittman's car. And where would that car be now? Home, if he wasn't out rounding up "lost sheep." Pittman lived in the Presbyterian manse three streets over behind the Dixie Dew.

I cut through several backyards and onto Iona Street, where I saw the two-story redbrick Williamsburg-style house with black shutters that had always been the Presbyterian manse. Hadn't changed a bit. I went to a lot of Presbyterian

Youth Club things there. Weiner roasts, scavenger hunts, volleyball games.

There had never been a garage. So where did he park his car? I walked up the flagstone walk between the two rows of boxwoods, thinking, thinking. And smelling. American box-woods are bigger than their sibling English ones and have a pleasant lemony herb scent. Nice, but I didn't have time to stop and smell the boxwoods.

When I got to the front door, I decided not to ring the doorbell. What would I say? I want to look in your car to see if I dropped something, but I can't tell you what? I walked around back to try to find the car. Maybe a garage had been added on over the years.

I was right. There in back of the manse was a double ga-rage and lucky, lucky day, both garage doors were up. I could pop in, check inside the car and no questions asked. No ex-plaining to do.

The garage was dark. Pastor Pittman's silver BMW was there, parked serenely next to a sporty Carolina-blue Miata convertible. His other car, a fun car, or Mrs. Pittman's? Hers, I decided. The dome light came on when I opened the door of the BMW. I didn't see anything on the seat. I crawled in to check the floor. I felt under the seat. Nothing.

Just as I started to back out, someone said, "You trying to steal my car?"

I started to rise up. It was Pastor Pittman.

"No, no, no," I said from my compromising position on my knees, butt in the air.

"Beth McKenzie?" He laughed. A nice laugh. He gently

shook his head side to side like he was saying to himself, Not again. Not this girl who keeps popping up in all kinds of places. Here she is on all fours in my car. "So," he said, "if it's not my car you're after, you must have designs on me, then?"

"No, no," I said again and felt my face flush. "Just looking for something."

"And did you find it?" he asked, leaning in so close I felt his body heat.

"Not yet. Just something I thought I left in your car, or dropped when we were at the motel this morning. I didn't want to disturb you."

"No problem. Can I help you look?" he asked.

"Thanks, but no." I straightened up. "It's not that important." It was, but not to him, just to me and Reba and maybe Ossie, and maybe whoever that was sprawled across the picnic table by the Interstate.

I thanked him and waved goodbye. He stood there shaking his head, looking totally confused, as though this town and some of the people who lived here were beyond his comprehension.

What next? Where next? The only place left where that wallet could possibly be was back where I had originally found it: Motel 3. Allison had played games with me.

Lied like a rug. And I sure didn't want to go back for more, but that had to be where it was. Should I go trucking over there now or put it off and maybe Allison would be a bit friendlier, forget she'd thrown a wallet at me? Cool down, calm down. Maybe she thought she was being cute—but I just didn't think so. I thought she was hiding something bigger than a wallet.

I decided no good would come of procrastination so I cranked Lady Bug and back we chugged to Motel 3.

At Motel 3, Allison had parked her cleaning cart in front of the room where Reba and the mystery man had their fateful picnic. The door was open, the crime scene tape taken down. That sure was some fast "collecting evidence from a crime scene" if indeed that's what Bruce had done.

"Knock, knock," I said as I marched right in.

Allison had the vacuum cleaner going and a radio playing reggae music, but she turned around. "You must like this place. You keep coming back like some warped boomerang."

I didn't answer.

She turned off the vacuum, came from behind the bed. "What now?" She stood with her arms crossed across her wide and blooming chest.

"The wallet, please." I held out my hand. "The real one this time."

"I don't know what on earth makes you think you have to have the damn thing. There's no money in it." She now stood with both hands on her hips. A defiant pose if there ever was one. A pose that said, you're going to have to knock me down and take it.

"Believe it or not, it's not money I'm after."

"I don't believe it. Everybody in this world is after money. The most they can get and get away with." She gave a long, lingering sigh.

"I need the pictures . . . the photos." I was tired of playing games with her.

"I should have buried the thing." Allison reached down and pulled the wallet from between the mattress and box springs. "Take it if you think it's going to do you any good. Been bad luck for me."

She handed it to me with a kind of good-riddance thrust.

I knew that wallet was not between the mattress and box springs when Bruce did the room for evidence. Even if he or someone else had done a cursory job, they would have found it. Anything between the mattress and box springs was an old, old cliché of a hiding place. Anyone would look there first. Allison probably had the wallet the whole time. But why?

This time I said, "Thank you very much," whirled around and left as fast as I could, got out the door before she changed her mind and tried to snatch it back. Life had sure seemed to toughen up Allison. Remembering the rumors I'd heard in high school as well as fairly recent ones, she wasn't somebody I wanted to trust. Not even with an empty wallet.

Chapter Eleven

This time when I went into the police headquarters I stopped to speak to Wanda Purncell, who only sighed and nodded me toward Ossie's office, where he was at his computer working. He sat bent to the screen, staring intently. Even the set of his shoulders said, I'm into serious business here. Don't interrupt me.

"I got it," I said and waved the wallet.

He looked up and blinked, like he was asking, Who are you? What do you want and it better be important?

I said, "Proof. You wanted proof the guy on the picnic table that Reba absolutely did not kill is not the husband who is missing. The husband of this bonko lady who's threatening me. Here it is."

He reached for the wallet.

I held it away from him, flipped it open to the photos. "This," I said and pointed to the photo, "is the woman who is threatening me. And *this* is Butch Rigsbee, who I think Reba kept calling God." I told him about the phone call at Motel 3 and my other suspicions that this woman was following me and meant to do me harm and that Allison said Butch Rigsbee had left, but his truck was the one Bruce drove here. "The one right out there in your parking lot." I pointed out the window, but Ossie didn't even look.

Instead he took the wallet, glanced at the photos, opened it all the way flat and felt in the compartment that would have held cash. "It's empty," he said, folded it back together and slid it in his desk drawer.

"That's evidence," I said, shocked at his nonchalance. "Aren't you going to tag and bag it?"

"Tell me something I don't already know." He turned back to his computer.

"I know this woman is threatening me. Threatening me with bodily harm. And her husband is missing. Missing. Maybe murdered." When I said it, my voice shook and I felt like crying. "She called me a hussy."

"So, are you?"

"Am I what?"

"A hussy." His voice almost sounded like it had half a chuckle in it. He gave a dismissive wave of his hand. "Little girl, go home. You are into something you don't know anything about."

"But . . ." I said.

He didn't even look up.

I let myself out and when I walked by Wanda's desk she gave me a look of pure sympathy and an uplifted finger of a wave that seemed to say, Honey, you just got a taste of what I work with every day. Goodbye and good luck.

Near the back entrance I saw Bruce Bechner's office. Hmmm, I thought. Maybe Bruce would be the one to get his mind on what was going on in Littleboro since he didn't have wedding jitters.

I opened the door and poked my head in. No Bruce. The office was empty except for a desk, a file cabinet, a one-cup coffeemaker and a whole windowsill of African violets in a profusion of purples and pinks and whites.

Out the window I saw the white van and on Bruce's desk lay a set of keys that looked like a jangle of truck keys.

"Hmm," I said, out loud this time.

I picked up the keys, went out the back door and jogged over to the truck. I knew Ossie could see me from his office, but my latest encounter with him told me he wasn't interested in anything I said or did. I'd bet anything he still had his nose glued to that computer screen.

I tried one of the keys in the rear lock and heard a rumbling noise as the gate lifted. Nearly scared me to death. I jumped back. Who knew that was the right key and that it worked the lift gate? The gate rose very slowly until the whole interior of the truck was wide open. Wide open to dark and more dark. Empty. There was nothing in that truck bed but a small stack of white boxes. I climbed into the truck bed and opened one of the boxes. Rows of dozens of new orange prescription bottles. Empty ones. Was Butch hauling pharmacy supplies?

So what was all this fuss about?

I closed the boxes, jumped down and pushed the button to lower the gate, all the while checking to see if Ossie or Bruce had seen me or heard something.

All was still. All was quiet.

I slipped back in the office to lay the keys exactly where I found them on Bruce's desk. I tiptoed in and was ready to lay the keys very carefully and without a single jangle when I felt a big, heavy hand hot on my shoulder. "Ohhhhhh," I said and pivoted into a tall and wide masculine body. Bruce Bechner.

"Hey there," he said. "Admiring my babies?"

I held my breath, backed up and very slowly laid the keys on the desktop. Not a single jingle jangle sounded. Whew.

"Ba-babies?" I stuttered.

"My violets." He smiled and lifted his chin. "There," he indicated. "On the windowsill. The light is perfect. Aren't they amazing?"

"Beautiful," I said. "Just beautiful."

He walked to the window, lifted up a fluffy pink African violet, said, "This pretty little girl is my Apache Primrose. One of my best sellers. At home I got two basement rooms filled with these violets in every shade of pink, purple and white. Some double, triple, some big, some small. Every week mama and me ship out dozens . . . all over the country. You'd be surprised how popular these things are."

"I'm sure," I said. "You really must have a green thumb."

"Not green." He placed the potted African violet back on the sill, "They're easy to grow."

I told him about the wallet I'd just given Ossie, that it was proof the man Reba *thought* she killed was not the one she was engaged to, who was a Butch Rigsbee who sounded like one of Allison's regulars and whose presence in Littleboro was unaccounted for.

He scratched the side of his face, but listened intently, thanked me and headed down the hall toward Ossie's office.

In the parking lot, I jumped in Lady Bug and scooted back to the Dixie Dew. Those keys on that desk were too easy. Too deliberate. They were either meant for somebody to find or simply there because Littleboro's "trained professionals" were totally inept.

Either way I'd found something, but I didn't know what I'd found. Certainly no body and no money. But I had recovered that wallet and turned it over to Ossie and that was one step toward finding out what was going on with this latest crime caper, maybe even a murder, in Littleboro. Not good stuff.

❊┼┼❊

Chapter Twelve

In the Dixie Dew kitchen Ida Plum poured me iced tea and put the pitcher back in the fridge. At the Dixie Dew we don't use the regular pound-of-sugar-per-tea-bag recipe. We leave it unsweetened and offer a sugar syrup, and always have fresh lemon at the ready. Mama Alice used to say, "We boil water to steep it, ice to cool it, sugar to sweeten it and lemon to spike it."

"I think one of our guests may be a judge for the festival. Or both of them," Ida Plum said. "They seemed to know each other."

Festival. I was so involved with Reba and her God thing and the missing Butch Rigsbee that I'd pushed the whole shindig out of my mind. Not only did the Green Bean Festi-

val have Scott gainfully employed for odds and ends but all
of Littleboro was buzzing both pro and con. Who would
come to our little town to celebrate the green bean? Who
cared? Who even liked the stuff? We might as well salute
something that had more guts and glory, like the black-eyed
pea, for gosh sakes. Or as Ida Plum had said, "Creasy greens.
Now they are something special. Or collards."

Littleboro's lady mayor, the Honorable Calista Moss, had
hatched the idea for something to put our "precious little village" on the map: a Green Bean Festival. What did we grow
in Littleboro that grew better and more abundantly than
anywhere else? Green beans! There was to be a cooking contest, a parade and as many activities to do with green beans
as she and her committees could come up with.

Last week Mayor Moss announced she was throwing a
wingding of a fund-raiser, something she called a trashion
show. What this had to do with celebrating the green bean,
I didn't know, but it was a gala event. Our Miz Mayor said
she expected a lot of "in" people would come. I guess they
would have to be the "in" people. I sure didn't know anyone
here in Littleboro who would go. After the committee meeting when I told Ida Plum, she thought this was the craziest
idea she'd heard yet. She had to hit her sides she laughed so
much.

"Trashion," I told Ida Plum, "is your kind of thing, right
up your alley. Making something out of nothing. Making do,
recycling. Taking something that would be thrown away and
turning it into, in this case, a wearable outfit. And having a
fashion show with models to show off the creation. Malinda
plans to wear a strapless ball gown made from several

purple plastic table cloths decorated with white polka dot prescription bottle caps."

"This I'll have to see to believe," Ida Plum peeked over my shoulder at Miz Mayor's registration form. "People wearing trash. I heard about people talking trash and people called trailer trash and just plan trash, trash, but taking garbage and wearing it? You gotta show me because I don't think it can be done. That mayor's going to be the laughingstock of Little-boro before all this is over."

"Trashion," she turned on her heel and went back to the kitchen. "Umph, some people around here don't have enough to do."

Chapter Thirteen

Scott and I don't talk business unless it is Dixie Dew business and lately that had been at the bottom of his list. I worried my gazebo was not even on his to-do list. I had also resolved not to nag. A gentle prod was as far in that direction as I planned to go, even if I could see some panic in my future when the Dixie Dew hosted Ossie and Juanita's wedding "on the green" with no gazebo in sight. I could do that—all cash for the coffers—but not happily. Ossie wasn't anywhere near my list of favorite people, but I did want this wedding to be sweet and beautiful, if not perfect, for Juanita's sake. I knew there was no accounting for taste when it came to choosing a mate, and besides, it was none of my business. Juanita would have to live with her choice, not me.

I had no idea what the trashion show had to do with green beans or what exactly the funds raised were to be used for. The cooking competition I could see, though I wondered what in the world one could cook with green beans besides the ubiquitous casserole with fried onions and mushroom soup. My vision for cooking creatively with green beans was mostly limited to the Thanksgiving casserole, but Mama Alice cooked them with fat back and potatoes. I ate the potatoes.

Other planned events were the crowning of Miss Green Bean, maybe a street dance or two, some music groups, some craft booths around town. Anybody who had something to sell that people had been living perfectly well heretofore without would be hawking their wares. Oh, this Green Bean Festival was going to be a hoot. Last week Malinda and I had been laughing about it, daring each other to run for Miss Green Bean.

"Can't you see 'Miss Green Bean' on your résumé some fifty years from now?" Malinda had hooted, both arms raised. "Or in your obituary?"

We then composed an imaginary obituary for *The Mess*.

I began, "Miss Vita Sue Hanly, age ninety-eight, died quietly in her sleep at the home where she was born and lived all her life . . ."

". . . excepting her four undergraduate years at Woman's College, where she majored in Interior Design, minored in French," Malinda added.

"Miss Hanly was an accomplished botanical artist. Her watercolors have been reproduced on note cards and sold widely," I continued.

Malinda and I laughed again. Miss Hanly would have had the note cards printed up herself and they would have gathered dust beside the register at Gaddy's Drug Store. When had anybody in Littleboro ever written a note card except for funerals or weddings, and then the paper was always plain white?

"Miss Hanly was crowned Miss Green Bean at the first Littleboro Green Bean Festival, which she said was one of the highlights of her life," Malinda said, finishing her imaginary obituary.

Poor thing. That's Littleboro, I thought. They never forget. And they don't let you forget either. The past is always present in Littleboro.

Together Malinda and I had visualized this woman on her deathbed with a crown of green beans (either dried or plastic) adorning her tight little white curls, or whatever sprigs of hair she had left.

And Scott, when he heard about the festival idea, had said, "My gosh. Green beans. They aren't even sexy. Peaches are sexy." He rounded his hands in the air like the shape of a peach. "Plums. Grapes. I could go for that. Pears? Even a pomegranate or two, but beans! Beans, beans, they're good for your heart. The more you eat the more you—" Ida Plum snapped the dish towel at him before he could finish the rhyme and shooed him out the door.

My Dixie Dew kitchen was a dropping-in spot for Malinda on her way to work at Gaddy's Drug Store, and Scott, if he happened to be "passing," as he said, between whatever renovating job he had going and Lowe's or Honeycutt Lumber in Aberdeen or, like today, building booths at the fairgrounds.

If he had spent the night, which he did on an irregular basis, and was there at breakfast when Ida Plum came in, she never said a word. Just lifted an eyebrow, turned her back and began doing whatever needed doing in the Dixie Dew kitchen, shrugging her shoulders as if to say, I know what you two are doing and you can't fool me a bit.

Malinda's friendship livened my life, distracted me from adding up figures and looking at them in the red most of the time. What was I doing in a town that didn't have a future? It had lots of past. I was surrounded by it. Big old falling-down houses that would take somebody pots of money to restore and not a lot of brains if they thought they could do it. But sometimes people like Calista Moss and her Mr. Moss showed up, bought the big old white house on the hill next to Miss Tempie's estate and began pouring money into it. People with big bucks. People with deep pockets. One house getting new life and next to it, Miss Tempie's castle was falling down more every day. Kudzu had already claimed most of it, and her handyman was in jail somewhere.

Only a big old gray-blue barn still stood on Miss Tempie's property. It listed a bit to one side, but still stood. Funny how barns can stand even after some houses go. Barns built of cheap lumber, never heated or cooled, mostly open to the weather, and they stayed tough. Barns are honest structures. And sometimes, like Mayor Moss's barn, they get reinvented, repurposed and lead a glamorous new life.

The Mosses had showed up one day "out of the blue" and started throwing money into the old Hemming house on the hill next to Miss Tempie's kudzu-covered estate. They had a front lawn that took a hardworking landscaper on his John Deere all day to mow. And that was just the front yard.

I'd been in the house once or twice for some committee meeting or other. The first time I went in, I just stood in that living room gazing up at the ceiling. All the moldings and details. The things I dreamed of having at the Dixie Dew. And the fireplace! Marble, with scenes of stags and hunts carved in the mahogany mantel. Thick, thick rugs in maroons and black. Elegant antique furniture, the real stuff. Not like all the *real* real stuff I had at the Dixie Dew that my grandfather Buie had made and some sentimental pieces that had been passed around in the family. Nothing elegant, just old. I never saw the rest of the Mosses' rooms but I could imagine the decor.

Malinda and I had to admit Scott had a point about the festival. Green beans were not sexy, but that was all Littleboro had. No peaches, no plums, not even any vineyards. And there were already a couple of vineyard celebrations, the toasting of the grape going on around the state. Ida Plum had been to some, and could talk about "the tasting of the grape." But green beans? Kale would have had more appeal. Kale has a lovely leaf and I could think of a lot of ways to cook and eat kale. I could think of some artsy-craftsy things to do with leaves of kale. Stitch them together to make a sort of sun hat. Or a cloche. Roll them into beads, dip in wallpaper paste, let dry, string for jewelry. Spray with Krylon and decorate a wreath for doors. Spray gold, make a fan. But green beans? I wasn't even close to any craft ideas.

"Beans," Ida Plum had said. "We'll be the laughingstock of festivals. Beating out even Miss Liver Mush over in Shelby."

"Not in my book," I said. "I've only tasted liver mush once in my life and that was the last time." I shook my shoulders in a shudder. "Yuck. I'd take a bean over liver mush any day and time. And fields of green beans instead of acres of hog farms like they have in Smithfield."

I had to admit our honorable mayor was a cut above most of the women in Littleboro. For example, she wore shoes with kitten heels every day, not just to church, and shopped at Talbot's—and places of the same expensive conservative ilk or above—in Raleigh. She had come to grace our village when I was living in Maine, and I didn't know exactly where she came from or when. She'd done the ribbon cutting (pink, of course) when I opened The Pink Pineapple Tea and Thee here in the Dixie Dew. Class. I needed some class and she added it. Got us on the front page of *The Littleboro Messenger.* Not that I had crowds breaking down the doors in the days or weeks afterwards. She did take some of my business cards and said she'd pass them out whenever she could. I'd take all the good publicity available out there anywhere. Dark, gray, bad stuff had seemed to hover over the Dixie Dew at times. First my grandmother's fatal fall, then Miss Lavinia Lovingood in my Azalea Room the second day the Dixie Dew was open for business.

Ida Plum wiped the counter and said, "Scott is building some new freestanding booths for the festival. Those old ones at the fairgrounds rotted away years ago."

I hoped he was building better "convenience facilities." I couldn't remember the last time I went to a fair in Littleboro. Did we still have a county fair? When I was growing up it wasn't much, a flimsy Ferris wheel, couple of spinning rides, church booths selling hot dogs and some displays of big pumpkins, watermelons, things that got blue ribbons. And the homemaking arts. All those jams and jellies and food canned in jars that had been sterilized in oversized pressure cookers. I remembered seeing gleaming jars of perfect green beans arranged like art and wearing fat blue ribbons.

I remembered, too, the county fair was the first time I'd ever seen an outhouse. This one was a two-seater: had two holes cut side by side in the sitting place. I remembered pointing to it with Mama Alice, who laughed, which made me laugh.

I told Ida Plum about this. She said what was funny was calling them convenience facilities. "Why not call an outhouse an outhouse? You call a horse a horse, not a cow. What are we doing to the language these days? Of course our mayor doesn't want a lot of those little plastic tents set up all over the place for booths," Ida Plum said. "You got to give her credit. She's got taste."

"I bet she won't let the fairgrounds have any of those plastic convenience facilities either," I said. Personally I thought the purple ones were kinda cute. I'd vote for purple, but I'd bet if the things came in green, Mayor Moss would order them that color to coordinate with the theme of the festival.

"So who is tasting the Green Bean Cook-off?" I asked, as I stirred honey and lemon in my jasmine tea.

"Surely not Mayor Moss." Somehow I couldn't see her photo in *The Mess* with a fork in front of her face, maybe a pucker of pure yuck on her lips. "Who would want to taste whatever concoction somebody could come up with made mainly of green beans?" Just the thought made my next swallow of tea less than delicious. I remembered the green stain on Reba's "victim" on the picnic table, the sour taste when I did CPR.

"Our judges." Ida Plum went to the oven, and came back with hot lemon scones on a blue-checked tea towel. "The two staying here showed me their cards. Professionals, graduate degrees from some cooking schools, chef here, chef there. A food writer and a retired home economics teacher from Care-lock U. I'd say between them they know foods."

Carelock University was a little bitty college set in the north end of the county—three brick buildings, a gym and a li-brary, all established by Miss Idabelle Lucier from "Yankee Land" over a hundred years ago. She was reported to have said, "Those Southern girls are so beautiful, but unless they get some education, they are doomed to lead simple lives." The reason the college was as far away from the town of Little-boro as it could be was that the founding fathers didn't want all those rowdy female students tearing up things, not to men-tion being too much of an influence on "our innocent young people." Over the years there was not only a definite town-and-gown feeling, but almost an invisible wall.

"My, my," I said. "If they're judging scones, you get a triple-A rating for these. Lemon curd the secret ingredient?"

Ida Plum ignored my question, let a smile curl up her lips on one side. "The woman who came in right behind them didn't look like a judge of anything except of humankind in general. Had her nose so far out of joint, if she followed it, she'd end up in Alaska."

I laughed. "Our third guest at the Dixie Dew?"

"She's an odd duck if there ever was one." Ida Plum took the plate of scones away from my side of the table, turned and put them on the counter behind her. "That woman—she, or maybe he, is a big one."

"Heavyset?" I asked. Not using the word "fat," of course. That was not polite. My grandmother would have called some large person heavyset. You never ever referred to someone as "fat."

"Not that." Ida Plum paused. "More like muscled. Like solid all over. As if she was a weight lifter or a lady wrestler of some sort. But what would somebody like that be doing in Littleboro?"

Lady wrestler? Oh, my. Fear jumped on the back of my neck and grabbed me around the throat. Mrs. Butch Rigsbee, the woman in the photos in the wallet in the motel room. Could it be her? And here she was a guest in my bed-and-breakfast. A woman under my roof who had just hours ago threatened to find me and kill me. Yikes. Double yikes!

My tea and scones didn't feel so comfortable in my stomach anymore.

"Odd woman," Ida Plum said. "Checked in and an hour later checked out."

"What?" I asked. Checking out had been the joke batted around town when Miss Lavinia, my first guest at the Dixie Dew, had died.

"Stayed in her room about an hour," Ida Plum said, "came downstairs and said she'd changed her mind. She had to be going."

"Going where?"

"Didn't say," Ida Plum said, "just asked me to give her a refund. I tore up the credit card receipt and threw it in the trash, hadn't actually charged it yet."

"As you should have. How in the world could you charge for an hour? Unless, of course, you were Motel 3." I started to laugh. "Did you check the room? Had she taken a nap or something?"

"Not a thing out of place that I could tell. She must have washed her face. One washcloth was wet, and she'd hung it across the towel rack to dry, real ladylike."

"That's all?"

"And she raised one of the windows," Ida Plum said.

"That's really odd. What was her name? And did you find out where she was from? What she was doing in Littleboro?"

"Real closemouthed." Ida Plum stood and put the cream in the refrigerator, then closed the door and leaned back against it. "I didn't get a word out of her, come to think of it. I even asked her if there was some problem with the room."

"Credit card," I said, suddenly realizing. I dashed to the trash can, started going through it. Paper towels, coffee grounds, tea bags. Finally I found what looked like a credit card receipt. Or pieces of it.

"And now it's not only shredded but those wet coffee grounds have probably erased any information. Damn," I said. "And double damn."

At the desk in the front hall I opened the guest register book, ran my finger down the page and read the last entry in all caps, "KATE SPADE, IN PERSON IN THIS DUMP," followed by three question marks and two exclamation points. Mrs. Butch Rigsbee's idea of a joke I guess.

Ida Plum didn't ask why I was so interested in this weird guest and I didn't explain. It didn't seem quite the time.

"Don't blame me." Ida Plum shrugged. "Just doing my job and what has increasingly become more of *your* job."

I held the limp bits of paper in my hand and wondered what in the world was going on in Littleboro. People who checked into a place only to wash their face and leave? People who made threats against other people's lives? Now she was not only here in Littleboro but *loose* in Littleboro, probably looking for her husband's motel lover, the one who answered the phone when she called. Looking for me? Even the Dixie Dew did not feel so safe anymore. And I wasn't the one she was looking for, but did she know that?

"What kind of car was she driving?" I went to the window thinking, hoping I might see an unfamiliar vehicle. "Or was she on foot?"

"Why are you so full of questions?" Ida Plum asked, as she picked up our plates and headed toward the dishwasher. "I had no reason to be suspicious of anything."

"You aren't suspicious when a guest checks in and leaves after one hour?" I repeated, "One hour?"

Ida Plum raised both arms in the air. She had her back to me and I read the body language that said she was a bit perturbed. Ida Plum was not often perturbed.

"I only work here," Ida Plum said, her voice tight and strained.

She came back to the table, picked up the plate that was empty of scones. "And you . . ." She paused. "You aren't telling me all I need to know."

That's when I knew I had to tell her about Mrs. Butch

Rigsbee and how she'd yelled threats at me over her husband's cell phone. So I did.

"In it again, aren't you?" she said. "Why can't you stay out of trouble? Why? Why? Why?" She raised both hands in the air and went back to the sink.

Chapter Fourteen

Needless to say I didn't sleep much that Saturday night. Not only did I have the catering job to do for our Miz Mayor and her trashion event, but I did keep reminding myself that the lady wrestler, Mrs. God or Mrs. Butch Rigsbee or whoever she was, wasn't sleeping under my roof. Somehow I knew she was loose somewhere out there in Littleboro or staying somewhere she could watch my every move. Watch and wait. I bet that was her idea. Then she'd kill me one way or another and I never even laid eyes on her husband. I didn't know which was worse, being hunted by somebody out there in Littleboro or somebody holed up somewhere just waiting for the perfect opportunity to do me in. I finally drifted off.

Sometime in the early, early Sunday-morning hours I

dreamed there was an ambulance coming down Main Street, wailing its lungs out. Was it residue from yesterday morning with Crazy Reba and her boyfriend, that body on that picnic table? But then the wailing seemed to come closer and closer, louder, louder still until I thought it was coming up my porch and through the walls right into the Dixie Dew. That's when I sat bolt upright in bed and saw, through the dark and my pulled shades, red and blue flashing lights. I knew then this was no dream. This ambulance was real and right outside my front door. I grabbed a robe and slippers, flew out the door and dashed down the porch steps. There in front of me was a replay of the scene from yesterday: two men and a woman in white uniforms, unloading a stretcher, lowering it to the ground and the lights on the ambulance going around—red, blue, red, blue. But who, who were they loading?

"Stand back, ma'am." One of the guys put his arm out like a crossing guard. "Don't want to crowd her."

"Her?" I tried to get past his arm but he held firm. He'd had experience with the likes of me. But I was no gawker. This was in front of my house. Who was she? Who was flat on the sidewalk? Couldn't be Reba. Ossie had her locked up tight and was probably sitting on the key. Or sleeping with it under his pillow in Juanita's heart-shaped red velvet bed. She'd invited the whole town in for an open house (with refreshments) when she remodeled her beauty shop and redecorated her apartment upstairs. That bed had been talked about for weeks, giggled over behind Juanita's back. "Tacky" was the word most used to describe it.

"I live here," I said.

That's when Verna, who must have heard my voice, piped

up, "Let her through. She's my neighbor." Verna reached both arms toward me.

"Beth McKenzie, honey. Lock my house, then find Robert Redford." I saw the EMTs give each other a look that said something like, We got us a live one here. Should we just drive straight to the loony wing?

One of them held Verna's arm, checking her pulse. Another listened to a stethoscope on her chest. Verna said to him, "You think living with Robert Redford is easy?"

The attendant rolled his eyes.

"Well, it ain't," Verna continued. "That rabbit's got a mind of his own. One minute he's on his leash hopping down the sidewalk pretty as you please, next minute he's got my feet tangled. Down I go, topsy over teakettle, my ass in the air. Excuse me, Lord. And off that rabbit goes dragging that leash behind him. I'm flat on my back and hollering, 'Bob, Bob Redford, you come back here.'"

The attendant straightened up and motioned for another attendant to unbuckle the straps on the stretcher, get it ready to load up Verna.

"If anybody who don't know me, they'd think I was crazy. Well, I'm just lying here on the sidewalk looking up at that dusky sky, thinking not blue sky but ole peeking moon behind the trees, thinking Emily Dickinson and her blue beloved air, and then I felt something funny, but not funny. Pain. Why had it taken a while to kick in? Was I knocked out cold? Anyway, my foot hurt. Hurt like hell. Excuse me again, Lord. Ankle? I tried to wiggle it and hurt worse. Had a bone popped and I didn't hear it?"

The men lifted Verna onto the stretcher, buckled her in.

She waved her arms and said, "Wait. I tried to lift my leg and didn't get it very high. When was the last time I lifted my leg? Then I remembered an old joke my daddy used to tell. He worked in Miller's Hardware forty years."

I just stood there while Verna went on and on. Telling a joke? Maybe she'd hit her head when she fell.

"Name the three parts to a woodstove." Verna laughed.

"Me?" I asked. "I don't know."

"Lifter, leg and poker." Verna haw-hawed.

"I don't get it," I said.

"It's supposed to be a dirty joke," she said. "They all laughed down at the hardware when Daddy told it."

"Just relax," one of the men said, but Verna kept on.

"I wiggled my leg. Foot just flopped. Hurt. Five thirty in the morning, where was anybody? Where was a paperboy? Used to be that little Gurley boy, Nestus—I always liked his name—used to walk by, come up and lay my paper on my porch. All I had to do was crack open my screen door, reach down and there it was. I didn't even have to put on a wrapper. Then Nestus grew up, went to college and old Mr. McNutt took over the route. He'd drive and his wife would roll and throw up papers out the passenger window. She had a good throwing arm, could get it almost to my porch sometimes. Now I don't know who is doing what, little newspaper there is. Sometimes it's in my boxwoods. Or my lilac bushes, or stuck up in one of the dogwood trees. I've had to get a ladder to get my paper down."

"Lady," one of the men said, "we're ready to shut these doors and get you some place you can get some help." I thought his expression meant mental help as well as physical.

Verna was still in her story and she wasn't about to stop in the middle. She held up her hand to stop them closing the double doors. "Now here I was flat on my back and wet from the sidewalk dew creeping into my blouse and britches. Where was anybody? Everybody? I hollered until I was hoarse and prayed somebody wouldn't come running by, stumble and land on top of me. When I heard a car pass, I raised my arm and waved. Nothing. They drove right on by."

"Lady." Two of the attendants stood holding open the doors. "We gotta roll."

"Wait a minute," Verna said. "I'm not through." She reached up, grabbed the lapels of my robe, pulled me closer and whispered, "I was in a state, I tell you. I tried to roll on my side and couldn't. Sidewalk was wet and slick. Sticky wet. I heard somebody's feet fast, fast. Running. Help. I raised both arms. Hel-up. Hel-up. Don't step on me. Hel-up."

"That was enough to stop anybody in their tracks," someone said. A man in blue running shorts had stepped up beside me.

"He's the one." She pointed. "He called 911. Bless the Lord." She blew the man a kiss as the EMTs started to shut the doors. "Find Robert Redford," she called. "Beth, find him!"

The EMT guys revved up the motor and started down the street. I guessed they'd take Verna to Moore Country Medical, then, if her ankle really was broken, she'd go to rehab at The Oaks Nursing and Rest Home, where my grandmother had been those weeks and months after she fell and before she died.

"Is this a scavenger hunt?" the man beside me asked as he

bent over to tie his shoe. "If so, I haven't a clue." He stood up and looked around, held up an imaginary list in front of him and read aloud, "Find body on sidewalk. Stop and call 911, move on to big blue mailbox for next clue." He smiled, a big beam of a smile.

In the excitement I hadn't even noticed anybody around me. This guy didn't look or sound like anybody I knew, certainly not anybody in Littleboro. Looked like custom-made running shoes, I thought, though I wasn't an expert on running attire. My, my. I looked up into the face of the most handsome man I'd ever seen: white-blond hair that fell halfway across his forehead and heavy eyebrows over startling green eyes.

Of course I stuttered introducing myself, almost forgot to extend my hand. When I finally did, he took my hand between both of his almost as if he planned to raise it to his lips and kiss it. Of course if he had I probably would have wet my pants.

"Miles Fortune." He smiled. "And I confess, I'm an addict."

I was startled for a moment. What kind of addict? I didn't know what he meant. For an addict, he sure had nice hands. Smooth, soft and long, long fingers with beautifully manicured nails, which surprised and amazed me. A man with expensive hands.

Scott's hands were tanned and rough, with short but knowing fingers that built things and painted things. Working hands. I loved working hands. They were honest and dependable. Mama Alice always said you could tell a lot about a person from their handshake. Never trust anybody with a limp one, she'd said. Or a cold fish of a handshake. But she never told me about anybody with a sexy handshake.

I stepped back.

"Running." He laughed. "I'm addicted to running. Have to get my run in before I do anything else or I'm a mess for the day."

He ran his fingers through his white-blond hair. "After being on the road all night, the first thing I had to do when I got here was my run. And it was as good a way as any to see a little bit of the town."

"Oh," I said, which probably sounded as silly as I felt standing here in robe and slippers in the fast approaching daylight. And I just happened to be wearing my rattiest robe, the one with a coffee stain down the front. I pulled it closer.

"Had a late flight from L.A., then found an all-night car rental at Raleigh-Durham, drove like the dickens and now have to find breakfast and a place to stay."

"I have breakfast," I said and pointed to the Dixie Dew behind me, which didn't look all that welcoming or friendly with no lights burning. I hadn't even turned on the porch light. I almost said "and a bed," then realized how provocative that might sound.

"It's a bed-and-breakfast," I said.

"Okay," he said. "I'm in the right place."

I told him to finish his run, and by the time he got back I was dressed in one of the two last dresses I owned, a green and pink shirtwaist that matched (if you squinted) my tearoom tablecloths. I had bacon cooked, a breakfast casserole in the oven and the table set. Plus coffee, always coffee. I liked for the smell to waft up the stairs and get my guests mosey-ing on downstairs.

While my two lady guests were eating, he signed the guest register. He put on his credit card two bedrooms. He said he'd take the Lilac Room and didn't give me a name for the per-son who would use the Daffodil Room, which Ida Plum had just cleaned. He did tell me he was with the festival and that he had no idea what a green bean was. He grinned, "Call this a mystery guest."

"Some kind of wild herb?" he had asked. "Like ginseng?" I saw the cutest dimple in his left cheek when he smiled. I get weak-kneed over dimples.

I extolled the virtues of the ubiquitous green bean casse-role that was a must at every Thanksgiving meal, then I told him about the value of green vegetables, vitamins and all that. He listened with his head cocked to one side as if he didn't believe a word I was saying but he liked the way I talked. I've read guys love a Southern accent and I've got a real one. That's one thing I never lost all those years in "Yan-kee Land," as my grandmother called it. Somebody once told me that if you lose your accent, you can never go home again. I never lost mine and here I was, born and bred and back in Littleboro, North Carolina, the Tar Heel state. Home sure stuck to me.

He finished the paperwork and then took his leather duf-fel up the stairs, climbing the steps two at a time. Again, I said to myself, "My, my."

Chapter Fifteen

I served Miss Isabella Buckley and her prize pupil, Debbie Booth, who wrote the food columns for *The News & Observer* and didn't look a thing like her little head-shot photo in the paper—Debbie turned out to be prettier, younger. They were judges for the green bean cooking contest. I was nervous about them judging my B and B food, but they loved the breakfast casserole. It was the standard eggs/milk/cheese thing, but I always added a jolt of red pepper and some ribbons of kale for color. And grits, I do grits in a silver compote with a lid. When you serve grits, they have to be hot. Grits can be country plain or dressed-up fancy. Anybody who has never had shrimp with grits hasn't lived, Mama Alice used to say.

Miss Isabella had retired from teaching home economics at Carelock U ages ago and moved to Glen Aire, a continuous care retirement community in Cary. She had to be nearly eighty, but prissy as ever in her blue voile dress with a lace collar and her little pearl button earrings, the screw-on type. Miss Isabella didn't strike me as someone who would ever allow piercings to her body, not even her ears.

Debbie, on the other hand, was the opposite of prissy. She wore green jeans (maybe in honor of the festival), a cute sweatshirt that had little red chili peppers stamped all over it and red sneakers. She looked as if she couldn't wait to get to this judging business, her red-blond curls bouncing. I bet somewhere on her body she had a tattoo. I tried to guess what it would be. A single red rose? No, not the type. A butterfly? Again no, not the type. I finally decided she'd have a tattoo of a small skillet and the words BON APPETIT above it. Or a tomato? A luscious, ripe one with an exclamation point. Very tasteful, but fun.

She and Miss Isabella left soon after breakfast, saying something about the Liberty Antiques Fair and that they'd be out until late.

Mr. Hollywood, the L.A. runner, had been up and down the stairs a dozen times, cell phone to his ear. He'd eaten my breakfast like a vacuum cleaner on suction, whooshed it down, then asked for a mug, more coffee, and gone out to swing on the porch. After about a five-minute swing I heard him spring up and saw him sprint down the walk. How much relaxing can you do in five minutes in a swing? I could tell he was not from the South. And he sure acted like he was in some high-pressure stress, stress, stress business. He needed a good swinging on a cool front porch shaded and scented with wisteria more than anybody I'd ever seen.

I cleaned the dining room and kitchen, realized the house was quiet and started in on the canapés for the trashion show. Baby cornmeal tortillas spread with garlic cream cheese then rolled around freshly washed raw okra pods. When I sliced them the little okra wheels looked like tiny flower mosaics. They crunched delightfully. I sneaked one myself just to "taste test." Yum.

I mixed up a pimento cheese dip that I'd serve warm though my grandmother was rolling in her grave. *Warm* pimento cheese. Then I did some cold cheese things, made a dip or two more, some slices of raw turnips which I wrapped in bacon for Angels on Horseback. The original recipe used water chestnuts, but this was Littleboro and our homegrown turnips were just as sweet and crunchy as canned water chestnuts and organic.

I had cheese straws in the freezer. Any good Southern kitchen always had cheese straws on hand for all and every emergency. Of course I had ubiquitous brie and crackers.

Sundays in Littleboro tended to have a peaceful feeling, quiet with almost no traffic. People went to church, ate a big Sunday dinner and took well-earned naps. Kids played in the yards, but were told to play quietly: "It's Sunday."

A fund-raising on a Sunday afternoon was a new thing for Littleboro and I wasn't sure how it would go over, but it wasn't my worry. All I had to do was make the food, show up and serve.

I had all my canapé stuff ready to go when Scott picked me up at one o'clock. He sat my insulated hampers in the back and as he drove, reached over and held my hand. Ah, I thought, and tried to send the thought his way, see how well we work together when we have a common goal. See how compatible we are as a couple. I bet you and Cedora never rode together in such companionable silence. "Isn't this nice?" I said.

"Very," he said and kept driving.

At the trashion show Scott helped me take my food carriers in the back door to the kitchen, then he unloaded his speakers and music equipment, went to the barn to set up and I got myself organized in that big barn of a kitchen with its land of granite countertops and gleaming refrigerators. Almost a wall of them! And an AGA stove. I drooled. This was a dream kitchen but it wasn't mine. My own at the Dixie Dew was like a '60s model. All white, anemic-looking and just barely adequate.

The bar was in the barn and Mayor Moss had hired two people to staff it. I was only to do the food, thank goodness. Wine bottles and ice and all that are heavy to haul.

I watched the audience arrive. People who looked like "out of towners," not from around here, but probably her friends from whatever big city she had come from. I had seen a helicopter on her back lawn and lavishly dressed people alighting from it. Really, I said to myself. This whole event was "big doings," as Mama Alice would have called it.

The out of towners, definitely not Littleborians, were dressed to the nines, mostly in black. Elegant, designer black but some of the men wore golf pastels and lightened up the whole picture. A few of the women wore hats! Either large, lacy "picture hats" or small flips of feathers and a veil. So NYC, so Paris, so Milano. I hoped somewhere in the crowd Pearl Buttons, our mysterious society columnist for the local newspaper, *The Littleboro Messenger,* was taking note. Nobody knew what the real Pearl Buttons looked like. She (or it could be a he?) seemed to be everywhere, her eyes and ears on everything going on in Littleboro. There had never been a photo beside her column in *The Mess.*

Mayor Moss, also in some sort of sleek black dress, stood at a podium at the head of the freshly built runway (I wondered if Scott had built it? He seemed to be doing everything but building my gazebo!), held a microphone and explained that wearables could be made from things like plastic garbage bags, bottle caps and metal soda tabs, cans and foil wrappers, paper products, anything that could be recycled. I'd been amazed and impressed when Malinda said she was going to be one of the models. Nobody had asked me to model, but then I was doing the food, little nibbles and dips, and I'd be busy. Plus one did not get paid to model and I was being paid to do food.

I had a feeling from the get-go that Malinda was going to be a hit in her long, swirling, strapless "dress" of purple plastic tablecloths covered with white 3-D polka dots, which were really prescription bottle tops. I'd helped her attach about a million of those bottle tops. We didn't dream it would take so many. Last week we were putting it together in the living room at the Dixie Dew. At eleven o'clock that night, making that dress, we ran out of bottle tops. We only had half that voluminous skirt covered. Panic time.

"There's a box of old caps in Gaddy's storeroom," Malinda said. "Let's go get them. I have a key." She jangled her ring of keys fetched from her purple purse that was made from a plastic place mat. That purse was the first thing we made. Easy. Fold in two thirds, stitch up the sides and let the top part flap over. Instant clutch purse. And it was shiny. "Dollar Store," I said, "we did you proud."

We walked downtown and Malinda unlocked the front door of Gaddy's. We didn't turn on any lights and after we got in Malinda locked the door behind us.

"Anybody passing by sees these lights on, they'll stop and I'll have to sell them a bottle of aspirin or a pack of gum. Anything that could have waited until tomorrow." Malinda led the way through the store with a flashlight she kept in the cash drawer. "Never any cash left here. Last one out takes every cent and drops the deposit bag in the night slot at the bank."

She was standing atop a ladder trying to reach the box on the top shelf when we heard the front door rattle. It sounded as if someone was trying to get in, then we saw beams from a flashlight sweep around the store, stop and stay on the entrance to the pharmacy counter. The light stayed there what seemed like a long, lingering time.

Neither of us moved. Did we breathe? What was going on?

"Mr. Gaddy?" I whispered to Malinda. "Some emergency maybe?" I imagined a child with a fever and no Tylenol. The parents would call Mr. Gaddy at home and he'd dress, drive over and unlock the store for them. That's what we do in small towns. We call on each other when there's an emergency.

"He's got a key," Malinda whispered back. "He'd come in the front door like we did."

The lights went away as did the footsteps.

Malinda handed down the box and we started to leave when a voice said, "Stop where you are."

We stopped.

"Stay right there."

We stayed stock-still.

The voice sounded very male and very guttural. I knew that voice. It made my toes tingle and not in a good way. Suddenly all the lights clicked on and there in front of us stood Ossie DelGardo with a gun drawn and pointed straight at Malinda and me. "What's in the box?" he asked. His gun hand didn't waver.

"Bottle tops," Malinda said. "You want to see?" She opened the flaps and Ossie stepped closer.

"Just bottle tops?" He peered in, then with the hand that didn't hold the gun, riffled through it. "Bottle tops," he said and stepped back. He holstered his gun and held the front door for us to go out. "You two must have a story to tell, stealing prescription bottle caps at two in the morning."

"What did you think we were doing?" I asked.

"With you"—he grinned at me—"I never know."

Malinda tried to explain trashion and how she'd be wearing a purple tablecloth studded with these bottle caps. I watched his eyes glaze over. He shrugged his shoulders and grimaced, as if to say, Two more crazies in a town of crazies.

"And what were *you* doing?" I asked. Mr. Ossie, the bigshot city cop, on the job as town watchman? I had imagined him napping all day in his office and sleeping (or not) at Juanita's at night.

"Only my job," he said. "I check the downtown, every lock, every night. I walk my beat."

Then he turned and walked one way, Malinda and I walked the other back to the Dixie Dew. At three a.m. we were still going crazy making those white bottle caps look like 3-D polka dots.

"This is the winner," I said. "It better be. We just got the Ossie DelGardo seal of approval. Ha ha." After that I yawned and crashed on the couch and Malinda rolled up our creation, picked up her purse and went home. I knew she would win. Or at least if I'd been placing bets, I would have bet on her.

Today before the models lined up at the trashion show, Malinda and I did a fist bump. "Break a leg," I said.

"Drop a tray," she said.

Minutes later, I watched Malinda swish up and down the runway in the middle of the barn, get catcalls and whistles. She hammed things up, waving and throwing kisses. She looked stunning. Tall, radiating confidence, her mahogany skin glowed. She wore her signature large gold hoop earrings. With her hair in a topknot bun she looked even taller, more regal. Our Malinda had always been a "looker."

Mayor Moss's barn was long past anything ever thought of as a barn. No animal would dare step a hoof on those polished hardwood floors that I'd heard had been used for dancing when Miz Moss imported a big-name band for one of her parties. Designer chandeliers hung from the rafters.

I hoped Malinda would get the first-prize trophy—not that

anyone would really want the thing since it was made of re-cyclables, too, a tall plastic bottle of some kind with Mardi Gras beads and odd costume jewelry glued on at random, but a trophy is a trophy and from a distance and with a squint, it might look impressive. And Elvis would be impressed his mama won a fashion show, even if it was a trashion one.

Someone from the library wore a pantsuit made of pages from an old *Oxford English Dictionary* glued onto some thin fabric, then cut and sewed. The model's paper hat sported a jaunty white feather from a quill pen.

Students from Littleboro High's home economics classes wore dresses made of plastic bags or fast-food wrappers. They carried purses made from juice boxes and gum wrappers. One darling girl wore a white tutu made of industrial coffee filters. She got second prize, a smaller trophy made of bottle caps stuck to sculptured pieces of milk cartons sprayed with gold glitter.

Malinda got the grand prize and the crowd went wild, clapping and finger whistling. Malinda gave a gracious bow in her royal attire, held the trophy aloft like it was really a legitimate prize. I bet her mama would just shake her head and wonder what would happen next in Littleboro? Me, too.

As I packed up my leftovers in the kitchen, I heard two people outside the back door talking. Two of Mayor Moss's guests, I supposed, hiding out for a place to smoke.

I heard one male voice say, "There's not a soul in this dead burg with an ounce of sense enough to figure it out."

"It" what? I wanted to ask. It? "It" could be anything.

When I opened the door to see who had been talking, there was nobody there. But they had left their cigarette butts, one

of which was from a cigarillo. I knew Allison smoked ciga-
rillos, but what I had heard was two male voices. Or I thought
they were male voices.

Could one of them be Mr. Moss? I'd never met him. Miz
Mayor referred to Mr. Moss often as being "away on business" and that he traveled "so much" she could never depend
on him to be where she needed him.

I got paid for catering, which I had not made of expensive
foodstuffs, just time-consuming, cute, fun and cheesy things.
Easy peasy. Scott had played the keyboard background
music, jazzy at first, then something with the right beat for
the models to stomp and sashay up and down the runway. I
was glad the mayor had decided to keep some things local.
That was in the spirit of things, this fund-raising business,
support Littleboro and all that. Mayor Moss gave us both our
checks at the same time, kissed Scott on the cheek and hugged
me. "Thank you. Thank you both. I couldn't have ever done
this without you."

As Scott and I walked to his truck I tried to see the figures
on his check but he folded it and tucked it in his shirt pocket.
Nosey me. I only wondered if he got paid more than I did.

On the way home neither of us said much. For one thing
I was so tired the bottoms of my feet ached and I felt like I
had bits of Brie in my hair. I knew I smelled like cheese, which
is seductive only to a mouse.

Scott drove, hummed some tune I didn't recognize, then
stopped in front of the Dixie Dew and parked. He got out,
collected my trays from the bed of the truck, came around
and opened my door, handed them to me. "Good night," he

said. "Sleep tight and don't let the bedbugs in tonight." He laughed, leaned over for a soft, wet, sweet, swift kiss, then was gone. I just stood there, disappointed and tired. Maybe even more disappointed than tired and I was really tired.

Chapter Sixteen

I unpacked, washed, put back my coolers and trays in the pantry/office and made myself a sandwich of leftover pimento cheese spread. I like mine cold on either rye or dill bread. Plus I put lettuce and tomato on it. In a rare dash of bravery I'll add a slice of Vidalia onion . . . one slice that's big enough to cover the whole bottom layer. When I was in high school, Gaddy's Drug Store, which wasn't Gaddy's then, used to offer toasted pimento cheese. With chips and a pickle. Toasted pimento cheese is the spread that went from mill worker's lunches to get a bit of education. Warm pimento cheese as a dip is pimento cheese that's gone to cooking school under the tutelage of some fancy chef in a black, button-on-the-side, name-embroidered coat with little shoulder pockets that hold personal thermometers and tasting devices. Those kinds of chefs.

It wasn't until nearly dusk I remembered Robert Redford. The missing mister bunny.

I had to round up that rabbit, who surely couldn't have hopped very far. I knew though that I had to find him. I only hoped nothing happened before I did so. Somebody strange to Littleboro could see him and immediately think barbecue or hasenpfeffer. I can live with a lot of baggage but a whole knapsack of guilt is tough to tote around. Didn't want to add any more to what I already had. I *had* to find that rabbit or Verna would never forgive me.

Somehow I kept thinking Robert Redford had to be in or near Verna's house. But shortly after I finished clearing out the breakfast things, I had checked outside, around, about and underneath the Dixie Dew as well as both yards and saw no sign of him. I had ruled out inside because I couldn't figure out how he'd get himself inside. But, knowing Littleboro, some kind somebody could have found him, knew who he was and that he lived with Verna and taken him home, opened the door and let him inside. Then I got rushed for time and had to start on the doings for the mayor's shindig.

Frankly I forgot about him until almost dark. That's when it hit me. Plus a big white rabbit should be easy to see in the dwindling twilight.

I went next door to Verna's, had to part my way through towering shrubs that had grown untrimmed into scraggly trees, through backyard grass gone to seed so high it fell over, then up Verna's back steps that looked as old and rickety as the rest of her house. I walked very carefully, lest one board be so thin from rot I'd fall through and there I'd be, one leg dangling and the rest of me hanging on to whatever I could grab to keep from falling the rest of the way.

On her screened-in porch I threaded my way past boxes and newspapers piled to the ceiling, an old wringer washer, tin washtubs on legs, a clothesline still hung with dresses and nightgowns, and long-legged bloomers that had been out there so long all color had faded. They hung in a line of tan-colored depression.

In the back hall, I peeked in the kitchen, which didn't seem quite as cluttered as the rest of the house. Then I saw an open door just inside the kitchen, some steps down, and darkness. A rabbit could have stood where I'm standing, started down those steps and hopped the rest of the way into what I now guessed was an old-fashioned root cellar.

"Rabbit," I called. "Robert Redford, honey." Secretly, I liked the intimacy of calling Robert Redford "honey," as though we (the movie guy, the famous one) and I actually knew each other and I could call him "honey."

I felt for a light switch and flicked it on. It was either a forty-watt bulb or so covered with dust and grime it didn't help all that much. Calling the rabbit again, I started down the steps while a thick dark smell got stronger and stronger. A smell like the bottom of the earth.

Halfway down, I heard the root cellar door slam shut behind me. A hard, final sort of *clunk* sound. *Clunk,* like the door to a jail cell. "What?" I yelled. "Wait. I'm down here."

Then I heard a bolt slide into place.

"Help," I yelled, ran up to the door and began to beat on

it. *Wham, wham,* wham. A hollow desperate sound. "I'm in here!" I yelled.

The door was metal and my *wham, wham, wham*s only echoed back, rocking but not loosening. Probably this metal door was the only thing in the house not headed toward rot and decay.

I banged and yelled and banged some more. Listened for footsteps of someone coming back. Nothing. Maybe whoever shut that door and locked it had known I was down here and had done it on purpose. But who? Surely it was an accident. There was no one in Verna's house but me. Maybe a breeze blew the door shut? Except a breeze wouldn't have slid that bolt into place. Not long ago I had been locked in a mausoleum on purpose, only then I had Robert Redford shut in there with me. This time I was alone.

Behind me I saw the last bit of natural light coming from the small window near the ceiling. "Hey," I yelled. I saw feet and legs walk by very fast. "Help!" I yelled. Then I thought, Whose feet were those? Whose legs? "Hey," I yelled again. "I'm down here." The feet were quickly out of sight.

The window was too high for me to reach and bang on it. And too high for me to climb out.

I went all the way down to the bottom of the steps where I saw a water heater that must have been in Noah's Ark, and a furnace that took up most of the wall and looked medieval. The water heater clicked on. The furnace looked so rusty it probably had not worked in years.

I felt my chest tighten, my breathing get shallow and fast. Panic. I must not panic, I told myself. There had to be a way to get up to that window.

If there was a ladder here, I could climb to the window, break it with something and climb out. No ladder I could see. If I could find even some rickety old table, I'd chance a climb on it. A table of any sort I could stand on. No table.

But there was something: the whole wall at the end of the root cellar was floor-to-ceiling shelves filled with jars of canned vegetables and fruits. At least I wouldn't starve. But how old were those canned goods? I bet Verna hadn't had a garden or gone to a Farmers' Market for fresh vegetables in a lot of long summers. I'd be taking my life in my hands to touch anything from any of those jars even if I could get them open, which I doubted.

So here I was locked in a dim, earthy-smelling root cellar that had one very secure metal door out and a teeny tiny way-up-high square of a window. I could yell my head off and nobody would hear. And nobody would have a reason in this world to come check anything in this cellar. If it was winter somebody might be scheduled to deliver coal for the old furnace. But there would be big doors that opened out so coal could be unloaded in. I looked. No chute, no big doors, so the furnace must not be coal. Or wood. Or the first gas one ever made. This one was a monster of a furnace and I didn't dare try to break loose some pipe to hammer at the window even if I could get high enough to do so. Didn't think that was the route to try.

I told myself I would not start to cry like a six-year-old. Big girls don't cry. They pull up their jeans and take on the task at hand.

I was locked in the last place anybody would come to look.

I should have left Ida Plum a note. I should have packed my cell phone somewhere on my body. I remembered some commercial for something that ended with the line "Don't leave home without it." Maybe that should apply to cell phones, but I was only going next door! Who would think to take their cell phone if they were only going next door?

I mentally kicked myself for ever, ever coming down those stairs in the first place. Dumb move. If I ever got out of here, Ida Plum would scold and scold. But now, just thinking about her voice, her scoldings made me tear up. Wimp, I told myself. I'd take the scoldings if I could just get out of here. "Lord," I said to the ceiling, "if you get me out of here, I promise—" What? Anything. Everything. Whatever.

I looked around again. Water heater, furnace, wall of canned food.

Floor-to-ceiling jars of green beans, of course. This was Littleboro. Corn, tomatoes, okra, lima beans and a mixture of all four called vegetable soup, which my grandmother made at the end of the canning season. Soup mix. Fat lot of good all this was going to do me now. Then I touched one of the shelves. Metal, like the door, and probably the newer of anything in the house.

A metal shelf would hold me. No rot. But this was a set of shelves and I could not make a ladder of them. Even if I emptied them and propped them against the wall under the window, I couldn't climb them. They'd be flat against the wall. If I leaned them against the wall to try to make them into a sort of makeshift stairs, I'd fall through.

I felt under the closest shelf. A plastic clip held it in place.

I could take out all the clips, then I'd have individual shelves. And boards, not shelves, but boards to make stairs. Boards are what you build stairs with.

Row by row I unloaded the shelves. I stacked a platform of jars wide and long, laid a few shelves across it. I'd made myself a base to make a set of stairs. Stacked more jars on top of that, then another shelf, until I had stairs. Steps up. Up, up and out that window, I said to myself. I stood back and looked at my creation, my inspiration, my salvation. I could climb to the top, break the window and crawl out.

Slowly, slowly, the jars rocking a bit under me, I took one stair step up, then another, higher, higher.

Now I held my breath, reached out and touched the window. I felt a latch. I wouldn't have to break the glass. The latch was rusted as heck, but I pushed and pushed on it until I felt it give. The window opened. I breathed good, clean air and smelled sweet, green, growing grass. I gave myself a mighty hoist, pulled myself up and through, crawled out that little window that was just wide enough. I belly flopped onto God's dear earth, stood and brushed myself off.

"Rabbit," I said, "wherever the hell you are, you are not worth it."

It was now almost pitch-dark and I was exhausted. I limped across the backyard and through the wall of overgrown hedges to the Dixie Dew, a bath to get off the grime and mold, years of accumulated dirt. All I wanted was my soft, clean bed and a good night's sleep. Maybe whoever at the trashion show had called this a "dead burg" inhabited by dumbheads had a point. Root cellars be damned.

Chapter Seventeen

Monday morning Ida Plum came in the back door saying she'd been by the jail to take Reba some underwear but nobody was there. "Gone," she said. "That cell was as empty as my pocketbook." Ida Plum liked to work Sundays but I had been the one to work yesterday. I had to *make* her take time off during the week to compensate. She said weekends were lonely for widows.

She was earlier than usual and we didn't have to start doing breakfast yet. Breakfast was at eight a.m. and not a minute before. No self-respecting guest would cruise downstairs and stand outside my dining room's French doors before eight a.m. Not unless they'd alerted me verbally the night before or when they checked in or left a note on my desk or bed-room door.

Ida Plum said the door to the jail cell in the basement of the courthouse was not only open, but also hanging loose on its hinges. If Ossie had assigned someone to stay with Reba, they'd left. Had somebody sprung Reba or had she jiggled the door and found the whole thing rusted to the point where mere touch could make the door fall open?

The question hung between us when Malinda popped in on her way to work at Gaddy's. Not a lot of business this early, Malinda had said, but somebody had to be there on pharmacy duty. Plus she could catch up on paperwork in the quiet.

"So where do you think she is?" Malinda asked after Ida Plum repeated her story about Reba being out and on the loose. Malinda put whole wheat bread in the toaster, opened the refrigerator for some of the mock strawberry jam made with strawberry Jell-O and figs. Tastes better than the real thing. I'd made jars and jars of it last summer with the bounty from my grandmother's fig tree. Not a bush, this fig was a tree that almost blocked the gate to the backyard. I loved figs raw, washed with dew and resplendent on a plate for break-fast. Or with cheese for a four o'clock snack. I loved figs plucked straight from the tree to my lips. I made the jam for guests at the Dixie Dew because it was such fun and so very, very easy.

"Anybody try looking for Reba at her tree?" I asked, pour-ing coffee into blue mugs. Dixie Dew guests got china cups and saucers. Kitchen people got mugs, beakers the British called them. They actually kept coffee hot longer.

"Looked empty when I drove by," Ida Plum said. "Not a

thing was flapping from the limbs." The three of us shook our heads. Reba liked to air her laundry on the limbs. Clean or dirty, she flew it like flags.

We drank coffee, standing at the center island, until I said, "If you two will sit down, I'll tell you what happened last night and how I came very close to not being here this morning."

"Tell," Malinda said. "I just hope it doesn't involve slime pits." She was referring to one of our former unpleasant explorations.

"No slime pits," I said, "just a root cellar from hell."

They took chairs at the table and waited while I told of my latest escape, my triumph over terror—not to mention how I never planned to darken another root cellar the rest of my sweet little newly renewed life.

"Nothing broken?" Ida Plum asked politely, but her tone said "you idiot." "Oh, you give me such worry and grief and I wish your grandmother were here to scold you. What in the world ever possessed you to go into that house?"

Malinda rolled her eyes. She knew me and she also knew if I'd called her she would have gone in with me. Malinda was always open for an adventure and Littleboro didn't offer a lot of them. I tried to describe Verna's house inside.

"So old Verna is a hoarder." Malinda laughed. "Who would have thought it? Or who would have thought otherwise? One look at the house on the outside and you'd know it. My mama makes sure her front walk is swept every day. She's even taught Elvis to handle a broom. She says a lot more people see the outside of your house than will ever see the inside and you better keep it clean."

"Good boy," Ida Plum said. "And good mama." She patted Malinda on the head. "Both of you."

"I had to make my bed every morning before school," Malinda said, spreading jam on her toast. "My mama believes in tough love."

I wondered what kind of mother Verna would have been if she'd had children. Or what it would be like if that house were filled with the ghosts and voices of children and children's children instead of crap? What I saw sure was crap. To the ceiling. Wall-to-wall crap. Front-door-to-back-door crap. Downstairs-to-upstairs crap, though I hadn't gone upstairs. Some things you know without seeing.

"I can't believe Verna lives in such a mess." Ida Plum poured us more coffee. "Nobody could, would live that way if it's as bad as you say." She raised one eyebrow at me. "It's not healthy."

"It's worse," I said. "A fire hazard. Mold. Dirt. It's where dirt goes to die. Couple of dump trucks need to haul that unbelievable houseful of god-awful away to the nearest landfill."

All this had gotten us off the subject of Crazy Reba's jailbreak and my crawling-out-the-window caper. "You don't believe me?" I said to Ida Plum. "Come on. I'll show you."

Malinda stood, brushed crumbs off her white lab coat. "I'm not taking a chance on getting near any of that . . . bleeping awfulness." She hesitated long enough I knew she wanted to say the word that was the perfect description of the contents of Verna's house. I also knew it was a word Ida Plum considered beneath both Malinda and me to use. Not to mention Ida Plum's own vocabulary. So I didn't fill in the blank for her.

She waved goodbye and was gone in a flash of white.

Ida Plum looked at the clock. "We got time if you are bound and determined to show me what I think can't possibly be as bad as you say."

She liked to challenge my imagination at times. Rein me in, she'd say, when I got too carried away or too excited. "Hold your horses," she also liked to say. Maybe that's what I should have said to Reba when she was hysterical, except that guy's body was enough to make anyone hysterical. I was surprised I could be so calm myself. But then this wasn't my situation. The crusty, hairy, smelly guy on the picnic table certainly wasn't the man in the driver's license photo. And DMV photos didn't lie, or get "enhanced" in any way, did they? A real puzzler, with Reba, me and Mrs. Angry Truck Driver Wife all involved. Life just couldn't stay simple, could it? It was so complicated right now it made me dizzy. Or the dizziness could have been from mold in that root cellar, and here I was going back into the house of mold, but this time I was staying upstairs.

Chapter Eighteen

Before our foray next door, just in case some Dixie Dew guest should decide to wander downstairs before the appointed hour, I made more coffee and put it on the warmer in the dining room. Ida Plum took in the toaster, bread and jam. I felt we had the bases covered for the next fifteen or twenty minutes, which was longer than I wanted to be in Verna's house.

We pushed our way through hedges that hadn't been trimmed in years, grass up to our knees, stepped past the window that had been my escape from the root cellar and on up the rickety back porch steps. At least there were rails on each side, rails that seemed loose from the very steps they were supposed to anchor. They wobbled under my hands. Verna could have grabbed one and gone tumbling over if she ever used them. I guessed she'd decided to go and come from the front door long ago.

The screen door was only half-screened with the lower part loose and curled. And the back porch was full of old clothes and stacks of yellowed newspapers. Cans, bottles and jars gathered in a corner, unwashed. The ones I'd seen earlier in the garbage can had been clean.

Ida Plum held her hand over her nose and mouth. I led her to the kitchen, which in some ways was not as bad as some of the other "awfulness." It was full of empty frozen food boxes and plastic containers. Here the containers had been washed and stacked up according to shape and size. That was interesting. A bit of order. But the stacks reached the bottoms of all the cabinets and covered the countertops. Verna had made an attempt at recycling, bless her untidy little heart. We wove our way down a narrow path into the next room and the next.

For all I knew, whoever had locked me in the root cellar could be back in the house. But with Ida Plum we were two against one. Between us, with me still smarting about being shut in such a place, my anger would boil up and we could take the rascal. If it had been meant as a prank, and I didn't think it was, it wasn't funny. The person could have been planning to come back later and let me out. Or not! Ever! I shivered at the thought. So here I was back at the scene of the horror, but not quite. With Ida Plum I felt confident, come hell or whatever else. I didn't say this, but I squared my shoulders and we pushed on, threading our way through what seemed like a tunnel. I kept my arms close to my sides for fear that if I brushed against a stack of stuff it would come tumbling down on me. I'd be as buried in this rubble as I almost was in the root cellar.

"How does she live in this house?" Ida Plum whispered.

"I don't know," I whispered back, even though I didn't know I was whispering. Or *why* we were both whispering.

"Where?" Ida Plum said in a normal voice. "Where does she live in this house? Which room?"

"I wish I'd brought a flashlight," I said. The hall was dark and several of the rooms so full we couldn't push open the doors. In a way I was thankful we couldn't get in or even see in. This house was a landfill inside! One's own personal landfill and Verna was living in it.

"She must sleep upstairs," I said, and started up a path narrowed by stacks of books on each step. "Careful." I reached a hand back to Ida Plum.

The upstairs hall landing had a bit more room to move once we got past some bureaus and chests. On one hall chest a lamp burned. A flicker of hope, I thought, in this upper level of Verna's hell.

Three doors down we saw a door that seemed to be slightly open.

"There," I said. "That must be her bedroom."

Ida Plum said, "She surely can't come back to this house. With an injured ankle, she'd never be able to climb these stairs."

We heard something that sounded like faraway music, very dim, very faint. We looked at each other.

"That room?" I pointed. "It must be coming from there."

We edged closer. On tiptoe.

I eased the door open wider and saw someone sitting upright in bed, a huge old four-poster, tester bed, with a crocheted netting canopy on top. The woman in the bed looked like one of those pictures in a child's storybook of Little Red Riding Hood, the grandmother or the wolf in ruffled nightcap and bedclothes. A small TV flickered on a dresser across the room.

The person in the bed turned toward us, waved an arm as if to say, "Come in. Come in."

It wasn't a wolf in grandma's clothing. It was Reba!

"Reba?" I croaked out. "Reba?"

Ida Plum grabbed my elbow. "Is that you? Reba?"

Reba sat like royalty, a dozen pillows propped behind her. Had it been Reba who shut that cellar door and ignored my knocking and calling? The Reba I knew, the old Reba, would have opened that door in a minute.

This Reba was eating something. Something white and tall that looked sticky. She licked her fingers. "Good," she said. "Good cake."

It looked like her wedding cake, the one I'd baked to practice for Ossie and Juanita's *real* wedding. Reba's was going to just be for a party where she could wear her white dress and we'd all pretend there had been a wedding. All she'd know was party and cake, but here she was helping herself to the cake ahead of time.

The cake I had slaved over for two whole days, making icing roses and swirls and scrolls and scallops. Even if we knew Reba's wedding was never going to come off, I figured we could eat cake and I'd know what had and hadn't worked when it came time to make the one for Ossie and Juanita.

Never hurt to practice something that in the past I'd mostly only watched my grandmother do.

"How did you get here?" I asked.

Reba walked two fingers down the faded wedding ring quilt, sewn in a beautiful old pattern of pinks and blues. I thought, How appropriate. Of course Reba wouldn't know the pattern. I was glad I had not made the cake chocolate.

Reba slid the covers back and got out of bed. "You want some cake?" She wore one of Verna's long nightgowns and a ruffled shower cap on her head.

"When did you get here?" I asked. Reba's could have been the footsteps I heard when someone shot that bolt in the lock and trapped me in the root cellar.

"I found the key, the key, the key and unlocked. I unlocked." She clapped her hands. She was into locks and keys these days. Like a child locking and unlocking a door, it was a game to her. I wondered if this was the first time she had unlocked a house to get in. Mostly she went in unlocked doors and until lately that had been most of the doors in Littleboro.

"I put cake down, unlocked the key." She danced around on bare feet.

Maybe that was when I was in the root cellar. Had she been the one to bolt the door? Locks and keys were one thing, but a bolt was another. And if she hadn't done it, who did?

And she had sometime gotten into the Dixie Dew and stolen her wedding cake. I had baked five layers, iced them, had the whole kitchen at the Dixie Dew white with powdered sugar and every surface tacky as glue. Then I decorated. I made white icing roses, sixty of them. Now half of them were smeared across Reba's face and hands and how many were on Verna's quilt? I didn't want to know. I only knew I wanted to reach over and shake Reba by her shoulders. But of course she had no idea all that had gone into that "good cake." At least she was enjoying it.

"Where? Where did you get that cake?" I asked.

Ida Plum stepped closer to the bed. "I put that thing in the freezer yesterday. No sense wasting good cake and all that work. Somebody in Littleboro would be getting married sometime."

"You're staying here?" I asked.

Reba got back in bed, pulled up the quilt and said, "I like this bed. It's soft and smells good." She patted the covers with the hand that didn't hold cake, then licked her fingers. Oh, Verna was going to have to have that quilt dry-cleaned of cake crumbs and icing.

"Don't you miss your tree?" Ida Plum asked.

I knew she was thinking about sticky icing and maybe whatever else Reba might decide to deposit in this house. Whatever she did, she wouldn't mess it up more than it was already.

"Hearing the birds? Fresh morning air? Sunshine?" Ida Plum continued.

"Birds on tee-vee," Reba said and took another bite of her cake.

Ida Plum and I looked at each other and shrugged. I was sure glad to be alive and aboveground. Which might be more than Mr. Butch Rigsbee was at the moment. Would Reba even know what I was talking about if I asked her? God, I wanted to say. God in the big white truck? Do you know where he is?

I didn't ask. She was hyped up on cake and I didn't want to go prodding into her time in jail and the business on the picnic table. Let her enjoy just being alive.

I knew I could bake more cakes. I could pipe more icing roses and decorate more wedding cakes unless Mrs. Lady Wrestler found me and hacked the daylights out of me with a chef's knife or something. I put my arm around Ida Plum, said, "Let Reba eat cake. Let's go." And we did.

Chapter Nineteen

Ida Plum and I sneaked in the back door at the Dixie Dew as quietly as we could, in case guests were in the dining room waiting for breakfast. I surely didn't want to hear the sound of them banging spoons on my grandmother's cherry table, chanting something like "Coffee. Coffee. Coffee." Getting ready to riot. And I certainly wanted no dents in that table my grandmother had me polish a million times while I was growing up. No dents, please.

All was quiet.

We started stirring up muffin batter, grits for a soufflé and cracking eggs into a bowl. I remembered the first egg I ever cracked, Mama Alice at my elbow, and it went right into the kitchen drawer I'd forgotten to close. All over the flatware.

One egg could surely make a lot of mess, I learned, as I cleaned it up and tried again, this time making sure the drawer was shut. Tight.

Then, at the agreed-upon hour, I heard footsteps coming down the stairs: Mr. Fortune, Miss Isabella and that cute little Debbie Booth, all bouncy and excited.

"Grits," said Debbie, lifting the lid of the chafing dish. "God made grits for our Southern souls and palettes and anyone else who has the good sense to know good food." She served herself a healthy portion. I got the feeling if she had been at her own house and cooking these grits in cream, she would have licked the spoon.

They ate and praised and Mr. Fortune asked for seconds on the grits. "A kiss of garlic?" he asked, tasting.

"A nice smack," I said.

"Red pepper? A generous sprinkle?"

"You got it," I said. "Eggs, milk and a ton of sharp cheese."

"And the grits," Debbie Booth said. "Stone-ground of course. That's the rock-bottom backbone. Everything else is superfluous."

I told Mr. Fortune about a fun documentary he could probably find somewhere online about "a grits tree," an old black-and-white film. He made notes on the stiff white French cuffs of his green-and-white-checked shirt. I couldn't remember the last time I'd seen French cuffs, not here in Littleboro. Not ever on Ben Johnson, my ex, who wouldn't know a cuff of any sort if it didn't come on a wool shirt from L.L.Bean. I could swoon over French cuffs and silver cuff links. I have a low swooning point.

They cleared out for the day. Miss Isabella and Debbie

headed to a luncheon at our Honorable Ms. Mayor Moss's mansion, to which I was invited, too. Why, I didn't know, just as a committee person I guess, but of course I'd go. One must socialize when the rich extend to all us lowlies an invitation. Mr. Fortune said he was off for his daily run, then errands and a late-night pickup at the Raleigh-Durham airport. Maybe our "mystery guest"? He had never given me any information, not name, or gender. Our mystery guest was still a big mystery.

Ida Plum and I cleared up, cleaned up and washed up. I reminded her Robert Redford was still missing and I dreaded going by to check on Verna. He was the first thing Verna would ask about. It seemed such a small thing, and I'd tried. I'd truly tried. But he was still out there somewhere. Still missing.

"I've got a feeling he'll turn up where you least expect," Ida Plum said in such an offhand way I didn't know whether she knew something I didn't or was trying to cheer me up. Either way, I didn't feel much better.

The practical side of me knew rabbits were not as resourceful as cats. They don't find mice or lizards as my cat Sherman would have done and make meals of them in order to survive. And water? He could be dehydrated. Cats can jump up and help themselves to water in somebody's birdbath. I didn't see rabbits doing that kind of high hopping. I was getting more afraid I'd find his little "fur suit," as Miss Tempie had once described her dead poodle, Harold, the dog she buried in her family plot in the Littleboro Cemetery. I wanted Robert Redford to still be hopping around in his little fur suit.

I also knew I couldn't go to a pet shop, buy a big white

rabbit and try to tell Verna I'd found Robert Redford. Besides, I'd never find one the age and size of R.R. in a pet
shop, which made me wonder exactly how old R.R. was. I
had no idea how long Verna had been cohabiting with him
in that hoarder house. Maybe the rabbit would be so glad
to be out of it, he'd run and keep running. Or hopping.
Hippity-hopping like the Easter Bunny, with his red leash
flopping behind him.

When the Sunday edition of *The Pilot* newspaper came, Ida
Plum and I sat down to share it. I get my subscription by mail
and though it comes on Monday, a day late, I always feel *The
Pilot* keeps me up-to-date on what I need to know. I usually
read the books section first. Faye Dasen has been the book
person forever. I love her book news and reviews, but today
a small item on the front page nearly leaped off at me. I had
read it online, but somehow until I saw it in black-and-white
it didn't seem true. Here it was on the page.

"Mystery Man Found in Littleboro," I read, then read it
aloud to Ida Plum. "An unidentified man found unconscious
on a picnic table in Littleboro was taken to Moore County
Medical, where he remains in critical condition." On down
in the paragraph was a description of his red beard, his tattoos and a plea that anyone missing a family member or with
information should contact Ossie DelGardo in Littleboro.
The newspaper account had little more information than the
online version.

"He's still alive," I said. "Either Reba didn't kill him or I
must have saved him. Or kept him semi-alive until the Med-
Alert guys got there."

"Will wonders never cease?" Ida Plum said.

At eleven o'clock, freshly showered and dressed, I left for my command appearance at Mayor Moss's big luncheon. Two big events in two days were almost too much opulence. Littleboro wasn't used to such "goings-on." Me neither.

Ida Plum was on the front porch with a broom knocking down spiderwebs. "They appear every night and every day I knock them down," she said. Sherman scooted under a boxwood every time she raised the broom, peeked out, ducked back under.

"Don't say anything I wouldn't," Ida Plum said. "And don't do anything to get yourself on the front page of *The Mess* or *The Pilot*." She laughed. Around here gossip would give you the latest good and bad—mostly bad—news. Nothing like somebody gone wrong or doing wrong to set the tongues in Littleboro flapping at both ends. But it was only hearsay—until you read it in *The Mess.* Once something was in print, whether it was the rumor or the actual deed, now it was set in stone. *The Mess* only came out once a week but everybody already knew most of what would be in it. Black-and-white print told it all. Sacred as the Bible. If you said, "I read it in *The Mess,*" it was a fact.

Our mayor was celebrating the Green Bean Festival by giving a kickoff luncheon. Mama Alice and I always used the word "dinner" for the meal you ate at noon. Supper was the meal you ate late in the evening, close to night. Luncheon was for those who had nothing to do but go to one, like hoity-toity big-city people. I was curious as to who would show up. Committee people, volunteers who would scurry around like noises in the night so they could get admission to all the goings-on for free.

I had dressed in my "glad rags," as Mama Alice would have called my polished cotton print shirtwaist dress that was old, old and soft, but not faded. Polished cotton never faded, plus this dress had been in the back of my closet since who knew when. Years maybe. This one didn't match my table-cloths and tearoom valances. It had a black background with red peonies in bloom and sweet pea tendrils. I thought it somehow said "luncheon."

"Do I look okay?" I asked Ida Plum as I turned around for her inspection.

"You're not going to win any fashion parades," she said. "But looks like you got everything sufficiently covered."

I laughed and headed for Lady Bug.

Chapter Twenty

I wasn't late, but the parking area at the Honorable Calista Moss's estate was almost full. I squeezed in next to her huge white barn that she restored, where we'd had the trashion show. That barn was fancy enough for somebody to live in. A couple of somebodies.

Ida Plum, when she heard about the luncheon, shook her head as if to say, What will Littleboro come to next? Putting on the dog?

Today as I had driven up that hill with the lush lawn, big magnolia trees and the old Little house looming at the top, I couldn't help but remember Miss Tempie's house that was in ruins, the kudzu claiming it more every day, every inch, on the adjoining hill. One old Southern mansion going down to sticks and bricks, another, Mayor Moss's, getting new life by the dollar. Or many dollars. Mucho dollars.

Mayor Moss met us at the door, dressed in yellow linen with a matching hat and shoes. Where did one find yellow shoes? She looked like a human daffodil. She even wore a bright-green, yellow-and-blue printed scarf, which I am sure was hand painted, a one of a kind. She led us through the living room with rugs that had pile so lush and deep I felt I was sinking up to my ankles or needed oars to row my way across.

The dining-room table was set for twenty-two. I counted ten on each side, one at each end. The table glowed with gold-rimmed china and matching gold place settings. A long centerpiece of stargazer lilies, red gerbera daisies and cymbidium orchids told me the Betts Brothers florists had outdone themselves. This Green Bean Festival was providing some revenue for local businesses. Maybe our mayor was on to something after all.

There were place cards! Oh, the elegance. I was seated between Debbie Booth and Pastor Pittman. Somehow I couldn't seem to get away from the man. And what did he ever have to do with the arts and this festival?

"I'm doing the invocation," he leaned over and whispered. "Before the cook-off, bake-off, do-off thing."

Yes, I thought, all that green bean stuff needs to be blessed. Even blessed twice. Three times. You couldn't bless green beans too much to suit me. Maybe it would help.

Across from me were people I didn't know, but Her Honor Moss went around with one-sentence introductions: so-and-so from the newspaper (a man I'd never heard of, could he be the mysterious columnist, Pearl Buttons?), so-and-so from the school board, so-and-so from the arts council, some city council somebody, a music teacher, a dance teacher, a local watercolorist, me and Pastor Pittman, Miss Isabella, Debbie Booth and others, until there were twenty of us. Plus two. Calista Moss sat at the head of this very elegant table glowing under one of the chandeliers, each of which with enough crystal drops for a rain shower. The other end of the table was empty. She explained, "Mr. Moss may join us." She pursed her lips. "Or he may not."

Her husband must truly be a real mystery man. I don't think anybody had ever seen him. He certainly didn't show up at the famous trashion show. Unless that had been the male voice I had overhead outside the kitchen window. Maybe Littleboro had a male Emily Dickinson?

Before we lifted a soup spoon, the Honorable Miz Mayor read a poem as a blessing, something about moon and stars.

I looked at Pastor Pittman, who shrugged his shoulders.

The poem rhymed in places. Mayor Moss didn't say who wrote it. Didn't sound like anything Emily Dickinson wrote, not even slant rhyme. I hadn't lived with Ben Johnson all those years not to know a poem or two when I heard or saw it. He ate, slept and breathed poetry, just couldn't write any worth a darn.

There was an awkward moment. Was this a blessing, a prayer? No, it was a poem so everyone applauded. Then we started on our first course: a murky-colored sort of pale green soup that looked cool and tasty. Perky-faced Johnny-jump-ups floated in the cold soup. Who of us present would lift the little flowers to their lips and eat one? I took a bite, looked around. Everyone else was spooning soup. No one tasted a flower but me.

The purple and yellow flower was crisp and had a bit of a bite like black pepper. I liked it, but then I'd grown up sucking the honey from honeysuckle blooms, chewing sour grass in spring, breaking open maypops that grew on wild passionflower vines. I ate the seeds. Mama Alice taught me which wild plants are edible. Sometimes she even fried daylily blooms, squash and pumpkin blossoms. I liked adventurous eating.

The waitress in black slacks and black T-shirt, sporting pecs big as kettlebells, had her back to me. Didn't look like any waitress I'd ever seen, but she wore a white apron and little lace cap as she went around the table serving cornbread sticks with silver tongs from a large silver basket. Pats of butter in the shape of daisies had already been placed on individual bread plates. I bet if there had been a butter mold in the shape of green beans, the mayor would have it to carry out the motif.

When the waitress walked past me, I saw her face. That bleached-out hair, those snarling lips—none other than Mrs. Butch Rigsbee. Oh my God. In the flesh. In person. Here in this house! I wanted to duck down, get under the table. I had seen her photograph in his wallet and I knew it was her. But she had not seen me up close.

"Oops." The server dropped a corn stick in Debbie Booth's lap. "Hope it wasn't hot." She laughed, a high horsey laugh, stepped back and clapped her hands. Didn't even apologize.

Had it been meant for me? A small, innocuous gesture to remind me I was under threat? Or was I getting paranoid?

I still suspected some weird woman was on the loose in Littleboro and had her eyes on me. Would anyone actually drop a hot corn stick on purpose? Maybe she was just clumsy or simply an inexperienced waitperson.

Debbie quickly picked up the corn stick, tossed it back and forth between her hands, then blew on it to cool. "Not too hot now," she said and buttered it. "Just right." Perfect manners. Our Debbie rose above the situation. That's what Mama Alice would have called it.

Mayor Moss frowned, waved her hand to dismiss the waitress from the room. "New," she said to the rest of us. "Her first event. She's a friend of my chef. Just showed up unexpectedly and he insisted I put her to work."

The waitress, aka Mrs. Butch Rigsbee, leaned around the passage to the butler's pantry, stuck her tongue out and mouthed, "I've got my eyes on you." Did she mean me? Or did she think Debbie was me?

Her Honor didn't see the rude gesture or maybe she chose to ignore it. Her Honor was gracious. My grandmother would have applauded her, too, that she knew how to manage gracefully a sticky situation.

There was a silence in the room loud enough to reach the ceiling. We all held our breath waiting for what might happen next. That's when I thought I saw something move in the centerpiece. Something was in the lilies. The lilies moved. Something alive was in and among the centerpiece.

Two bright little dots of black eyes looked up at me.

Had an anole gotten in with the greenery? But these eyes were bigger, farther apart. Not an anole. At the Dixie Dew, Sherman brought the little green lizards inside regularly and alive. He was a hunter, but not too much of a killer. If I couldn't catch the anoles and put them back outside, Sherman managed to eat them one body part at a time, sometimes leaving the tails. Picky eater.

The mayor kept eating her soup and so did the rest of us. Cool and tasty. Good soup.

The little black dotted eyes in the flower centerpiece moved, disappeared, appeared again.

Did no one but me see them? I didn't want to say anything and cause any sort of commotion, like everyone screaming, jumping up and running from the room. All because of a lizard? Or it could be a snake. All I had seen were eyes and a wiggle in the flowers.

We ate amid companionable chitchat: the weather first and foremost, the festival, the trashion show, who had been where, doing what with whom. The corn sticks had gone back to the kitchen and our little butter flowers got softer and wider on the plates.

I smelled some sort of chicken dish coming after the soup and thought to myself, Please don't let the vegetable be green beans. Spinach, I can love. The ubiquitous broccoli lightly steamed. Anything but green beans. Knowing the mayor, and in keeping with the theme, she'd probably planned them first. I hoped dessert was going to be something gooey and chocolate. Please let it be chocolate.

"My wife sent over her Lemon Crème Cake," Pittman said, as if he'd read my thoughts. "It's to die for."

I hoped not, but no sooner had he said it than Miss Isabella screamed, "There's a turtle in my soup!"

She fell back in her chair, which landed on the floor with

a loud *kathump*. She lay flat on her back, both legs kicking in the air, arms waving frantically.

"There's a turtle in my soup!" Miss Isabella screamed. "It's alive. Alive! It looked at me."

"What?" the man from *The Mess* asked. He cocked his ear toward Miss Isabella. "What's in your soup? A fly?"

I didn't hear her say "fly." She said "turtle." Or I thought she said "turtle." I wasn't sure and it surely did sound odd. Everyone at the table looked at each other. Had she said "turtle"? I saw puzzled frowns around the table. No one knew what to do. We froze like people in a painting.

"Oh," said our honorable mayor, springing up from her chair, "my goodness. That must be *our* precious Nadine." She came around the table, plucked the box turtle from Miss Isabella's soup bowl, held it at eye level and said, "Why you smart little thing, you. Of course. You knew it's mock turtle soup. You knew, didn't you?" She laughed, picked up one of the thick monogrammed linen napkins from the table and wiped Nadine's feet, her little toes as dainty as a doll's fingers. "Smart, smart girl."

The turtle blinked as if to say, Where did all these people come from? A perky turtle. She looked intelligent, even.

"Those clever Betts Brothers must have put Nadine in the centerpiece. They know how she loves flowers." Mayor Moss held the turtle close to her chest, said to it, "Don't be scared." The turtle nodded her little head. "She is not fond of loud noises and that scream may have scared her a bit," Mayor Moss told the group. "But she does love the television in her room. Especially PBS and golf. Tennis matches make her nervous."

Mayor Moss walked to the French doors and opened them to a flagstone patio. "She's had her bath for today," she called back to the frantic Miss Isabella, still flailing on the floor. "And sometimes she gets a touch of baby oil on her shell to keep the shine. She's a perfectly lovely turtle."

With that she took the turtle out to the patio, patted her shell a couple of times, then released her at the base of an ivy-covered fountain. "Play sweet," Mayor Moss said.

I didn't know whom she expected the turtle to play with. A vole or two? A dragonfly? A lizard? And a turtle with her own room and TV? Who knew?

The rest of us stood looking down at Miss Isabella thrashing like a two-year-old having a tantrum. Who would reach down to help her up? Then as suddenly as she had screamed and fallen back in her chair, Miss Isabella went limp. Arms limp, outspread on the floor, legs limp, eyes rolled back in her head.

"Is she breathing?" someone asked. I think it was Dr. Rouse Wilson, the dentist. I'd been in his chair often enough growing up I should have recognized him across the table, but in a sport coat and Carolina-blue tie, he looked different. And, of course, he'd gotten bald. He bent over Miss Isabella, lifted her wrist and felt for a pulse. "Faint," he said. "I think we better call somebody."

"Who?" asked Her Honor, standing at his elbow. "What?"

A couple of people pulled out cell phones, fingers at the ready to punch in 911, and asked, "What's the house number here?"

"Stand back, everybody," said Dr. Wilson. "Give her some air." He went over to a large plant in the corner, broke off a leaf, and started waving it back and forth, fanning Miss Isabella.

Miss Isabella wasn't making a sound. Not a gurgle. Not a cough. The room was so quiet we could hear the paddle fans going *tick-tick, tick-tick, tick-tick.*

Chapter Twenty-one

"Wait," Dr. Wilson said. "I think she's coming around." He reached down and helped her up. Miss Isabella stood on her feet, wavered, rocked a bit, held the back of her chair for support. "I think it snapped at me." She pointed in the direction of the centerpiece. "That turtle. It hissed. It was awful. I definitely heard a hiss." Miss Isabella wrapped her arms around herself as though she had to protect herself against a turtle, or the memory of the one who had since left the room.

Calista Moss drew herself up tight as a folded umbrella. "Nadine does not hiss. She has never hissed in her life. And snapping is not in her nature. She is not a snapping turtle."

Miss Isabella shook her mass of white curls fluffy as a bag of cotton balls, put a hand to her forehead. "I don't feel well at all."

Dr. Wilson, who had been holding her elbow, said, "I think I'll take her to the emergency room, get her checked out."

Everyone around the table murmured that seemed like a good idea.

We took our seats. Now there were three empty chairs at the table.

"I'm sure Miss Isabella will be perfectly fine." Mayor Moss picked up her napkin and spread it again in her lap. "Nadine, I'm not so sure about. She's very sensitive. Gets frightened easily." She frowned slightly, quickly regained her smile, and set about finishing her soup.

Her Honorable's chef, with two sous chefs trailing behind, brought in three large silver casseroles and put them on the sideboard. Everyone was to serve themselves some sort of chicken that was creamy and crispy, mixed with water chestnuts and rice. If there had been green beans around I didn't see any, only asparagus. The third contained a squash casserole that I saw Debbie Booth analyzing in small bites and recording in her mind. I knew Debbie could write a food column and make plain old squash sound like King Midas's gold on a plate.

After everyone had filled their plates, the waitstaff cleared the sideboard of the main meal and brought in dessert trays piled with thumb-sized squares and rounds and triangles of chocolate cake plus little bitty parfaits. But no Lemon Crème Cake. Where was it? Had somebody absconded with it?

Pastor Pittman looked at the dessert tray, then at me, and shrugged his shoulders as if to say, Beats me. I even smelled it baking this morning.

Somehow I could see Mrs. Butch W. Rigsbee back in the kitchen, shoving that whole cake in some takeaway box and beating it out the back door, holing up somewhere to eat it, getting supercharged with sugar and planning her next threat to me. I, like Nadine, did tend to scare easily.

Mr. Moss didn't even appear for dessert. Was there really a Mr. Moss at all?

Outside a window I saw a shadow, someone or something move. Mr. Moss?

When the person came closer, I saw Miles Fortune holding a small camera to his eye. What was he doing here? He came to the window, put his face next to the glass and cupped his hands around his eyes, stepped back, took another camera shot, then came to the window again. He stared in at the luncheon party, stood staring a long time. I tried to get his attention by making a face at him, tried to mouth the words, "Go away. You're being rude."

He ignored me. Everyone else seemed intent on scraping the last smear of chocolate from their dessert plates. Debbie Booth licked her spoon. A minute later, Miles Fortune was gone from the window.

As we were leaving I saw a Rolls-Royce Silver Cloud heading down the driveway. "Oh, dear." Mayor Moss put her hand to her cheek. "That must be Mr. Moss taking Nadine to her psychotherapist. That woman's scream could make her jittery for days."

No one commented. What did one say: I hope she recovers?

I tried to imagine Nadine on the couch in a psychotherapist's office. The one-way conversation.

The first thing I did when I got back to the Dixie Dew was go straight to my pantry/office and on my computer I Googled Mr. Miles Fortune. Put in his name and there was his photo, killer smile and all. He looked L.A. laid-back. Posed casually, one leg laid lightly across the arm of a director's chair in his studio "near downtown Los Angeles." His biography listed a stint at Oxford, some studies at UCLA earlier, then most recently photography shows in London and Paris. I was so impressed I sat back in my chair. And here he was in little ole Littleboro.

While I was at it, I Googled Ossie DelGardo. Nothing. Not one line. I tried every site, every spelling of the name DelGardo. According to Google he didn't exist. Was he here under some assumed name? The idea sent shivers up my backbone. And this Ossie DelGardo was marrying Juanita, one of our own. That meant he'd be here to stay. Not good news.

I called Ida Plum to come look at the computer screen. As she bent over my shoulder and saw the nothing on Ossie, she said, "Sometimes those things don't know it all. And sometimes it's better not to know so much."

"Are you saying ignorance is bliss?"

"Not in your case. If I know you, and I have for too long, not knowing just sets your teeth on edge and you won't rest until you get the down and dirty."

"Well, I wish I didn't know so much about Miles Fortune. All that intimidates me to no end." I got up. "And the less I know and see Ossie DelGardo, the better off I am."

Then I Googled Butch Rigsbee and got nothing. I tried every variation of the name, every spelling. Nothing. What was this business of people who had no birth, no history? These nonpeople? They weren't even a name.

Chapter Twenty-two

I shut down the computer and started upstairs to change clothes. Ida Plum called after me that Malinda had phoned, said she was making posters for the return of Robert Redford and I could come pick them up.

I found Malinda standing next to the copier in the back of Gaddy's. This copier was so old it could have come over on the Ark. In Littleboro if something still worked, we used it until it didn't or you couldn't get parts for it. This ancient box on a stand shook and rumbled as it ran a page. "Look." She handed me one of the posters from the still warm stack.

She had found a picture of the *real* Robert Redford online and put it in the center with the word LOST and then "large white rabbit with red halter and leash answers to the name Robert Redford," followed by my name and phone number.

"This will get attention," she said as she held up the limp poster and waved it to dry.

"Do we want to offer a reward?" I asked.

"Not unless we have to," she said. "I think people who return lost or stray animals don't really expect a reward. They do it because they love animals."

Mr. Gaddy pushed his glasses tighter on his nose, came from behind the pharmacy window. "I'll give a twenty-five-dollar gift certificate."

"Thank you," I said. I'd always liked Mr. Gaddy. He'd flavored all my cough syrups and yucky medicines with coconut because he knew that was one of my favorite tastes, right up there with lemon.

In the bright light of day and a ceiling full of fluorescents, as opposed to the spooky night when Malinda and I had come for more prescription bottle tops, the drugstore looked like any small-town drugstore was supposed to: rows of over-the-counter health remedies, a magazine rack, the cosmetics aisle and of course the soda fountain/lunch counter. But I felt as if Ossie DelGardo's shadow, or the memory of him, lurked just outside the door, around the corner and into the alley.

When Mr. Gaddy was out of earshot I told Malinda, "I found the wallet. I showed Ossie the photos and told him how this woman was threatening me."

"And?" Malinda said as she straightened and stacked the posters. "What?"

"He didn't laugh. At least he didn't do that, but I could

swear he must have been thinking what fun he was going to have telling Juanita what a little scaredy-cat I am."

"What did you want him to do?"

"Take me seriously," I said. "Believe me. Treat me like I have some sense."

"I think you have to earn all that." Malinda put the cover back over the copier.

Since when had she gotten so philosophical? And just when I needed her to be on my side. I wanted total sympathy. But she did have a point. I hugged her, thanked her for all her work on my behalf and Robert Redford's.

I took a handful of posters and headed home.

Chapter Twenty-three

When I got there Scott was at the kitchen table eating a bacon, fig and Brie sandwich Ida Plum had made him. Pig and Fig. One of my favorites. "His mother doesn't cook," she said, and poured him a glass of tea. "I don't know how she raised him."

I thought how humiliating it must be to be an adult and move back in with your parents. I guess that's what Scott did when he came back. After Cedora, after another life. What had he done in California to occupy himself between music gigs and practicing, while his wife (?) Cedora was making herself famous? Build sets for some movie studio? Construction work? Is that how he learned to do all the carpentry and other stuff?

I wondered if Scott still slept in his childhood bedroom

at his mother's house, if it had bunk beds and wallpaper patterned with spaceships or boats or some cartoon character. Snoopy sheets and towels? I had lost a lot of years with Scott, as he had with me, and so far the only filling in the blanks we'd done had been in bed, not catching up on where we'd been and who we'd been with. He had been ahead of me in high school. I hadn't known him as much as I had heard about him. Then when I came back to Littleboro, he was the one to pitch in and help me patch up my house and try to turn it into a business. And occasionally try out one of my beds, with me in it. Just not often enough, and not enough to let me know where I stood. I didn't know where I fitted in his life, if at all. We were both trying to patch together our lives these days and we managed to get a little busy between the sheets on a few occasions, too few and too far between lately. Mostly, as most people did in Littleboro, I let things ride.

Ida Plum had told me she had *heard* that Scott married Cedora Harris, his high school sweetheart, the one the whole town said had "Talent with a capital T." But I didn't know if Ida Plum knew that for sure or it was just one of those things you hear but don't have confirmed. If it hadn't been reported in *The Mess*, then it didn't happen. I needed to check files at *The Mess* office. Maybe later when I wasn't chasing down a runaway rabbit. Or was the only one who seemed concerned about a missing, maybe murdered man Reba had called God.

I knew those files were not online, probably never would be, and to check would mean a whole day, or days, of my life looking through microfilm. There would be a lot of press on Cedora I was sure. I'd heard about her most of my life. Her voice. She sang like a red-haired angel and stood out in the

church choir any Sunday she decided to put in an appearance. She won some sort of state talent contest, then was a
finalist in the Miss America competition, but not the winner.
I remembered watching it with Mama Alice. The whole town
couldn't understand why *our* Cedora only came in as a finalist. It was probably the last Miss America pageant I ever
watched. Art school, then the Maine years with Ben Johnson
occupied my time. He didn't even own a TV. He really believed electronics were polluting the airwaves.

"Do you have a hammer?" I asked Scott. "I need a hammer and some tacks."

"Can't use one of mine," he said between bites of his sandwich. "My hammers are personally weighted to my hands
and body rhythms. These are healing, knowing hands." He
wiggled ten fingers, reached across and patted my hip.

I plundered in Mama Alice's junk drawer until at the back
I found a small hammer, then got some pushpins from my
check-in desk in the hall. I waved the hammer at Scott as I
walked past.

"Not so fast." He grabbed one of my belt loops. "We need
to catch up. Ossie knows Reba's out and he's okay with it. He
wanted to let her stay in the jail cell until he could get more
information on her situation. At the moment, the fellow Reba
thought she killed is in Moore County Medical, critical condition."

I knew that already. Front page of *The Pilot,* but I didn't
say that I knew.

"That's the latest," Scott said. "Word is the fellow could
go either way. Whatever Reba thought she did, Ossie said
there was not a mark on him. Could be pills or some combi-

nation of stuff he swallowed, or smoked. If he doesn't make it, his body will go to Chapel Hill for an autopsy."

"And Reba? What will happen to her then?"

"That's Ossie's call. Police business."

"And that's the way Mr. Ossie wants to have it," Ida Plum said, "with your nose out of it, Beth McKenzie."

"I have to find Verna's rabbit before it's too late." I pulled loose from Scott's hold on my belt loops. Since when and where had Scott gotten buddy-buddy with Ossie DelGardo? At the Breakfast Nook? Blue's Dinette? Service station? Probably at one of the guy hangouts in this town.

"Any chance Robert Redford is with Reba, wherever she is? Her tree?" Scott used his napkin, left it beside his plate. I saw Ida Plum had given him some of Mama Alice's secret-recipe sweet-and-sour pickles. The open jar was too near his plate so I removed temptation. I picked up that jar and screwed on the lid. People loved those pickles so much they couldn't stop with just one. The jar was half-full and I didn't know how many Scott had eaten or how many jars we had left. These were reserved for special occasions and special people. Ida Plum must have felt Scott Smith was one of those. I was still thinking on that one. Our relationship at the moment was just that, a relationship. More than friends, but not really committed to anything heading toward permanent. I didn't know whether either of us wanted that. We were in the middle.

"You don't worry about Miss Reba," Ida Plum told Scott, then she looked at me and winked. "We got her covered."

Scott reached over and did a tap dance with his fingers on my arm, lifted his face for a kiss.

"No hammer," I said and whirled around, "no kiss."

"Stingy with your affection, aren't you?" Scott grinned. "Why do I always have to earn your love?"

"Not earn," I said. "I've got scars and scabs you haven't seen from this battle of just taking things one day at a time."

"And I've got to build one more booth, reinforce the bandstand, then hang some banners and sheeting," Scott said. "If this festival thing happened more than once a year, it would kill us all. Work us to death."

"Worry us to death," Ida Plum said. She picked up his plate. "Even if some of us have to keep the everyday wheels turning." She looked at me, pointed to a bill on the counter: $240. The real plumber had come and gone. "He said these old houses are only patch-up jobs until the next fitting decides to spring a leak. I think he looked around and saw graduate school for his kids."

"Thank you," I said. And meant it. She was my rock, my steady ground to stand on when the world around me was crashing like ocean waves. "Mr. Fortune get back?" I asked, as I ran my hand over the hammer handle. I bet my grandmother's hands were the last ones to touch this hammer. Or had this hammer belonged to my grandfather, the furniture maker, the woodworker? I could almost feel a warmth in the worn smoothness.

"Who's Mr. Fortune?" Scott stood and pushed his chair in.

"The person who found Verna after she fell," I said. "And my latest Dixie Dew guest." I pointed upstairs.

"What does he look like?" Scott asked.

I wondered why he'd want to know and felt like saying

none of your beeswax, that old sassy grade school answer. Instead I said, "Oh, you'll know him when you see him."

Ida Plum laughed. "He's not only a mystery, he's picking up our mystery guest. Someone to do something with the festival."

Scott rolled his eyes. He knew something he wasn't telling.

I left Scott with his hand in the cookie jar and Ida Plum pretending to slap it. The cookie jar was in the shape of a giant green apple. It had been on my grandmother's kitchen counter as long as I could remember. And as long as I could remember it was never empty, most often filled with oatmeal raisin cookies baked from scratch, except when I came home last fall. There hadn't been a crumb in that cookie jar. My grandmother had been in the nursing home where she died after her fall. Sometimes I stocked the jar with packaged stuff, but not often, and sometimes I cheated and popped in some "almost homemade" oatmeal cookies with coconut and chocolate chips from the new Phoenix Bakery that had opened next to Gaddy's Drug Store.

I grabbed a box of tacks and headed out the front door.

Chapter Twenty-four

Reba was the first person I met outside the white picket gate of the Dixie Dew. She was humming some tune I couldn't quite name and carrying one of Verna's umbrellas that had a bent spoke. The sky was a perfect blue. Not one cloud sailed across it. Verna's umbrella had one side flopped down like a huge red bird with a broken wing.

Reba wore an orange chenille housecoat I'd seen on Verna's clothesline in the past. The tufts were gone in a lot of places and it was too short for her. She'd tied the belt in front so the back hiked up, where I saw some of the long-legged panties Verna favored. They had torn and ragged lace on the legs that came to Reba's knees.

If Verna was able to come home after some rehab, she

wouldn't miss that robe or the panties. I bet in that house she had a dozen packs of new panties ordered from some old-fashioned mail-order place in New England. I'd seen stacks of their brown catalogs on one of her tables downstairs.

"Think it's going to rain, Reba?" I asked, as I tacked a poster to the utility pole.

"Sometime," she said, and looked at a sky so clear and bright it blazed blue.

She was right. It was going to rain. Sometime. Just please not on our Green Bean Festival.

"Where you headed?" I asked as I walked and she walked beside me, holding the poor umbrella over my head.

"Not to jail." She punched the air with her fist. "Not to Mr. Ossie's jailhouse room. No sirree. Broke the door down." She laughed, jumped up and down and jiggled the umbrella with both hands.

I tacked up more posters. Reba held the posters to the poles with the tip of her umbrella while I tacked.

"You haven't seen Robert Redford anywhere, have you?" I tapped the poster.

"TV," she said. "On a horse, horsey, horse."

"I mean the rabbit named Robert Redford. The white rabbit."

She shook her head no. "No rabbit nowhere no time. Any-time." She walked on. Barefoot. Which made me remember her flip-flops. In my car parked in my driveway. With her wedding dress. The wedding, which started this whole busi-ness of God and him being dead and Reba killing him. She seemed to have forgotten the whole thing. Jail had been the most recent thing on her mind. I wondered how much wedding cake she'd eaten and if the rest of it was left in Verna's bed for rats and mice and who knows what else to find.

Reba skipped down the street like a child, the umbrella bouncing up and down. Oh, to be so innocent, so absolutely carefree, trusting in everything and everybody.

For a long moment I just stood and watched Reba skipping down that sidewalk, stopping to hop over a raised place or crack, and I wondered if maybe all of us who had been involved in the so-called wedding joke had learned a lesson. In our boredom and need for something to talk about, a shared experience, we had used her. Not something to be proud of. Now one man was missing and maybe dead, another one nearly dead, plus a wild and strange woman was after me breathing fire. Verna could have a broken ankle and Robert Redford was missing. Or dead? And people thought this was a quiet little town where nothing ever happened. Little did they know that underneath the appearance of peace and tranquility in Littleboro things went on. And on and on. The ordinary and sometimes, since I had moved back, the not so ordinary. Dead or nearly dead bodies kept blocking my way toward normal. Quiet small-town days and months and years. The kind I'd grown up with and wanted back. Peace and harmony. No crime. No Ossie DelGardo anywhere in sight.

We had births and deaths, but these days in Littleboro, we had more deaths than births. *The Mess* always had at least a half page of long obituaries and during the winter months, more. The obits said things like "Zelina Hatley passed at age 101 after having lived a good life in the community where she was born." Other deaths were ages ninety-six or eighty-eight, teachers, a barber beloved by the whole town, pillars of Littleboro. Gone. Buried on the hill. Not many moved in. People kept "dying off" as the saying went. The population was dwindling.

We had the usual seasonal things: the Easter egg hunt at Lemon Lake with "fewer in attendance than ever before" and an ominous note that this would be the last year unless attendance picked up. The annual opening of the town pool in early summer had the same ominous note. The town was dying natural deaths, mostly. Miss Lavinia's death in my bed-and-breakfast had been "unnatural," as was Father Roderick's and later Miss Tempie's final swat at the sensibility of Littleboro's "upper class." *The Mess* simply reported the facts, but everybody knew. We have always known how to read between the lines in *The Mess*. Between the lines was where the truth often hid.

With these thoughts tumbling in my head, I kept tacking posters.

Chapter Twenty-five

Tuesday came and I was no closer to any sanity than I was on Saturday when all this business with Reba and God and Ossie started. It was also the third day of the missing rabbit. Reba was wandering around barefoot. I should tell her that her flip-flops were still on the front seat of my car along with her wedding dress. I wasn't particularly looking forward to the Green Bean Parade Day, followed by the Green Bean Cook-off.

Normally I hate parades. Maybe I'm the only person in the world who does. They're boring. They're all pretty much the same: marching bands, some Miss Somebody of Something in a convertible waving and fake-smiling, the usual fire truck, police car, mayor, city council person, some horse people pulling up the rear, blah, blah, blah. Still, it had been a long time since I'd seen a real parade and since this was Littleboro, I knew the parade wouldn't be a big one or last very long.

This one would start at the fairgrounds, meander down-town, wind around the courthouse and end up back at the fairgrounds where Debbie Booth and Miss Isabella (if she'd recovered) would be judging the green bean entries. I as-sumed the mayor had rounded up a third judge. Somehow I could imagine Debbie and Miss Isabella coming back to the Dixie Dew looking a bit green around the gills. I knew I would if I taste tested all those green beans.

Ida Plum said she'd seen all the parades in her life she ever wanted to see and then some. She headed home and though she didn't say so, I had a feeling she'd stop by to check on Verna. I knew she wouldn't mention that Robert Redford was still missing; that sort of news could or would cause Verna to spring up, weak ankle, rehab and all, and start sprinting or hobbling down the street calling that rabbit. Ida Plum knew how to mind her Ps and Qs and she never carried gossip. At least not that much and not too often, just shared what she picked up at Juanita's when she went for her weekly appoint-ment to get her mass of cotton white curls washed, fluffed and sprayed to perfection. She always looked the same. I bet if you shook her awake in the middle of the night she'd look like she always did, every hair in its proper place. Several ladies who had been Juanita's regulars for ages still got modified beehives. Ida Plum said as they left the shop, they'd pat the sides of their beehive hairdos and say, "The higher the hair, the closer to Heaven." She'd laugh saying that.

I watched the parade from in front of Mr. Gaddy's, which

had closed, as had a few of the other stores along Main Street. Mama Alice told me that during WWII all the downtown stores closed every Wednesday at noon so people could go home and work their victory gardens. She said that's when it became prayer meeting night at churches, too. Now most of the stores I knew as a child were vacant, empty, yearning spaces. A few were occupied by consignment shops or antiques stores. Somehow the fabric shop and Juanita's Kurl Up and Dye had hung on, along with Bennett's Jewelry, which had been on Main Street forever. And of course Gaddy's Drug Store, and the S & T Soda Shoppe, which still had a soda fountain with the original booths and little metal chairs and tables and the best and world's biggest banana splits. So there wasn't much to close for a couple of hours and it was Tuesday, not Wednesday, after all.

At noon Malinda locked the door of Gaddy's and came out with her son Elvis. We each held one of his hands as he stood between us. He loved us to swing him back and forth and he'd giggle until Malinda made him stop asking. I personally thought at three it was cute and showed he was getting to be more little boy than baby these days.

"He loves a parade," Malinda said, "as long as they don't include a flyover. One Fourth of July some planes flew over a parade in Faith and he screamed for an hour. We had to leave."

"No chance of that here. This is Littleboro," I said. "And it isn't a Christmas parade, so Santa won't be throwing out stale Tootsie Rolls." This parade would be raggle-taggle whatever could be rounded up, shoved into a band uniform or dance costume and marched down the street.

"What do you bet You-Know-Who will be somewhere in it?" Malinda asked. "If she can still squeeze herself into her car."

You-Know-Who was Lesley Lynn Leaford from high school, whose daddy bought her a baby-blue Thunderbird convertible when she first got her driver's license. She drove all the cheerleaders in it for high school homecoming football parades. After that her life went downhill. The car became a classic and she became well padded with a couple hundred pounds. A town legend, Lesley Lynn Leaford. I hadn't thought of her in years.

Mama Alice had catered her wedding the summer after Lesley Lynn graduated from high school. She'd dated the groom since eighth grade. Their wedding was the talk of the town: twelve bridesmaids, parties, luncheons, bridal showers. She was feted so much Mama Alice and I laughed for years whenever we saw the word "fete" in *The Mess*. Hadn't been a wedding in Littleboro to match Lesley Lynn's to this day. Lesley Lynn divorced in a year and moved back home to live with her daddy and take care of him. Every day the two of them ate breakfast at The Nook, had lunch with John Blue and the crowd at the diner and they probably went to Apex for supper. People said they hadn't had a stove in that house in years. She never learned how to use one. But she sure knew how to use a knife and fork, people said behind her back.

"I figure she'll be right up front in the parade in that vintage car," I answered Malinda.

Ossie DelGardo started things off by blowing the siren of the police car. He didn't smile or wave, just cruised slowly down the street. The car and driver and siren seemed to be saying, Get out of the way. Get out of the way, you idiot people who have nothing to do but stand here waiting for something to happen. His set lips and thick eyebrows seemed to say this parade business was not in his job description and he considered it all a waste of his trained professional, framed-degree, expert time. Elvis pulled his hand away and waved. Malinda laughed. "He likes cars. Any car."

I thought of Crazy Reba, how she liked to ride. She'd get in the car with anybody. Look at the trouble she was in now. Not a dangerous business, just sticky. I knew when *The Mess* came out Ossie would be on the front page right in the center: badges, white hat and all. Ossie in his glory. Our hero on the trail of this mysterious man, John Doe, aka Mr. Nobody, found "at roadside picnic area." Only Reba and I and Pastor Pittman would know the truth. Or half of the truth. The other half remained. Where was the real Butch Rigsbee? Was Ossie even looking? He couldn't be doing much looking if he was leading a parade!

Now I just stood there as Ossie's police car passed, not waving or smiling, not willing to give him the pleasure of seeing me being friendly. We had crossed swords too many times for him not to know that any show of enthusiasm from me would be false. And I didn't play false. I played fair. I wasn't sure he did.

The Littleboro High School band came next with the usual bass drum behind a couple majorettes in white twirling their batons and high stepping in their tasseled boots. A bunch of clarinets, a trumpet or two, and some snare drums followed. They made a hardy and brave attempt to play a jazzed-up version of what I guessed was supposed to be "Carolina in the Morning." We jumped Elvis up and down to the music as they walked past.

Then came a dance troupe in pink tutus. Five little girls with their hair rolled atop their heads, wearing makeup and eye shadow with sparkles, pranced by. Two of them looked to be about the age of Elvis. I could swear several wore false eyelashes. And bright-red lipstick.

"My grandmother wouldn't let me out of the house like that," I said to Malinda. Not that I ever twirled around a dance studio when I was growing up. Piano lessons with Miss Tempie had been my Waterloo. That awful woman with her alcohol swipes on the piano keys and the ruler she used to whack my hands when I hit a wrong key.

A float from the First Baptist Church putt-putted by. A half dozen choir members in white sat stiffly in straight chairs and sang "Shall We Gather at the River." They didn't look up from their books. Several looked as if they had just eaten a pickle.

The First Presbyterian Church float followed. Pastor Pittman waved and waved. His wide smile and friendly wave seemed almost a beckon. He belied that old bit about Presbyterians being the "frozen chosen." The choir wore purple robes and sang "For All the Saints." I wondered what his choir members would think if they knew he'd been seen at Motel 3 and with me, of all people? He seemed to give me a secret little half smile at the mayor's luncheon and I made sure not to return it in kind. But the turtle incident would have taken anyone's mind off anything said or referred to about motels and/or Crazy Reba's latest escapade. That was old news. We were in parade mode now.

Where was Lesley Lynn Leaford? Some convertibles drove past with officials of some sort. County commissioners, I guessed. The fire truck. A van from animal control that had cats painted on one side, dogs on the other.

"Wonder where turtles and rabbits fit in their scheme of things?" Malinda asked. I'd told her about Nadine the turtle's luncheon adventure while we waited for the parade to start. "Let's take Elvis there sometime, let him meet and pet a cute turtle," she said. "I wouldn't object if he wanted one. Quieter than a hamster, doesn't have to be walked and Mama would be impressed Nadine likes PBS. Wonder what she thought of *Downton Abbey*?"

We laughed and Elvis let go our hands to play with some pebbles from one of the empty flowerpots next to the metal table and chairs in front of the drugstore.

A Boy Scout troop marched by. A tubby little boy carrying the flag was so drenched in sweat his hair looked wet.

A Rolls-Royce Silver Cloud drove past, but it had dark windows and we couldn't see who was in it. There was no sign on the side that declared a sponsor of some sort. It seemed to have gotten in the parade by mistake. Certainly didn't belong.

"Nobody I know." Malinda shrugged both shoulders.

I said, "But I saw that car at Mayor Moss's." I told Malinda how I had seen the car from the dining-room window. The car had backed from one of the five garages and quietly rolled down the hill toward the street. I'd wondered if inside those dark windows was the mysterious Mr. Moss. What was the purpose of this car in the parade, if indeed there was one?

People in parades smiled and waved, they didn't hide behind dark windows, anonymous. Could it be our mystery guest Miles Fortune was always saving a room for and buzzing back and forth to RDU Airport?

Our Mayor Moss came next in a white convertible draped in green bunting. She wore a green dress and matching hat big as a forty-eight-inch pizza box. Kate Middleton had nothing on our girl. Miz Mayor even wore green gloves and waved and smiled like a pro. I wondered if, in another life, she had been a prom queen or sweetheart of some fraternity at some swanky East Coast college. Someday when I had nothing else to do I'd Google her.

A floral truck painted with every flower that ever bloomed drove by with the Betts Brothers' logo squeezed between the roses and ivy garlands. Ronnie Betts waved from the driver's-side window, his brother from the passenger's side.

"Still no Lesley Lynn?" I peered down the street. The parade was almost at its end. Only one more float, a car or two and the horses.

The last float was done in black and pink. Black crepe paper with big pink satin bows. I mean big! At least three feet wide. On the float sat a shiny black beauty shop chair and on each side, in black smocks with pink slacks and pink bows in their hair, stood Juanita from Kurl Up and Dye and her assistant, Tina Marie. Their hair matched their pink slacks. They waved and smacked the world's biggest pair of scissors open and closed like a huge menacing bird, which didn't make me want to avail myself of their services.

Then with the last *clop, clop* of hooves and few *plops* of horse patties, the parade was over. "No Lesley Lynn," I said. "What's the world coming to? Did she die and nobody told me?"

Malinda didn't answer. As a pharmacist she'd know about prescriptions going to somebody by the bucketful, but by professional oath and just plain good sense and integrity she didn't answer. I'd read nothing about Lesley Lynn in *The Mess* since I came back to Littleboro. She must have moved, left for a life of her own if her father had died. Nothing to hold her here.

About that time Malinda's mother pulled up to the curb in a red Toyota Prius and Malinda buckled Elvis, kicking and screaming, into his car seat. "Bye." She blew him a kiss. He snuffled and blew one back.

"Nap time," she said as we walked toward the fairgrounds. "He gets cranky and we sure don't want to be chasing and losing him at whatever is going on." "Losing" reminded me Robert Redford was still out there somewhere, probably hungry and thirsty.

"No one has called about the Robert Redford posters," I said.

Malinda sighed. "Rabbits eat clover. I bet he's not starving."

We walked on, not talking, not looking forward to what we were going to see at the fairgrounds.

Chapter Twenty-six

Turned out there wasn't much. Well, this was the first year of the Green Bean Festival and Mayor Moss was fairly new in town. When I asked how in the world she ever got elected, Scott said, "She's the only one who ran. It was unanimous."

The question was why anyone would want the job. The answer had to be that Mayor Moss was maybe an ingénue, a fresh-from-somewhere sophisticate who wanted to play politics. I didn't think she was one of those "let's dive in and raise the burg into the twenty-first century" types. And she wasn't an Ossie DelGardo, who acted like he thought anybody with a Southern accent was a yokel too dumb to walk and chew gum at the same time.

At the fairgrounds entrance was a ten-foot-tall sculpture

of a giant green bean wearing a top hat and holding a cane. He was outlined with blinking green fairy lights. Mr. Bean, I supposed. Should we stop and salute him like he was some sort of dignitary? Malinda and I let out a huge laugh at the same time. "And who says green beans aren't sexy?" I asked. "That's about as phallic as you can get."

Then I turned around to see if Mayor Moss or any of the committee happened to be within hearing distance. No one was close, but as sure as I'd said what I was thinking, which was, Whose god-awful idea was this? than the originator or the sculptor would be right behind me and I'd be left with egg on my face. Or in this case green bean mush.

Actually, there was almost nobody around.

Clyde Edgemont had a display of used cars and there was a vintage Carolina-blue Thunderbird among them. Could it be Lesley Lynn's? Nobody was around to ask, so we walked on.

We passed by a couple empty booths, old and weathered but shored up with some new lumber, which told me Scott had been there with hammer and nails and hope.

One booth advertised Green Bean Burgers and I thought, "Why not?" If kale was the current green rage, then green beans might be next. Some men in green aprons and chef's hats flipped burgers. Across the top of the booth was a sign: HOPE ETERNAL COMMUNITY CHURCH and the letters WWJE.

"WWJE?" Malinda stopped to read them.

I grabbed her arm and pulled her along. "What Would Jesus Eat?"

"Of course." Malinda clapped her hands together. "Of course."

Down the almost bare midway I saw a booth swathed in green lights, making it glow a green bright enough to make you shade your eyes. GET YOUR GREEN IN the sign, decorated with a string of little lights in the shape of green beans, read. Wow. I had seen strings of lights in the shape of red chili peppers, but itty-bitty green beans was a new one.

In one of the occupied booths, demonstrating some sort of juicer machine big as a steam cleaner, stood someone who looked like Mrs. Butch Rigsbee. That woman sure moved in fast and moved around a lot. First serving luncheon at Mayor Moss's and now here slinging smoothies. She wore a green tank top that displayed her deltoids and biceps with tattoos of vines and snakes. You couldn't hear her spiel above the roar of the machine juicing and crunching. I saw a basket full of jars of canned green beans, another basket of some bananas, pears, cherries and avocados and decided there was nothing that could make a green bean smoothie delicious.

I knew I sure didn't want to taste anything this woman would whip up. She had threatened me on the phone and intentionally dropped a hot corn stick in Debbie Booth's lap at the mayor's luncheon. I didn't feel safe around her, not one bit. I grabbed Malinda's arm to try to hurry her away from the menace.

Malinda didn't budge.

"Come on," I said, my voice a little sharp. I pulled at her.

Mrs. Rigsbee's helper, in a green smock with a cap made of green felt leaves, leaned out from the booth. She was pressing upon passersby, which in this case was only me and Malinda, small white cups of a sample smoothie. "It's our pear, peanut butter and green bean flavor," she said.

I waved her hand away, but Malinda took one. "Peanut butter? Gotta be good." And before I could say "don't" she had downed the stuff.

"Not bad," she said. "But not so good either." She tossed her cup into the trash and shook her head. "I think I can live the rest of my life perfectly happy without ever tasting another. You put it up to your lips and down it goes. No stopping it. Like a green oyster." She shuddered and wiped her hand across her mouth.

I steered Malinda toward the Agriculture Building.

The Agriculture Building smelled the way I remembered: aged dust and fresh sawdust. The spaces where 4-H and Home Extension people used to put up educational displays and instructional booths were mostly bare. Toward the back we saw Miss Isabella leaning over a row of brightly lit food items. She had a clipboard, wore an apron and a hairnet, and waved a tasting fork. Someone followed her and it wasn't Debbie Booth, but Miles Fortune in the most elegant suit I'd ever seen on a man. It shouted custom-made, perfectly tailored, and he wore a green-and-white-checked shirt with a tie that changed colors. He reached over to check the label on something that looked like pond scum, all green and frothy piled in a dish. "Blended Italian Garden Salad," he said when he saw me. "I'm not touching it."

"Green beans are the main ingredient," Miss Isabella said. "Herbs and garlic. Not bad. It's an interesting idea."

The woman must have a stomach of iron, I thought. Wonder how many food competitions she had judged all these years? And lived!

"These brownies I can go for," Miles said. He broke one in half and handed pieces to me and Malinda.

"We're not doing desserts yet," Miss Isabella snapped. She looked as if she'd like to take her trusty clipboard and wham the three of us on the head. But she didn't. She focused back on the array of dishes in front of her to be judged.

I wondered when and where and how Miles Fortune got pulled in to being a judge. I thought he had people to see about something or an airport run to Raleigh. He must have read my mind because he turned to me and whispered, "On hold."

"So who hornswoggled you into risking your taste buds in this crazy business?" I asked, but he had stuck a tasting fork into something that looked like an ordinary green bean casserole for any ordinary Thanksgiving table. He didn't answer, just shook his head.

"And where's our cute little Debbie Booth?" I asked.

"She started out fine," Miss Isabella said. "We finished the appetizers and soups, then she started feeling woozy, sick to her stomach. She just had to taste that god-awful-looking and smelling smoothie sample . . . so devoted to her profession. I didn't go near that booth, but bless her soul, that girl is something else when it comes to food tasting." Miss Isabella sighed. "Somebody took her back to your place."

"The Dixie Dew?" I asked. My next thought was, Oh no, not again. Shades of Miss Lavinia. It could never happen again. Fate would not deal two deaths to my budding business venture. No way. Then I calmed down. Maybe Debbie had a slight stomach bug, nothing to panic over. Food judging had to be risky business. I wouldn't want to do it, not in a million years and not if they paid me, as bad as I could use the money. It would be money or my life on the tasting fork.

Malinda and Miles had moved down to more entrées, more casseroles, cheesy-looking noodle things, then I saw cakes and what was left of the brownies.

"A flourless chocolate cake," Malinda said, eating a piece out of her hand. "But made with green beans."

"So where's the green beans?"

"Who cares?" said Miles Fortune cutting himself a slice.

I figured if you can put kale in everything you cook and bake, zucchini in bread and cakes, then green beans can go in, too. Just puree the hell out of them and mix well. They don't actually have much taste in themselves and nobody would know. Chocolate can cover up anything, maybe even poison.

Our Miz Mayor came rushing up to be the third judge. Somewhere, somehow, in mere minutes she had ditched the parade people, zippered herself into another darker shade of green linen sheath dress. Maybe she'd changed in the back of her car or the nearest "convenience facility." She clamped on a huge matching green hat as Miss Isabella handed her a clipboard, apron, tasting fork and bottle of water.

"Stand back," Miss Isabella told Malinda and me, then pointed Miles and Ms. Moss to the first dishes on the table. "Start right there," Miss Isabella said, "we're behind."

I loved how she ordered the mayor around and how Miz Mayor scooted to the end of the row in her kitten heels, sawdust billowing little tan dust clouds after her. Malinda held a napkin tightly to her mouth.

Had the smoothie gotten to her already?

"I need a convenience facility, a comfort station," she said with half a laugh. "In a hurry." She looked a bit green around the gills, as Mama Alice would say.

I looked around for Porta-Potties and didn't see anything that looked like one. Probably the mayor had banned plastic ones from the festival. Back in my childhood the Littleboro fairgrounds had wooden "johnny houses" out behind the animal barns. Surely those had been replaced years ago. I had no fond memories of having to "go" in one of those dark, smelly, spiderwebby wooden booths. Mama Alice would always say, "Why in the world didn't you go before we left the house?" And I'd protest, "I did, I did."

Now I saw a small, tall johnny house gleaming with unpainted fresh lumber. One of Scott's recent projects for the festival?

A sign beside it read, MODEL ORGANIC SOLAR CONVENIENCE FACILITY—USES NO WATER, NO ELECTRICITY. On the roof bubbled a solar tube. "Look." I took Malinda's hand and pulled her toward the door that actually had a half-moon shape cut in it, plus a couple of stars. I laughed and lifted up the wooden bar that held the door shut. This "model" didn't have a doorknob, and inside you pulled the door shut with a long string of leather with a knot tied in the end. I guess you held it to hold the door closed. What a showcase of simplicity.

Malinda bent over the hole carved into the sleekly finished pine board. "Close the door," she said.

I pulled in a length of leather string and held it while her smoothie rushed upward and out and down the hole. Then

I handed her some sheets from the roll of tissue on a loop of string tied to a nail on the wall. Simplify, simplify must have been the order for whoever built this. And built it well, with the freshly cut pine boards notched together in golden smoothness.

I love fresh lumber. This little johnny even smelled like cut pine. I ran my hand over the wall. Nice, beautiful wood. Was this the way of the future? Used no water, no electricity. Little carbon footprints all the way around.

After Malinda "tossed her smoothie," she wiped her mouth, said "yug" a couple of times and that she felt better but thought we ought to head home.

I took her arm and we walked slowly, slowly toward the Dixie Dew. I thought to anyone looking who didn't know us, we must have looked like two little old ladies out for a stroll, old friends who had known each other all their lives and were now depending on each other for balance and staying up-right, keeping each other safe and alive. And that's what we really were. Well, alive at least. Safe, I didn't feel so good about.

Behind us at the fairgrounds the judges were still judging and heaven knows what else was going on. What green bean rumpus was afoot?

As we headed toward the Dixie Dew I wondered if Debbie Booth was alive and well or at least on her way toward get-ting up from her sickbed and back to judging. If she had her green on and was jumping with it. Please God, let her be okay. Please, please, please.

And thank you, Jesus, that Malinda's malady was only temporary. So far.

Chapter Twenty-seven

Sherman sat on the Dixie Dew porch washing a paw. When I went in the front door he followed me up the stairs to the room where I hoped Debbie Booth was recovering from her "stomach bug."

I tapped lightly on her door, called, "Debbie, Debbie Booth."

No answer. My heart was choking me it was so huge in my throat. I called louder. Knocked again. Harder.

This time I heard a little moan.

"Are you all right?" Oh, thank God she was alive.

A muffled reply. Oh, she was alive.

"May I come in?"

"Wmumffered."

I didn't know if that was a no or yes or help or yes you can come in. I tried the knob. Locked. All I knew was that she was alive!

I heard the bed creak and footsteps padding across the floor, then Debbie opened the door a crack and stuck her curly head out and said, "I'm okay. Just had the throw ups and sit downs." She still looked cute, but not her usual perky self. She was pale and wan.

"Oh, dear," I said. "Anything I can do?"

"I'm feeling better. Really. Just weak as water." She gave a thin little half smile.

"I'm so sorry," I said. "Would you like me to bring you up a cup of tea? Some toast?"

"Later, later," she said. "I'm going back to bed." And she shut the door.

I was relieved down to my little toe. Shades of Miss Lavinia Lovingood were not being repeated. She was alive! Whew. I wiped sweat beads from my forehead and went downstairs to bed.

That night every time I closed my eyes I saw white rabbits jumping over a fence, looking back at me with fear in their eyes. Hundreds of rabbits, all leaping, looking back. Some of them wore masks that looked like the photo of Butch Rigsbee only with long flopping ears. Where was the man? If he was dead, his ghost was trying to tell me that. It said nothing while bigger-than-life white rabbits hopped away with blue backpacks on their backs.

I'd heard Miles Fortune and Miss Isabella come in, though they did so very quietly, politely. Then I heard the clink of spoons against china cups as one or both of them must have made a cup of tea or cocoa. I left the dining-room kettle always plugged in and a basket of teas and cocoa beside it on the sideboard for guests to help themselves. I thought if Scott or Malinda had been around we would have shared a nice touch of sherry, a glass of blackberry wine or a good-night toddy with rum and cream. I didn't need any tonight. Things were quiet, if still mysterious. For example, where was the person for whom Miles Fortune was reserving my extra bedroom? He was paying for a room nobody was using. But most of all, where the hell was that damn rabbit?

I must have hit the pillow hard, eyes already closed and the rest of me close behind. Rabbits, rabbits, rabbits all night long.

Chapter Twenty-eight

I woke with a start, damp with sweat. The clock read six a.m. I pulled myself up, feeling creaky as a hundred-year-old. I pulled on yesterday's jeans and a clean T-shirt and in break-neck speed went to the kitchen. I brewed coffee, telling my-self, "Think, think, think. If you were a rabbit where would you be?"

Where there's food, of course. If Robert Redford was like Sherman, he thought food first thing in the morning until last thing at night. Food, food, food. Pellets. Rabbit chow. Robert Redford couldn't live on fresh clover forever. He'd come home!

Of course. But I had looked under every leaf and limb and shrub in Verna's yard. I'd looked under her house, *in* her house as much as I could, and there was not a trace of Robert

Redford. But if he came home, or had come home, he wouldn't be able to get in. He couldn't open the front door, and though there were steps to the back porch, I couldn't see him hopping up them to push in the screen door.

Finding Robert Redford was not the most important of my worries, but a nagging one that kept my mind off being paranoid about Mrs. Butch Truck Driver Rigsbee and her threats on my life. I still felt safe in Littleboro most of the time. I had family (Ida Plum was close as family) and Scott and Malinda. And if Littleboro was the kind of place Reba could sleep outdoors and wander the streets any hour of the day or night she took a notion, then I could shake off my concerns for my own safety.

Reba! If Reba was in and out of Verna's house, she might let Robert Redford in, but I couldn't quite see Reba under a roof, any roof, for very long, even if she did have cake to eat and a plush antique canopy bed to sleep in.

I left a note for Ida Plum to put the coffee cake in the oven and pour the juice, put out the fresh fruit, that I was going "rabbit hunting." I'd set the table the night before. I didn't have to tell Ida Plum what to do, but I felt better leaving the note, acting as if I were in charge of things. Going into Verna's could be dangerous. Stuff was piled so high there was only a narrow path through rooms and there was always a chance something could topple and avalanche, bury me under six feet of collected crap. This way, at least if I didn't come back in a reasonable amount of time, Ida Plum would know where to look and order some steam shovels, bulldozers and bucket trucks to dig and claw their way in to find my body.

I even thought about taking a rake or shovel with me. This was not a jungle so no bush knife was needed unless I ran into vermin. A hard hat might have been nice, and I should have remembered to bring a flashlight. Though it was daylight, old houses tended to be really dark inside.

At the front door of Verna's house the first thing I checked was to see if it was locked. No. The knob turned, the door opened, and I was in, which meant Reba was probably out. Roaming? Gone back to her tree. That's the first place Ossie would go looking.

I called, "Reba?" No answer. The whole house was quiet as a tomb. Not an easy or good metaphor.

I eased my way into the hall and bypassed the living room, not that I could have gotten in it anyway. The French doors had stuff piled next to them so close I knew I'd never get the doors open. The dining room was the same way.

I squeezed myself down the path. At least I could see the ceiling, which looked as if it needed painting and replastering. The huge patches of lattice showing through where the plaster had fallen looked worse than the ceilings at the Dixie Dew, missing pieces of miniature scrolls and swags and swirls, before Scott and his crew remolded and repaired the plaster and painted them with beautiful creamy white paint.

On the path to my left was a sort of den, I supposed. Somewhere behind stacks of newspaper, magazines and books there was probably a fireplace. On the far wall there was probably a window or two now covered with "stuff." I might not be the neatest person in the world, but I knew for sure I could never live like this.

Two bedrooms across the hall looked as if nobody had been in them in years. The beds were covered with clothes piled to the ceiling. The floor was wall to wall with boxes of shoes. My Lord, there must be a couple hundred pairs. Some boxes were stacked on top of each other, some were open, and shoes were scattered like some big department store fire sale. Hell had to be a shoe department with every pair on sale and when you found the perfect shoe that fit, you couldn't find its mate. Digging and digging through hundreds of shoes to find one that matched.

The word "Hell" made me think of fire and how this place could go up in minutes. Old timber, heart-of-pine flooring, plus Verna's collection of stuff. This place was a fire hazard. If I reported it to some town department, could it be declared a fire hazard? Condemned? Would Verna have to move? Where would she go? As far as I knew she had no family. No sisters, therefore no nieces or nephews. Cousins? Cousins didn't usually take cousins in.

I was getting more depressed the longer I stayed in this house, but I kept going until finally, in a small room at the back of the hall, I saw a recliner chair and some quilts. There was a tiny TV on a table close by. This must be where Verna spent most of her time, perhaps even sleeping in that chair. The bathroom was just around the corner.

I felt awful that I had not checked on her, but I'd been up to my ears with all I had to do to get the Dixie Dew Bed-and-Breakfast up and running and try to get The Pink Pineapple tearoom off the ground. Not that I'd had that many events yet, just the occasional call for a tea or two with sandwiches, which I could whip up in no time. And I always had scones in the freezer, some cakes of various kinds. I could have made the time.

In the kitchen I already knew what I'd find: all those plastic containers from frozen dinners that Verna had washed and stacked in rows on her counters. Plus the boxes they came in, all neatly stacked on the table by the window where the curtains hung heavy with dust and gook from a thousand days and nights.

Verna's kitchen had one of those old porcelain sinks with the drain board, and, miracle of miracles, there wasn't a dirty dish in it. Sparkling clean. Underneath the sink was not a cabinet but a sort of skirt. The fabric, a print of pansies, gathered and strung on a wire, concealed the dark underneath.

I had to get out of there, but I couldn't go without one more attempt at finding Robert Redford. I couldn't figure out how to call a rabbit. For cats you call, "Here kitty, kitty." For rabbits, do you call, "Bunny, bunny, bunny"? That didn't sound right, so I whistled. I put two fingers in my mouth and whistled. I was so out of practice the sound came out more a sputter and a lisp.

But what do you know? The curtains under the sink parted and two pink eyes sparkled up at me.

"Robert Redford?" I stepped back in utter surprise.

He hopped out and I swear he grinned at me as if to say, You found me. Okay, you're *it*, your turn. Now you go hide. I swear that rabbit smiled.

I looked behind the curtains and saw a huge bag of rabbit chow, a water dish and his litter box. Self-contained rabbit hutch. Reba must have outfitted him and said, "Now rabbit, you stay there. Be home," then gone off and left him.

She had told me she hadn't seen Robert Redford when she helped me tack up posters. She may have meant she hadn't seen him that day, or she could have said it with her fingers crossed behind her back to cancel out the lie. All I knew was at this moment I had found Robert Redford. I hugged up that rabbit and even kissed his warm pink nose, laughing and crying a little.

"Oh bunny, honey, you're all right. You're all right." I held him close, felt his little heart racing right up close to mine. He was all warm and fuzzy and really sweet, nuzzling my neck and chin. He was all right.

He was going to stay all right, too, and I was going to know where he was because I was taking him home with me to the Dixie Dew.

Chapter Twenty-nine

Robert Redford was kicking, trying to wiggle out of my arms. He still had on his red harness and leash, so I put him down and let him walk—hop—to the Dixie Dew's front steps, where he let me pick him up and carry him inside.

Inside we were greeted with cheers from Ida Plum, Scott and Malinda, who had stopped by on her way to work and said, "Today's got to be a better day than yesterday." She did the thumbs-up victory sign.

Ida Plum just gave us a puzzled look and took Robert Redford in her arms.

Miss Isabella and Miles Fortune smiled, looked up from their breakfast, but kept eating as if they were enjoying these odd locals, who had such strange customs of shouting and cheering when someone came in the door carrying a big rabbit. Odd, but harmless in a quaint way.

Robert Redford got passed around for hugs and petting as I told his tale of adventure. Not that I knew all of it, but I simply guessed that he'd hopped home after Verna was taken to Moore County Medical. After eating his fill of clover and spending a night out in the dark and dew he must have been on the porch when Reba broke out of jail and came to Verna's house for asylum. She'd let him in.

"And cake," Ida Plum said taking her turn with the rabbit again.

"Cake?" Scott's eyebrows raised. He looked at Ida Plum.

"Reba found her own wedding cake in my freezer and stole it," I said, taking back Robert Redford, who now wanted to nip at my hair. We headed toward the kitchen.

As I walked through the dining room I saw something that almost made me stop in my tracks. An empty place at the table, Debbie Booth's. Miss Isabella and Miles Fortune calmly continued their breakfast and gave small, indulgent smiles as the troop of us passed by. Where was Debbie Booth? I needed to check on her.

First I had to put out a water dish for the rabbit on the mat beside Sherman's own yellow bowl, then pour him a portion of cat chow in another bowl. Sherman moved over and the two of them sat eating side by side as though they'd been doing things this way for years. "Good kitty," I said and patted Sherman's black head.

"Good rabbit." I patted Robert Redford's white one.

Back in the dining room I got down to the panic of the day, Debbie Booth's place at the table. "Debbie Booth? Anybody know what's keeping her?" I tried to keep the concern out of my voice.

Ida Plum and Scott shook their heads no. "I'll bet she just wanted to sleep in. Recover from seeing and tasting all those green bean concoctions. I know I would," Ida Plum said. She brought in more coffee and nudged me toward the kitchen.

"What?" I asked as I watched Scott pick up his retractable ruler from the kitchen table, flick it in and out. "I got work to do." He grinned. "That is if you want a gazebo anytime soon."

Did I? Did I? Just the word "gazebo" coming from his lips gladdened my heart. So there was hope, but was it possible in time for the wedding? I could have kissed him soundly and more than once but first I had to see the real thing sitting in my back garden. I'd been hoping for the gazebo long before this green bean thing came upon us and had the whole town going ditsy. The fact was Mayor Moss had deep pockets and I didn't. Scott had a business to run. The gazebo he'd have to build for love and delayed payment until my bank loan came through. Miz Mayor had tied up Scott to build a fashion runway, fair booths, shore up the Agriculture Building and who knows what else. That model solar convenience facility? Was that his idea, too? All this he had done for the mayor in addition to a big restoration project he had going in Pinehurst.

Back in the dining room I refilled coffee cups. Neither Miss Isabella nor Miles Fortune seemed concerned about our missing Debbie Booth. They ate in companionable silence and seemed intent on their personal plans for the day.

Maybe they saw Debbie Booth as one of those self-sufficient

types who gets into a situation and lands on her feet, perky and smiling, waving both hands in the air as if to say, What was all the fuss about? I am fine. I am perfectly fine. But I knew she had not been in good health last night. My question now was whether to wait a bit and see if she came down to breakfast looking a bit peaked but otherwise upright. Or what? It was early yet. I debated whether I should wait or play busybody and go upstairs.

I decided I couldn't dillydally any longer. I almost raced up the stairs. Ida Plum heard me and came behind me, hard on my heels. We screeched to a halt outside Debbie's door. There, just as I had left it last night, was her cup of tea and plate of toast. Untouched. Not a good sign.

"Debbie," I called. "Are you all right?"

No answer. Nothing. Not a sound.

I knocked. Waited, knocked again.

"Debbie!" I called louder.

Ida Plum opened the linen closet to get the master key so we could unlock Debbie's door and go in. But when I tried the door, it was unlocked. We tiptoed in. What I saw made me gasp and reach back for Ida Plum's cool hand.

Debbie Booth, so young, so curly haired and cute, lay flat on her back in bed, her skin the color of wax. She wore green polka-dotted baby doll pajamas and had a few curlers in her hair. Curlers. This was a revelation. I had thought her hair was naturally curly.

I froze. Ida Plum stepped closer, checked Debbie's breathing, then her pulse. She held out her arm to stop me from coming closer. She pulled the sheet up—*all* the way up and over Debbie's head—and we left the room.

"911. They'll call Eikenberry," Ida Plum said. "Then I think we better call Ossie on this one." She closed the door and made sure it was locked.

I was near panic, gasping for air, couldn't believe I'd seen what I'd seen. Not again. Not in my precious Dixie Dew. Two. Two dead people in one house. *My* house! First Miss Lavinia Lovingood and now Debbie Booth. I grabbed my middle and Ida Plum grabbed me. "Don't you pass out on me now," she said. "Or scream. Or anything else."

I stopped at the top of the stairs, took some deep breaths, felt color come back to my face, neck and hands. "What about Miss Isabella and Miles Fortune?" I whispered as we came down the stairs.

"Miss Isabella's luggage is already on the porch. She paid and checked out when she came down for breakfast," Ida Plum said.

"What about Miles Fortune?"

"He said earlier he'd taken his daily run before breakfast this morning and was going over to Raleigh for new running shoes," Ida Plum told me. She went for the phone.

I went outside to wait for the inevitable. What in the world had killed poor Debbie Booth? Yesterday she was throwing up like she had a stomach virus or food poisoning. I'd had a touch of food poisoning once or twice. I felt like hell for a few hours and maybe overnight, weak the next morning, but it didn't kill me. Just made me miserable and resolve not to buy seafood from the back of a pickup truck even if it did say STRAIGHT FROM THE SEA and the driver swore his fish and shrimp had been swimming only hours ago. If it was something Debbie ate, it had to be either at the fairgrounds or before. I knew nothing she'd eaten at the Dixie Dew had anything in it that would make her sick. In my mind I went over what all I had served for breakfast yesterday. The rest of us had eaten the breakfast casserole and muffins and we were fine.

Then I remembered how Malinda had gotten sick at the fairgrounds. The smoothie? Malinda had thrown up almost immediately after drinking it. Miss Isabella mentioned that Debbie had gotten a smoothie and gone back to the Dixie Dew feeling sick right after that. But it didn't make sense. Malinda had the smoothie, thrown up and been okay. Debbie was dead. Did the Dixie Dew have a curse on it? Sometimes I really did wonder.

Chapter Thirty

While Ida Plum called 911, I waved Miss Isabella off. She and Debbie Booth drove to Littleboro in separate cars and as she left, she said she hoped Debbie was enjoying her "lie in" this morning. Last night she thought Debbie had looked a bit under the weather and Miss Isabella had told her to rest and sleep late.

I thought, Oh boy, she sure is sleeping late. God bless her little recipe-loving soul. I just nodded and wished Miss Isabella a safe trip.

Miles Fortune had jogged out after Miss Isabella, cocked his head as he heard the wailing sirens approaching, but shrugged, hopped in his rental car and sped off. "Hurry,

hurry," I said under my breath. As the sirens got closer Miles disappeared down the street in the opposite direction.

I sat in the porch swing holding Sherman. Robert Redford sat at my feet giving himself a bath. "Funny rabbit," I said. "You're a good boy. You're home." He looked up at me, twitched a whisker. He seemed perfectly happy here. He had people and he had Sherman. I didn't worry he'd bound away looking for Verna or try to go next door. He seemed relieved to be found.

I didn't have long to wait for the world as I knew it to come crashing in. Ossie DelGardo had beat Eikenberry to the Dixie Dew. He roared up in the police car, blue and red lights flashing, parked right smack dab in front, got out, slapped on his white cowboy hat, slammed shut the car door and came striding up my walk like he owned the place. And me.

"You," he said and pointed his forefinger like a dagger toward my heart.

"Me?" I said meekly. Sherman jumped down and disappeared in the boxwoods. Robert Redford hopped under the swing.

"You," he repeated. "As I have said more than once, I did not move to this godforsaken nowheresville burg to *work* and you're making my job *work*."

"It's not my fault," I said and started to say more, but just clamped my lips shut and held the door for his majesty's grand entrance. Ossie looked down as if he expected a red carpet, then glanced to both sides like he waited for trumpeters to sound his arrival. He wiped those snakeskin boots on my doormat. Okay, so that proved he wasn't raised in a barn, and I'd give him points for manners.

Ida Plum would raise him up some notches in her rating, which had always been higher than mine since my rating of Ossie was zero. I thought he acted like this town was beneath him, that he was too good for the likes of us Littleborians. That he'd like to wipe his feet on all of us. And here he was engaged to one of us: Juanita, who was a Littleboro institution. I thought she must be doing hair on the third generation: grandmother, daughter and granddaughter. I hadn't been in her shop since my seventh-grade disaster of a perm. I came out looking like a brunette Little Orphan Annie. Every hair on my head was curled and the curls curled. Now I just took the manicure scissors to my bangs and whacked the end of my ponytail when it got to brushing my butt. "Simplify, simplify" was one of the idioms I got from Ben Johnson. I remembered Juanita's beauty shop had plaques of sayings on the walls, things like HAIRDRESSERS ARE A CUT ABOVE and WE ARE BEAUTICIANS, NOT MAGICIANS. A little humor always helps no matter where you find it.

Bruce Bechner came right behind Ossie. It's like the two of them were joined at the hip. You saw one, you saw the other one. Bruce tipped his hat to me and said, "Ma'am." He went in after Ossie, who squared his shoulders and strode ahead like he was ready to take on a Roman army if that's what waited for him inside.

I hugged myself. None of this was good and I feared the worst as I pointed upstairs. What were Ossie and Bruce doing up there? Taking photographs? I hadn't noticed a camera, but then some cameras were so small one could be in a shirt pocket and Ossie and Bruce had whizzed right by me. Checking for fingerprints? Poking in Debbie's lingerie drawer? I thought the worst.

Ida Plum poked her mop of white cotton-ball curls out the door, dish towel slung over her shoulder. "In case you have forgotten, this is still a business. You have one guest and another to come. And breakfast dishes to clear up. I've got linens to do."

About that time Eikenberry very quietly pulled up in his long, gray hearse, parked right in front of the Dixie Dew and came in. He nodded his good morning. And as was his way, his look seemed to measure me up and down and sideways as if he were fitting a coffin for me. In his dark, spiffy suit, white shirt and shiny purple tie, he went upstairs. Purple tie, I thought, what's the world coming to? Is it his little attempt at modernism in a very conservative, traditional business? That purple tie would lead to a lot of speculation and gossip in Littleboro. Did he now have a girlfriend? Been on a vacation to some exotic place with palm trees? Was something different in his life? Any change around Littleboro got the gab going.

I went inside. In the dining room I cleared away breakfast things, then carried dirty dishes into the kitchen and loaded the dishwasher.

I had forgotten to eat breakfast and despite the continued thumping and shuffling of heavy footsteps upstairs, I heated a cranberry muffin and poured myself a mug of the last dregs from the coffeepot, then just sipped and nibbled as I read today's copy of *The Mess*. Sure enough, on the front page was a picture of Ossie in all his glory with details of his finding the unidentified John Doe on the Interstate. Moore County Medical still listed him in critical condition. In bad shape, we called it in Littleboro, but hanging on. Was I the only one who knew this John Doe was not the God Reba thought she was marrying? And if this wasn't her God, who the heck was he? Where was her real fiancé? Wasn't her fiancé Bruce Rigsbee? Reba's fabrications could surely get tangled, woven and rewoven. But I had seen her little love nest and the wedding feast and it was real. When she called me on that cell phone, she'd said she killed God. This mystery guy was still alive, so had she killed Butch Rigsbee, the one she had been calling God? I felt as mixed up as if I were Reba.

I flipped pages over to the society news and there popping off the page was our illustrious Mayor Moss posed ever so prettily with her arm around a few of her luncheon guests. I was not in the picture, nor was Pastor Pittman, but we were mentioned in the "also attendings." Pearl Buttons gave the menu, the names of the flowers in the table centerpiece, and the names of the china and silver patterns. She described the day as having been "weather perfect with a Carolina-blue sky and multitude of fluffy white cumulous clouds." I surmised she must be paid by the word, bless her. And she did love her words, whoever she was. And how did she know all these details unless she was at the luncheon in person? Somebody at that luncheon was a paid snoop and gossip.

Chapter Thirty-one

I was trying to think of all the names of everyone at that luncheon table when I heard footsteps coming down the stairs. Heavy, hard-hitting feet. I heard Eikenberry say, "Dead," as he opened the front door to go out.

Ossie followed. "Dead," he said.

"Chapel Hill," Eikenberry said. "That's where she goes."

A few minutes later Eikenberry came back in and he and his assistant loaded up poor little Debbie Booth onto their stretcher and carried her lightly out the door of the Dixie Dew. They carried that stretcher so effortlessly it looked as if she weighed little more than a tray of feathers.

"You'll hear from us," Ossie said as he left, tipped his hat.

"I'll want you in for some questions so don't plan to go anywhere."

I think I nodded or swallowed or maybe started to say something and it came out as a weak gurgle.

"I'll talk to you later," Ossie said.

It sounded like a threat. Then he mumbled something about fingerprints and how things had been speeded up lately, mumble mumble. Something about he'd see me in his office for a "follow-up," which didn't sound good. I wanted to avoid Ossie's office like it had a contagious virus.

When I went upstairs there was yellow crime scene tape across the bedroom door where Debbie Booth had slept her last sleep. DO NOT ENTER. CRIME SCENE. DO NOT ENTER. There was no way I ever planned to enter that room again. Ever. Except I knew if I stayed in the B and B business I'd have to. But I'd never tell the incoming guest who had last slept in that bed.

I set about cleaning Miss Isabella's room, which didn't take much doing. The whole room was as neat and clean as if she'd never been there. She'd even made the bed. Habit, I supposed, but I'd have to strip all the bedding and wash it for the next guest.

I thought about Reba's room at Motel 3, how she and her "man" had made it almost a home: food, champagne, unpacked their clothes and hung them up. I still could see in my mind the suit and shoes and I'd noticed then that they didn't seem they'd fit the guy on his back on the picnic table. Who was he? All I knew was that he surely wasn't the "God" who apparently owned the big white truck and made regular stops at Motel 3. Also, where was all that stuff from the motel room now? In Ossie's crime lab? Did he even have one? And Reba? Was she still hanging out at Verna's next door or had she gone back to the group home or her good old tree? Reba, Reba, I thought, you and I get in such situations.

Such messes, Ida Plum would say.

I stripped the bed, put on fresh pink sheets, plumped the pillows, did the bathroom, vacuumed and dusted. Whoever Miles Fortune was bringing from the airport could have this room or the room across from his.

I didn't even know if the mystery guest was male or female, not that it mattered. All rooms rented at the same rate and I was glad to have any guest. Even a runaway rabbit who, the last time I looked, was snoozing next to Sherman in the blue living-room chair, Sherman's favorite napping spot. Cat and rabbit looked content.

Ida Plum brought a stack of fresh, warm sheets from the ironer to the linen closet.

"Wait," I said.

"What in the world?" she stood holding the stack of pink.

"I just need one good smell to remind me of Mama Alice and sweet childhood dreams on sun-dried sheets and summer and Littleboro when all was right with the world."

Ida Plum waited while I took a deep breath of sunshine and memories then said, "You enjoy your sniffing. I've got to leave early."

I didn't ask why or where or what for. Ida Plum had her own life and she sure was closemouthed about it. I knew only as much as she wanted me to know which wasn't all that much. There was a daughter in California Ida Plum flew out, ever so reluctantly, to visit. She said she could never live in a place where they dried okra instead of frying and eating it, that those people didn't know good eating when it was set in front of them.

After lunch I checked the computer to see if any reservations had come in. My website had already brought in a few and I really owed Scott for dragging me into social media, plus he had designed a site that made the Dixie Dew look homey and sparkling fresh.

Oh, miracles of Photoshop! He put up photos of the porch, boxwood-lined front walk, porch swing, dining room, bedrooms, the biggest and best bathroom. I oohed and awed, clapped my hands when he ran it by me. "Big bucks," he said. "You owe me big bucks." I must have grimaced because he leaned over and pulled me in for a long kiss. "Down payment," he said.

There were several comments from people who had been guests here, comments like "Soft beds, great breakfast," "small-town charm" and "Be sure to taste the local barbecue." No complaints were listed, which made me give a sigh of pure relief. And no mention of a recent "unpleasant situation." Relief on that one, too, but the last e-mail asked if there had been any "sightings." I read the word twice. As in ghost? Not here, I thought. I've lived in this house all my life and there have not been any unaccountable noises or incidents.

The writer went on to explain she or he had read that a lot of older houses, especially in the South, were haunted and they were especially interested in staying in a B and B that had its own ghost. I e-mailed the writer back to say I was not aware of any at the Dixie Dew but to please come and stay.

Perhaps between the two of us we could scare up, conjure up, a ghost. Miss Lavinia, I wanted to say, you could help me out a little here. Tiptoe in and go through some walls, rearrange some furniture, bang clang some doors or crash some pictures off the wall.

I went upstairs to "deep clean." Ida Plum did the daily beds, dusting and general housekeeping but sometimes I liked to go behind her and really clean. Run a dust mop under the beds to make sure all the dust bunnies were rousted out. Under the dressers, nightstands. Wipe down the baseboards and windowsills. Really, really scrub the tubs and sinks. Run my fingers over the top of door facings, wash light fixtures, wipe even the tops of the bulbs in bedside lamps.

By the time I'd done the first three bedrooms and started across the hall, I thought I heard a door slam downstairs, felt a whoosh of air blow past me. Ida Plum? She'd left before lunch, taking some comp time since both of us would be working our tails off Saturday. Scott? He'd be out at the fairgrounds building booths, probably working in the dark to the pitiful beam of a floodlight until midnight. Malinda? She would have yoo-hooed up the stairs when she came in and noticed nobody in the kitchen.

At the top of the stairs, I called down, "Hello." Nothing but silence answered. I called again, "Ida Plum?" Maybe she'd forgotten something? Nothing.

Cleaning supplies in hand, I opened the door to what had been Miss Lavinia's room, the room where she died. There was a creak, a sort of wooden floor, *old* wooden floor kind of creak. I whirled around. There was nothing behind me. Nobody but me, my brushes and pail in the hall. But across the room I saw the white wicker rocking chair by the window. It seemed to be going back and forth. Or did I only imagine it?

I quickly closed the door and put away my cleaning stuff. Maybe just thinking about ghosts had got me seeing things. I did not need a ghost in this house. I did not want a ghost in this house. I had all I could do to keep up with, and work with the living, in my life.

Before I went downstairs, I stood in front of the closed door to my pink Azalea room, said out loud, "Miss Lavinia, honey, you finished your business here in Littleboro, didn't you? I can't help you. Go away now."

When the day doesn't go right (and when does one ever?) I find a good soak in almost-too-hot water helps. I called Malinda on her cell phone to see if she was okay and told her briefly about Debbie. She had taken the afternoon off to be with Elvis, who was cranky and running a slight temperature, probably from too much parade excitement, she said, and was already in bed.

Epsom salts take some of the bruises away, or at least soothes them a bit. And some drops of lavender oil. Then you keep adding hot water as it cools until the tub gets really full and you have to climb out or drown.

So that's what I did and wished with all my heart that poor little Debbie Booth was asleep in my nice bed upstairs. Or that she had packed her blue roller bag and waved goodbye to me on the Dixie Dew porch this morning, full of a hale and hearty good breakfast. Instead she was either on a slab in a cold morgue, or on her way to one, and I felt awful about it. And awful about me and my bed-and-breakfast business.

Would there be whispers among the bed-and-breakfast crowd? What if this made the headlines in the next issue of *The Mess*? I might as well put out a "for sale" sign, but who would buy it? Next thing after the gossip could be a tale about the Dixie Dew being haunted and then a team of ghostbusters would descend on me.

I twisted and turned, a thousand thoughts and worries diving in and through my mind. Near midnight I turned on my light, picked up a book and tried to read when I heard a key in the lock, then the front door open. I waited. The door closed, the lock clicked in place, then I heard one set of footsteps that sounded male. No little spikey heels, no giggles with it. Only one person had come in. Those flat male footsteps went up the stairs.

I listened hard for a second set and heard only silence. Either Miles Fortune had come back from the airport alone or he was carrying somebody upstairs and the footsteps didn't sound heavy enough for two. Whatever in the world was going on? Why was he making all these airport runs that didn't seem to result in bringing anybody back with him?

What did I know about the man, really? Nothing. Only what I read on his professional website and that he was friendly, very good-looking and dressed like a *GQ* model. The ultimate *Gentleman's Quarterly* model. He seemed to know bits and pieces about the Green Bean Festival and seemed connected somehow to Littleboro, but I didn't know how or what or who with or when. And what had he been doing spying on the luncheon at Mayor Moss's on Monday? My mind was still circling with questions when I went to sleep.

Somewhere in my dreams I saw Ida Plum being crowned Miss Green Bean. She rode on a single float, regal as Cleopatra, held an okra stalk like a spear and waved her other hand that wore Reba's hunk of a diamond ring. Then she took off the ring, threw it into the crowd and rode on.

Chapter Thirty-two

Thursday morning Miles Fortune came to breakfast looking rumpled, his hair mussed and his running clothes wrinkled and ratty. This was not the *GQ* guy I'd seen the past few days.

I poured him coffee. He grunted. He downed his juice, shook his head as if to clear it, then went to my buffet and ladled his plate with grits and scrambled eggs. Ida Plum brought him whole wheat toast, brown and hot, from the kitchen. He mumbled something that sounded a little bit like "thank you," picked up his fork and began to eat like he hadn't seen food in a week.

So far the morning and the whole house seemed filled with a strange quiet. Maybe a respectful quiet for our dear departed Debbie Booth, except Miles didn't know about that, he'd left for Raleigh before Ossie arrived and apparently not returned until around midnight. I wondered if he'd even noticed the crime scene tape on the door down the hall from his room. From his foggy state I thought it was safe to assume he hadn't. I said nothing.

Ida Plum and I tiptoed from the room, whispered in the kitchen about whether we should offer pleasantries or not. We decided not. When I went in to refill his coffee cup, Miles Fortune had started out, had his hand on the front doorknob when I came in.

"Wait," I said. "I have to tell you something."

He turned around, smiled as though he expected something pleasant, some sort of good news. I thought he must be one of those glass-half-full people. Bless them. We need more of them in the world. Unfortunately, what I had to tell him was not good news. I ushered him into the living room, closed the French door and watched his smile quickly fade and his expression turn to puzzled.

"What?" he asked.

"Debbie Booth is dead," I said.

"No." His face darkened. "What? When? How did it happen?"

I told him nobody was sure how it happened. Her body had been taken to Chapel Hill for an autopsy, but my guess was something she ate. Ida Plum had agreed with me and even Miss Isabella said Debbie started feeling sick at the fairgrounds and just got worse.

"My God." Miles grabbed his throat with both hands. "When? What?" He started to make gagging noises. "I ate green stuff, too. I judged." He groaned and shook his head. "I must have been crazy to taste all that stuff."

"Wait," I said. "Miss Isabella said Debbie started feeling sick *before* the judging."

Miles put his hands on his flat, trim stomach.

"I didn't come here to die," he said, and groaned some more. "This sucks. This whole town sucks. My life sucks."

Well, I thought, so much for my glass-half-full theory. He surely is in a whole lot better than the spot poor Debbie Booth's in right now. He bent over, groaned again. I helped him to a chair.

"I'm sure you're fine," I said, even though he did look pale.

He leaned back in his chair and stretched out his legs. I went to the bathroom and brought back a wet washcloth to put on his forehead, then I patted his shoulder. Who knew he was such a baby? A real wuss. "I think if you ate whatever it was that Debbie ate, you would have felt it before now."

"I feel it," he said. "I feel it right now." He grabbed his stomach with both hands, bent over and moaned in agony.

"Relax, take deep breaths," I said, taking his warm hand. "You haven't been throwing up, have you?"

He closed his eyes. "I can't get sick. I'm a runner. Runners don't get sick. You run in rain, in sleet, in snow, in heat and the deep of night. You run, run, run."

I felt him relax. After a few minutes he flung the washcloth toward the ceiling, jerked himself up, shook himself all over like a wet cat, and said, "I'll be okay. I'll be okay. I must think positive."

He patted himself all over as though checking himself for

anything out of the ordinary. No bumps, no bruises, nothing broken. He smiled. "Nothing hurts," he said.

I stood holding the damp cloth I'd managed to catch. I was a bit startled. One minute he's moaning and groaning about dying, the next minute he acts like he's going to bolt out the door.

"Are you sure you're okay?"

He raised both arms in the air and started chanting, "Deep cleansing breaths. Deep cleansing breaths. Deep . . ." Then he was gone, letting the door slam behind him.

I heard footsteps pound across the porch and he was down the walk, out the front gate, gone. He sure hadn't shown much sympathy or concern for Debbie Booth and certainly not an ounce for me and the Dixie Dew. I guess he just had an L.A. kind of mind. Me, me, me.

Scott popped in at lunchtime, looking harried and hungry. He went straight to the fridge and started rummaging around. "Ham?" he said. "Swiss?" Then he went to the bread box. "And rye! Who could ask for more?" He waved two slices of bread in the air.

"Mustard." Ida Plum handed him the jar, plus one of bitter orange marmalade.

"Tops it off," she said.

He got the last of the coffee and I made more. "Tomorrow night's the big night." He winked at me and reached for my hand that held the coffeepot. "We'll find out who is Miss Green Bean. And the winner of the Green Bean Cook-off, do-off, send-off, end-off business."

I thought surely he'd been at the barbershop, service station or Breakfast Nook and heard about the demise of

Debbie Booth. I didn't ask because I really didn't want to know how far or how fast the bad news might have traveled.

"Miss Green Bean will be crowned," he said, chewing.

Whew. Maybe he'd read my expression about Debbie's death and decided not to go there. I sat down beside him.

"Who entered?" I asked. "How many contestants were there?" I couldn't see many teen girls who would want to wear a crown of green beans or even be willing to let it be known for the rest of her life that she was once a Miss Green Bean.

"Don't know," Scott said. He cut his eyes toward the cookie jar. He was as bad as Sherman with body language hinting for food. Ida Plum stepped in front of the cookie jar, blocked his view and folded her arms across her chest. "Some of the music and dancing might be pretty good," he continued.

"Debbie Booth—" I started, then stopped with a knot in my throat big as a coffee mug. I couldn't tell him.

Ida Plum came to stand behind me, put both hands on my shoulders. I needed stability, bless her. Scott ate his sandwich and didn't look up. When he had swallowed a bite, he said, "Heard it at the Breakfast Nook. Too bad."

"She was wonderful," I said, and started to cry. "I loved her newspaper columns and cookbooks and the fact that she was willing to come to Littleboro's First Annual Green Bean Festival to be a judge. She's big time. We're little bitty green beans in the gigantic pot of the foodie world. She could have been anywhere, gone anywhere and she came here!" Ida Plum handed me a napkin and I blew my nose.

"It's not your fault." Scott hugged me.

He didn't know that it might be my fault. That smoothie

could have been meant for me and somehow, at the fair-grounds, Debbie had gotten it first. Scott released me and drank a big swallow of coffee.

"I built the flats for the stage," he said, "decorated them with green bunting our Miz Mayor ordered from some fancy place, beautiful stuff, got about a thousand green balloons all attached." Then he started laughing as if a sudden thought had flashed across his mind, an image. He waved the hand with the knife that had been in the mustard jar. "Can't you just see it? Enough balloons and that whole auditorium at the high school could be lifted into the sky, Miz Mayor and our beauty queen sailing out into the biosphere."

"Not possible," Ida Plum said with a sniff. She was more practiced than me at holding back tears.

"And speaking of possible"—I regained my composure—"how's progress on my gazebo?"

"In good time, my sweet." He aimed for a kiss on my cheek, missed and hit my ear, eased past Ida Plum to the cookie jar, helped himself and shot out the door.

"Do we know anything yet?" I asked Ida Plum. "Green bean queens? What killed Debbie Booth? We're left out of the loop and speaking of loops, any news on Verna? Does she know Robert Redford is alive and well?"

"I told her"—Ida Plum put Scott's plate in the dishwasher—"when I stopped by last night. She seemed relieved, said she knew she could depend on you to take care of him. But she's worried about coming home. Says The Oaks and even their great physical therapy is just not home."

"Of course not," I said. "Too neat. Too clean. Too orga-nized." The thought of Verna coming back to that house depressed me. But what to do? I wasn't even related to her, just concerned. Plus I was the temporary babysitter of Robert Redford.

"*The Pilot* might have a list of the contestants by now, and the cook-off winners," I said as I headed out the door to the mailbox. When I brought it in, I raced Ida Plum to see who would unfold it first. And no news about the John Doe that our Ossie had "rescued" from the roadside picnic table. The man always got the front page. In this case, I guess no news was good news.

Chapter Thirty-three

Nothing about Littleboro on the front page, but that wasn't surprising. *The Pilot* is published in Southern Pines, our sophisticated neighbor. I liked to read news of the rich and world traveled who lived there. What was surprising was that *The Pilot* ever had anything at all about Littleboro.

Nothing about Debbie Booth in the obituaries—it was too soon. She'd make the next issue. I hoped her write-up would be all she'd want it to be. In the second section was a photo of some Boy Scouts hanging a rope bridge in the park in Carelock County. I wondered if their bridge was across the "moat" dug by Miss Tempie's handyman near her property, the moat that almost claimed Malinda last year with its slime and sludge. I hoped somebody had filled the moat in and this rope bridge was across a sparkling little tumbling-over-rocks creek along a wooded trail.

I flipped pages as Ida Plum, at my elbow, looked on. Nothing on page 2 or 3 or 4, but on the society page of *The Pilot* were pictures of Mayor Moss's luncheon and who all were "feted," the word that used to give me and Mama Alice hysterics. There were no details of the menu, the mock turtle soup and corn sticks, assorted desserts, and alas, Nadine the turtle was not mentioned here. Poor Nadine. Her moment of fame and glory had gone unrecorded.

Winners of the Green Bean Cook-off, nobody I knew, were pictured along with the judges: Miss Isabella, Miles Fortune with his teeth-whitening commercial smile and Debbie Booth. Must have been taken just before she fell ill and had to bow out. I looked closer at the photograph. Debbie didn't look her perky self, but had a rather distant and faraway gaze in her eyes. Poor girl. It was as if she was feeling her own mortality even then. The paragraphs below the photo said Debbie Booth was replaced at the last minute by Mayor Calista Moss.

The winning dishes almost made me pitch the paper right then into the recycling bin. Green Scene Canapés, Verde Verde Soup, Salad à la Littleboro, casseroles (of course), then desserts: the green bean brownies and the flourless chocolate cake. I really felt a bit ill just reading them. The same page had photos of jars of pickled beans, dried shucky beans and just plain canned green beans, some of which were arranged so straight they looked like works of art. *The Pilot*'s food photos were in glorious color. I could have shredded the pages, poured on some oil and vinegar and had a salad.

"Well," said Ida Plum. "That only leaves the crowning and the finale fireworks." She picked up the broom to sweep the porch, pushed open the screen door, turned back to me and said, "Isn't it too early for the fireworks?"

"A day too early, in fact," I said.

I walked out onto the front porch, looked at the sky where she was looking and saw red, red, red. And orange. And smoke. The sky was filled with smoke. Then I heard fire trucks. It sounded like more than one.

The whole western sky was ablaze. It looked like the whole downtown of Littleboro was on fire, all of Littleboro, burning like Hell.

"That's not fireworks!" I shouted. "That's fire!"

We started toward it, running.

People I didn't know came from houses I didn't even think were occupied. People came up side streets and back streets and stores along Main Street. Mr. Gaddy and Malinda came from the drugstore, grabbed my arm and we walked together, Ida Plum behind us.

The courthouse. My God, the Carelock County Courthouse was on fire! Two hundred years old, heart-of-pine timbers and walls and floors throughout. It would go up like a rocket.

Flames shot from the roof. I saw the clock in the cuppola melting, the rooster weathervane twirling frantically in the whoosh from the flames. Fire hoses covered the ground, hoses big as conduit pipes, water pulsing through them, shooting great streams of water on the red, orange, yellow and black dragons that breathed fire. As fast, as furious as the firefighters swung hoses around and aimed at the giant flames, more shot up, bigger, bigger. They filled the sky. The courthouse was burning, burning. All the records of Littleboro history, who begot who and married whom and died and were buried where, were going up in flames.

Ossie, in his good guy white hat, kept the crowds from getting too close. He worked the front of the courthouse. I saw Bruce taking care of the back.

Malinda clung to me and I clung to Ida Plum. We stood there in the crowd, stunned. The fire crackled and roared. We heard timbers drop inside the building. I thought of the portraits that hung on the courtroom walls: the one of Lord Carelock, of Judge Little, whom Littleboro was named after. The whole wall was filled with Littleboro legendaries.

Amazingly enough, the outside walls of the courthouse stood. Brick may get sooty and flame streaked but it doesn't burn. Brick buildings leave foundations and outside walls.

It seemed in no time the whole building looked gutted, a shell, a smoldering picture of destruction, the area around it sodden and black. Exhausted firefighters rolled up limp hoses, took off their hats, wiped their smoke-streaked faces and crawled into their trucks.

The crowd talked about what could have started such a fire as that. What would it cost to replace our courthouse, Littleboro's centerpiece, our icon? For as long as anyone could remember, the profile of the Carelock County Courthouse had been the symbol of our town. Some of the crowd wept. I choked, but told myself it was from the heat, the smoke. My eyes burned.

"Crazy Reba," Malinda said, suddenly clenching my arm tighter.

"What?" I asked. "Oh, she's not in the jail. Don't worry."

"It's not that," Malinda said. "I know she's not in there."

"What then?" Ida Plum asked.

"Birthday candles," Malinda said. "Reba was in today wanting birthday candles. No money, of course. I gave her all the packs we had. They were old and dusty. I didn't think they'd even light."

"You don't think . . . ?" I asked. Surely you couldn't burn down a building with birthday candles. Surely not.

But the contrary evidence stood before us, black and empty. Somebody, something had set it on fire. Then I realized I had not seen Miles Fortune in the crowd. I searched the crowd again. And it was a crowd. Families of all sizes, shapes and colors I didn't know we had in Littleboro. I waved to Pastor Pittman, and to Birdie from Calico Cottage. I didn't see a soul that could have been Miles Fortune, and he certainly would have stood out, even though not nattily dressed. Just his stature, his stance, his haircut would have identified him. Could he be a firebug? Had he been hanging around Littleboro planning this grand finale? *His* grand finale?

And Scott? Didn't see him anywhere. But it was a big, big crowd and he could have been anywhere in it. Whatever Green Bean Festival construction he'd planned for today wasn't happening. All festivities had come to a halt when the fire started and smoldered for hours.

The sky darkened toward night and the air hung wet and heavy as though full of sadness and sorrow. Even the statue of the Confederate soldier was black as the smoke had been, covered in soot head to foot, sword to scabbard.

There was no joy anywhere in Littleboro tonight.

Chapter Thirty-four

Walking home, I couldn't bear to look back, to even think of the skyline of Littleboro without that landmark.

Ida Plum had gone on home and Malinda back to Gaddy's to get her Jeep.

Back at the courthouse that still smoldered, firefighters rolled up their hoses, took off their blackened boots and hats, sat down on the curbs, weary heads resting in their hands.

In my living room when I got to the Dixie Dew I saw someone standing with his back to me. Miles Fortune? I brushed flakes of charred paper from my hair and my shoulders. Where had he been all this time? Not in the crowd watching the courthouse burn. I waited for him to say something.

He wore a short, monogrammed robe, brown suede, and he was barefoot.

"Oh," I said.

"I know you want an explanation or maybe more than one," he said, walked over to the fireplace, picked up a vintage vase that had been one of Mama Alice's wedding gifts. He toyed with it, turned to face me, put the vase back.

I picked up Sherman, but he squirmed loose and followed Robert Redford down the hall.

I sat in the blue chair and waited for his explanations.

"I was upset this morning," he said. "I apologize for my rudeness."

"You were fine," I lied. "I thought you were just not a morning person."

"No, I was horrible," he said. "I was upset about Debbie, but more than that my whole reason for being in Littleboro fell apart for the third time when she didn't show up."

"Who?"

"Sunnye," he said and wiggled his feet. I noticed he had elegant, long, white feet and carefully trimmed pink toenails. A man who gets French pedicures. "She was supposed to judge the Miss Green Bean contest. I was to make a documentary of her in her hometown. Local girl makes good, hits Hollywood like a cyclone, goes international, etc."

"Sunnye? Sunnye Deye?" *Bonk*. I slapped the side of my head. Of course. Cedora Harris, who had been Miss Talent-Running-Out-Her-Rear-End when she was at Littleboro High. Cedora, who went to Hollywood as Sunnye Deye and took our Scott Smith along, only he came back and she stayed. All this had been relayed to me by Ida Plum when

Scott first showed up to help renovate the Dixie Dew. How long had he suckled a broken heart before I came back to Littleboro? Did he still have stirrings toward a sweet songstress the likes of which I could never compare to nor compete with?

At this point in my life I had all I could handle trying to support myself in an on-again/off-again bed-and-breakfast business and deal with a couple of murders in which I was somehow, even indirectly, involved. For all I knew Ossie and his crew could padlock all the doors to the Dixie Dew and arrest me tomorrow. I'm sure he'd make up something! I could almost still feel the sharp arrow point of his finger and hear the way he accused when he said "You!" very loud and very direct when he came about Debbie Booth's demise.

Miles Fortune took the chair across from me, stretched out his long, bare legs and reached his arms toward the ceiling. Was he naked under that robe?

"I'm not sure what I'm going to do next. Where to go?" he said.

"Well," I said, "you were a pretty good judge in the Green Bean Cook-off." I tried to lighten up the mood showing on his long, mournful face. "Maybe you have some talent in that direction." I gave a little chirp of a laugh.

He smiled for the first time, a little weak, half attempt. "Not much pay in that, I'd think."

"So does that mean I can rent out her room?"

"Mine, too," he said, looking at the ceiling, his tone so mournful I wanted to get up and go hug him, except if he stood, his robe might fall open and Lord knows what he had, or didn't have, under it.

"There are no jobs in Littleboro," he said. "Especially for a filmmaker, unless you want to show a town standing still. The downfall of the old South." He yawned. "And I already got some of that. Great footage of the fire."

"You were filming the fire?"

"Standing on the roof of the library," he said. "I got some better shots than those of the burning of Atlanta in *Gone With the Wind*." His voice was excited now. Don't stand up, I thought. Just stay quietly seated until I leave the room. "I was covered with soot. That's why I took a shower," he said retying the belt to his robe. "This afternoon I got some great shots of houses in ruin, old Colonial types."

I thought of Miss Tempie's house, among others.

"And some tobacco fields out in the country. Barns," he said. "Nothing stands like those old barns. I got shots that will knock your eyes out. Those that show how the old South ain't no more."

So this explained his goings and comings and why we had no one in the reserved bedroom. Without a judge would there even be a Miss Green Bean? Poor Mayor Moss. Two missing judges, one dead, then the courthouse fire. And I was beginning to think maybe my Dixie Dew business was being done in by bad luck. Two deaths in two years were too many. If word got out in the trade, I would be done in.

"I think we've had a really bad day and what we need is a really good night's sleep." I stood to leave before Miles Fortune beat me to it. "That old cliché about things looking better in the morning just might have some truth to it."

But oh, my Lord, before I could get out of the room, he stood up, his robe swung open and I saw a flash of . . . silver satin boxer shorts. Whew. He retied his robe with great haste and flourish. He seemed totally embarrassed, but maybe no more than me.

"Good night," I said. "Sleep well."

"I'll try," he said. "Tomorrow. No false airport runs. No Sunnye Deye to jerk me around by my camera strap." Then he started singing, "'Sunnye days aren't here again. Tra la tra la.' Never could remember the real words."

"Good night," I said again from the back hall.

Here we were, the only two people in the house, him half-undressed and me still rocking from the day's events. I wanted nothing more to happen today. Nothing I couldn't handle.

Miles Fortune went upstairs to bed.

In the kitchen I made myself a cup of tea and felt the house settle in for the night in a soft, resting sort of slumber. I could have relaxed except the courthouse fire had me all in jitters. Butch Rigsbee could have set it. Nobody seemed to know his whereabouts. Or his crazy wife's. Nobody knew if he was alive or dead and Ossie didn't seem to care. I'd heard brides get jitters; maybe bridegrooms do, too. Makes sense, just not talked about because men wouldn't dare admit to such things.

For no more reason that I was restless and had so many questions hanging over me, I got in Lady Bug and drove out to Motel 3.

I parked down the road a little bit, then walked closer, but stayed in some woods where I could see, just not be seen. Something told me there were answers at Motel 3.

I heard the bulldozer crank, then someone driving it back and forth over the rubble of the landfill.

Allison? Her red copper-colored hair almost glowed in

the moonlight. Allison who had told me Motel 3's handy-dandy-man was the only one here who knew how to operate a bulldozer? Allison? What was this person driving the bull-dozer trying to cover up? And at night?

I saw the bulldozer lights shine on something white and sparkly, then the flash of white disappeared under the rum-ble, grumble, rumble of the bulldozer pushing dirt and debris. When had I seen something that white and sparkly? Bong! Butch Rigsbee's fancy Elvis impersonator suit. What I had thought was his wedding suit. But what was it doing now in this construction/destruction rubble unless there was a body in it? A body that was now under the dirt.

Did I dare call Ossie and say that I thought I knew where to find Butch Rigsbee's body? Ossie either wouldn't believe me or wouldn't care. He sure seemed to have a lot of other things on his mind.

Or should I come back in daylight and try to be sure? Ossie had accused me in the past of going off "half-cocked" on something or someone I found suspicious.

I decided I'd better make sure, so Lady Bug and I putt, putted home, not to sleep, not even to dream, but to toss and turn and worry.

Chapter Thirty-five

"I, for one, don't believe it for a minute," Ida Plum said the next morning. "Nobody, not even Crazy Reba, burns a court-house down with birthday candles."

That's when Scott chimed in. "Somebody down at the service station said that politician who's on trial for embezzling campaign funds and having that affair with a lady photographer had it set to burn up the sex videotape evidence they were storing at our courthouse. It has been all over TV."

"Ha. I bet he just wishes. A sex tape in the Carelock County Courthouse," Ida Plum said. "That beats all." She measured flour to make more biscuits.

"You mean our little Littleboro courthouse had that kind of national media coverage going on and I didn't know about it?" I asked. Which meant I really did keep my nose to the Dixie Dew grindstone closer than Ida Plum was making me believe. TV? We didn't allow them at the Dixie Dew. Maybe Ben Johnson's austerity had left a little bit of residue on me. All that noise and verbal spewing would pollute my peace and harmony, which was considerable when I didn't think about how much I owed fixing up the Dixie Dew and how much more had to be done and what it would cost.

Except for all that, I felt I had come back to claim my childhood and plant my feet in the rich soil of my ancestors. After all, some of them had fought and died for it: Great-Great-Great-Grampa Buie, who had fought in the battle of Spotsylvania Courthouse, had miniballs of gunshot working their way out of his body the rest of his life. But he had come home, miniballs and all. Then more wars, on down to my daddy, who died overseas in battle.

"That was what I heard at the service station." Scott shrugged.

We waited but he didn't add any detail, if he even *knew* any more details.

Instead he reached for the biscuits Ida Plum had put in the warmer basket. I could make muffins in my sleep, but only Ida Plum could make biscuits crisp on the outside, tender and butter-melting on the inside. A true art if there ever was one. "At this point, gossip and speculation are the only things we got," I said. "Is that right?"

"I believe that," said Ida Plum. She peeked in the dining room, then shut the door. "Where's our Mr. Fortune this good morning?" She looked at me as if I had answers, which I did, but I didn't want to talk about it in front of Scott. Surely he knew Sunnye Deye was to judge the Miss Green Bean contest, that his old love was to be back in Littleboro. Maybe he even knew now she wasn't coming. If they did keep in touch, where did that leave me?

I watched Scott refill his coffee mug as though he didn't have a care or concern in the world. Then when he went looking for fig preserves, I knew he was all right. I knew he was looking for fig because he went to my secret stash in the upper, upper cabinet by the pantry.

He found a jar I had half-hidden at the back, pulled it out and reached for another biscuit. For a moment I had a flash of an idea that I could offer a "stop by" breakfast for guys like him who wanted it fast and homemade.

Miles Fortune had not come down to breakfast before Scott left with an extra biscuit wrapped in a napkin Ida Plum handed him. "Bribery," he said. "I know it when I see it." He waved me a quick goodbye and left.

Ida Plum winked at me. "He's going to start on the gazebo. Let's do everything we can to keep him here, on the job, as long as we can. We can feed him lunch, too, if that is what it takes."

Sherman and Robert Redford ate side by side at their separate bowls. He would miss that rabbit when Verna came back home. I let them both out the back door. I didn't have to worry that Robert Redford would run off or roam the neighborhood. He and Sherman were almost always together. Buddies.

I knew keeping Scott on the piddly dink job of my gazebo wouldn't be easy. It was such a small job and he had some big restorations lined up in Pinehurst and Southern Pines, places owned by people with big bucks and deep pockets. I only had big dreams and flat pockets. He had yet to give me an estimate. What if I couldn't afford it right now? But I needed it right now. Juanita had already booked it for her wedding to Ossie. I would have to add it to my already too big bank loan that had this house as collateral.

That was one wedding I'd knock myself out making as close to perfect as possible. Not because I liked Ossie, but because this was Juanita's third and maybe there'd be a fourth in her future, more business for the Dixie Dew. Who knew? I couldn't imagine living with a man like Ossie more than a week. All wound up, going to wipe the world clean of crime and those who even think of committing one. Too focused for me. And I somehow had a feeling Ossie DelGardo was in Littleboro because of something he had done wherever he came from. His eyes were too dark and too close together. And he walked with a swagger, like he owned the town. Mama Alice wouldn't have trusted him farther than she could throw him. She could spot a phony from one meeting and a good look square in the face.

Crazy Reba's wedding was off. Dead and done. It was her dream and we'd all played along. A harmless dream that had made Reba so happy we couldn't bear to burst her balloons. Poor Reba. Where was she now?

It was ten a.m. before Miles Fortune came in from his run, showered and apologized that he'd totally missed breakfast and hoped he hadn't inconvenienced me in any way. He'd gotten pancakes at the Breakfast Nook. "Great pancakes," he said. "I haven't had pancakes in years."

I felt a bit envious and wondered if I should put pancakes

on my menu once in a while, even if they were not one of the things I liked to make. Crepes, yes. Pancakes, no. Crepes had possibilities. Pancakes were pancakes unless they were the Dutch Babies Mama Alice used to pamper me with when I was growing up. She poured batter into an iron skillet on top of the stove, let it set, then put thin apple slices on it, let it puff up and put it on a plate. So sweet you didn't even need syrup or honey.

"Not a problem," I said, but did offer him a cup of coffee.

Ida Plum had made his bed, tidied things, brought the towels down. "A laundry chute would be a dream in this house," she said as she walked by on her way to the basement. Washer there, ironer here in the kitchen. I liked it that way. Loved the smell of sun-dried sheets being ironed. We stored them in the linen closet with dried lavender. Did my guests notice? Did they write comments on the national B and B site?

"Just cream, no sugar." Miles Fortune waved away my offer. Scott would have said "Sugar. Give me some sugar," and leaned toward me hoping for a kiss. But Miles was cooler and besides he didn't know here in the South when someone said "give me some sugar" they meant hugs and kisses.

This Miles was a different man from the one half-dressed in my living room last night. He smiled his gleaming killer of a smile. He wore beige linen pants and a crisp blue pinstripe shirt with white cuffs, this time elegantly rolled to his elbows. I loved to see a man who could roll cuffs and still look perfectly dressed. And he smelled like a fresh shower, all soap, a hint of lotion. Confidence. He radiated zest, enthusiasm.

He stirred cream in his coffee. "Guess what I heard down at the Breakfast Nook?"

I shook my head. He could have heard anything and 90 percent of it wouldn't be true. But I waited.

"The fellow your Ossie cop picked up from the picnic table beside the road, the one who died—"

"Died?" I waited some more, listened harder. Now I was interested. Very interested.

Chapter Thirty-six

"Somebody who works down at the sheriff's department said the guy regained consciousness long enough to say something about a body. Helped bury a body? Something."

"Did he say whose body?" I kept my back to Miles, pretended to crumb the table. This had to be Butch Rigsbee. His body. Had Reba killed him? Oh my God, now she really may have killed him. As well as the fellow I "rescued" from the picnic table. "The stranger died?" I asked.

"Yeah," Miles said, "but get this. The guy said he wanted to get to the hereafter with a clean slate."

Knowing the condition of the body on which I'd done CPR, his conscience would be the only thing clean about him. "So who was killed? Who was the body?" I could guess, but needed to hear somebody say it.

"Get this. The stranger, his name was Swaringen something, hooked up with a woman who thought the dude was going to marry her. Some crazy lady. It's the funniest stuff I ever heard. Everybody at the Breakfast Nook was laughing."

They all knew about Crazy Reba and her wedding. Miles didn't. "Swaringen?"

"Somebody identified him." Miles was enjoying all this. This local color. This wild tale.

I could see he was already thinking what a great story this would make at some swanky party back in L.A., about all the loony local yokels in Littleboro. He'd have them all in stitches. He'd be the life of the party.

"Somebody from Motel 3. That motel that is no motel," Miles said. "Thank God I didn't have to stay there. Bedbugs and fleas would have been the least of my worries. The handyman might have been ready to do me in." He looked at the ceiling, still smiling. I'd admired that blinding white smile at first but now I hated it. So fake. Miles was such a phony. Why had I not seen it before?

Now I was distracted, a bit lost in Miles's story. Swaringen, the man on the picnic table, had been working at Motel 3, and knew something about a body. Could this be Butch Rigsbee? And how in the world did Reba fit in all this?

"What about this woman who was going to marry him?"

"That's even funnier. She came to the motel room with her wedding dress looking for the dead guy. Swaringen told her he was the dead guy's best man and somehow she got the idea she'd marry him instead since the dead guy wasn't there. He must have given her some song and dance."

So Swaringen had convinced Reba he was Butch's best man, "better man," and Reba was ready to marry anybody just so she could be a June bride. But had she really killed him? Or Butch? She had called me to come *save* Swaringen. She wouldn't have done that if she'd been trying to kill him. Plus there was not a mark on his body, and I had sat on a lot of that body. Did she know he might have killed Butch Rigsbee before she got there with her KFC picnic? Was Butch her original God fiancé? She must have bought into this Swaringen's story about being God's best man hook, line and swallow. She had said in all her hysteria that she'd killed a "better man." To her, anyone who drove the GOD truck was "God." This whole thing was getting too strange, even for Littleboro. And Miles was enjoying all this way too much.

"Where were our professional police in all this?" I asked. I tried to say "professional" without my usual sneer. At the moment my dislike for Miles was surpassing my dislike for Ossie. I didn't want Miles thinking I disrespected one of Littleboro's own.

Miles laughed. "Oh the talk was that Ossie and Bruce had been on the case from the beginning." He referred to them by their first names as if they were old buddies of his. I was getting angrier, but I wanted to hear the rest of his story. "In fact," Miles continued, "they'd seen that van parked at the motel earlier, went back and saw the clothes hanging in the closet. Knew they didn't fit Swaringen. They figured out something fishy was going on. Duh." Miles slapped his knees with both hands as though this was as funny as some comedy show. Oh, these locals. Oh, these backwoodsy types.

"It's not funny. People are dead," I said. I didn't want to think about how the morgue in Chapel Hill was filling up with bodies hauled in from Littleboro. Debbie Booth and now the Swaringen guy.

Miles stood to go, still chuckling. "I filmed the remains of the fire," he said. "Got my old-South-in-ruins image. It's perfect."

He was changing the subject but I'd heard enough about bodies for the moment and needed time to sort it all out. The mention of the fire shifted my attention back to yesterday, and the smell of smoke that still lingered outside my B and B.

"It's horrible," I said. "It's ugly. That courthouse was the symbol of our town. It was our icon. We're known for that silhouette of the courthouse with the clock tower on top." I was almost crying. Here he was celebrating, his life back in order, and my town was bereft. Black ruins, shambles, only the brick walls still standing.

Yes, he got the photos he wanted to tell the story he wanted to tell and it would be better without our Miss Sunnye Deye. But what he got wasn't true. Littleboro might not be booming but it certainly wasn't dead.

"And you are going to take this film back to Los Angeles and show the rest of the world this is the American South. See? This is what it looks like. They hang on to their past, revere it, worship it, even."

Miles Fortune pushed back in his chair, put both hands out toward me. "Whoa," he said. "I'm not making a statement. Just showing what I saw."

"You *are* making a statement and it's not true. You're not showing any of the beauty. Only the ruins, the ugly, the neglected." I thought how dismal the Dixie Dew looked when I'd first come home and how it looked now. Not perfect, but with white paint that glowed, a sturdy new roof, and gleaming copper gutters. Black shutters. My pretty tearoom that got an occasional lunch group of book club ladies. My bank loan in big figures that I chipped and chiseled away bit by bit each month. I was hanging on by the fringe of my living-room rug, which was so worn in places you could see the bare boards underneath. Threadbare. I knew what the expression meant. I wanted to ask if he was leaving. I wanted him to leave.

"All right if I stay on a few more days?" he asked as he started out. "It's not like my room's in great demand." He sounded a bit miffed. And who wouldn't be? I'd preached him my sermon, waved my birthright flag in his face.

I nodded. If I said a whole lot more, my anger would singe him. "Stay as long as you like." If he noted the sharp tone in my voice, it didn't show on his face or in the set of his shoulders as he left the room.

What I didn't say was, I hope you scare up a copperhead snake poking around in our "ruins."

Chapter Thirty-seven

I hoped I wouldn't do the same thing when I went back to Motel 3 to see if I could get some answers and try to get Reba out of some of this mess. Was Ossie out looking to re-arrest her?

I cranked up Lady Bug and away we went, even though I didn't know what I expected to find at Motel 3. It was the only place I knew to go, the place where it started with Reba and her wedding supper and Allison playing keep-away with the wallets.

What I saw and heard was Allison on that bulldozer, running it back and forth across the rubble. When she saw me, she aimed that yellow dinosaur in my direction and roared straight toward me as fast as it would go.

Was she trying to run me down? Not if I could help it. I dodged out of her way. She braked the bulldozer to a squeaky stop where it kept on puffing and snorting out black goop until it finally chugged to a silence. Then it seemed to me like that yellow monster sat there and sulked, pouted that it hadn't got the chance to run me over.

Allison climbed down and came over, stomping dirt off her boots, slapping more off torn black leather jeans two sizes too small. Her sweatshirt read TOM CAT'S KITTEN but she didn't look like anybody's kitten to me. "They could have cleaned me out," she said.

"Who? What?"

She took off her hard hat, shook out her hair that now had reddish-pink and blazing-blue streaks in it. More and more it had a look of flames, burning bright down to her coal black roots.

"Ossie and Bruce." She waved her hand toward the rubble.

"You mean when they checked the scene, bagged evidence, that sort of thing? Like they do on TV?" I wanted to start our conversation on a quiet note. Mama Alice always said you can catch more flies with honey than vinegar.

"They only took the rinky-dink stuff out of the room, the prescription stuff. What was left"—she waved an arm toward the rubble—"was the rest of his mess. Butch's clothes, his god-awful tacky suit and shoes and stuff. I told them to take it all. Take the whole pile. Of course they didn't. Wouldn't. Would have saved me a lot of paying by the hour to rent this hunk of junk." She slapped the bulldozer's hood. "Yeah, that bastard. Been using me as a stop-off place between here and Florida."

For what? I wanted to ask, but didn't. Instead I asked, "Using Reba, too?"

"Yeah." Allison clapped her hard hat, smothering the flames of her hair. "All for his dirty business."

"What kind of dirty?" I asked, but she had already walked away, hopped back on the bulldozer and cranked up with a roar that shook the ground under me.

Could Reba be in over her head? Caught up in Swaringen's death and Butch Rigsbee's, too? At least Ossie had the body of Swaringen, but where was Butch's body? I looked harder to try to see that flash of something white I saw last night that I thought might be Butch's suit. Only rubble. No sequins, no white suit.

Allison was into something illegal with Butch the crook along with the murder of Swaringen? Who was the real killer or killers in this business?

I didn't know. So I started home to think on it all, back to my own business. Minding my own business for a change. I wasn't doing much good at anything else.

I got almost to Lady Bug when I saw a flashing of lights, turned to look and noticed the lights going on and off in the office of Motel 3.

I walked over. The door was open, so I went in. That whale of a monster TV was going like crazy, the sound was off, with some black-and-white Western playing. Who was watching it? Allison was on the bulldozer, and there were no cars except mine in the parking lot.

The bedroom door was cracked, so I eased it open all the way and saw somebody in Allison's bed. I walked closer, found myself tiptoeing even on the carpet.

I pulled back the sheet and saw a body. Male. Nude. Butch Rigsbee. Or the dead body of Butch Rigsbee. He was so stark white, his hair looked even blacker. A shock of black hair and a cadaver's smile pulling back from his still sparkling teeth. "Ohhhhhh," I said.

The smell of Old Spice shaving lotion in that room was strong enough to knock me down. Somebody must have emptied a whole bottle in here. I pinched shut my nose, held my breath and turned to leave. To call Ossie. To get out of here before I screamed or threw up or both.

"Don't move," a voice behind me said. Allison?

I had not heard the bulldozer stop, but it must have. I felt her behind me. "He's dead," I said. She started to cry. I felt her crumple, heave deep sobs. Then more sobs. "I know," I said, turned around and held her, let her cry all over me.

"He was not coming back." She finally sniffled.

Well, I could have told her that.

"From Florida." She swallowed a big sob with a wet gulp. "This time. He had a floozy, been seeing her all along." Allison cried more. "They were going to Cuba to live."

"You killed him?" I said.

"I had to. He said he was leaving me. All these years. After all I did for him." She screamed now, leaned over and began to pound both fists on Butch's body. "He said he loved her. *Loved* her! Not me."

I slipped out of the room to call Ossie DelGardo. This time I told him matter-of-factly what had happened, that I was standing next to the room where there was the very dead body of Butch Rigsbee.

I started to close the door, but not before I saw that Allison had crawled into bed and lay there holding Butch Rigsbee's body, sobbing, sobbing like her heart would break.

My next phone call was to Pastor Pittman. I told him to come to Motel 3. That Allison had killed her lover and would need to talk to someone. Pittman is usually a good listener and probably had a lot of counseling bones in his background.

Then I waited for Ossie. This time he would believe me. I had the body to prove it.

Chapter Thirty-eight

Ida Plum is a good listener, too, and this time she didn't scold me for putting my nose in where it didn't belong. She did say she hoped things in Littleboro would calm down after this. That she could do with a little bit of normal for a change.

I thought, So could I. Some everyday, run-of-the-mill ordinary.

But first we had a wedding to cook for. And I was still seething inside when I thought about Miles Fortune and his camera, how he was going to show L.A. all these local yokels.

A kitchen is a good place for therapy. You can get out a lot of frustration, anger and, yes, even grief in a kitchen.

You can beat, chop, sear, broil, whip, scald and more.

When I'm upset I beat up a great cake batter, the fluffier the better, and I bake, bake, bake. I bake breads, rolls, muffins. I steam and sweat and wear down all the worst feelings. The nerve of that man Miles Fortune, poking around to reveal the decaying underbelly of the South. And here's Scott, hammer and nails, paintbrush and ladders, trying to put things back together again. War, I thought. Like me and Ossie. Opposite sides. He sees the ugly, the crime, the undoers, and me, I see the trying-to-do, fix up, clean up, paint up, do up. Make it better. I'm the polished cotton print in the tearoom; Ossie is the dark shadow on winter's eve.

And here I was baking a wedding cake for him. Ordered by Juanita. Seven layers. Plus the groom's cake in the shape of a police badge, Juanita's idea. So I did the sheet cake first, carved it in the shape of a badge, put it in the freezer to ice later, to have ready for the rehearsal dinner the night before the big "I do." I was not hosting the rehearsal dinner. The bridal party was going to some fancy digs in Pinehurst. All I had to do was make the groom's cake for that one. The Dixie Dew would hold the reception in the back garden after Pastor Pittman did the service in the gazebo, which was now only the gazebo in progress.

Occasionally I looked out to see if something, anything was rising in the garden. All I saw so far was stacks of lumber and no trace of Scott. I was reminded of my first days trying to fix up the Dixie Dew when the contractor Verna had recommended ordered materials and more materials and didn't show up to do anything with them. Just ran up my bill at Lowe's and elsewhere. That's when I got lucky and Scott came into my life. Maybe even saved my life, as well as my living, and pried me loose from the clutches of Ossie DelGardo more than once.

I mixed icing by the gallon, listened to a radio talk show on NPR, Frank Stasio's *The State of Things*. Radio and newspapers keep me going. I trust them, believe in them, don't need experts who are not experts pontificating on themselves. World news from the BBC I can handle; I don't need the shock pictures. And I love music, bluegrass to classical, one to get my feet going, the other to soothe my soul.

Ida Plum had left to get her hair done but promised she'd come back and help clean the kitchen. "And fill me in on the latest news," I had called, as she got her purse off the hook in the pantry.

When Ida Plum got back, smelling strongly of perfumed hair "hold it" varnish, she announced, "The latest is that Lesley Lynn Leaford is back in town."

"What?" I stopped Mama Alice's trusty old KitchenAid mixer midswirl. This was news indeed. "I thought she died."

"No. It was her daddy who died."

I scraped the sides of the mixing bowl.

"Not only back in town," Ida Plum thumped one of my already baked layers onto a dish towel, "but."

"Skinny and worth a million dollars?"

"Two of the two." She put the cake pans in the sink.

"So, which one first?" Ida Plum loved to make me pull details out of her. She could be as bad as Verna, drawing out a good story.

"The million dollars." Ida Plum stacked bowls and stuff in the dishwasher.

"Daddy?" I asked.

"None other. Left her *beaucoup* of the stuff." She pronounced the French "boo coos."

"Who'da thunk it?" I made icing rosettes, which I thought too much with the scrolls and swags, but whatever Juanita wanted Juanita was going to get. Maybe marriage would sweeten up Ossie. It couldn't go the reverse.

"Not only money. Tina Marie told me she almost didn't recognize Lesley Lynn."

"Well my, my," I said. "Like how?"

"How what?"

"She didn't recognize her how?"

"Seems not only had she lost a couple tons of weight, but had found some world-class plastic surgeon and availed herself of his or her services."

"My, my," I said again. Our own Lesley Lynn Leaford. "So that could have been her car I saw at the fairgrounds in Clyde Edgemont's display. It would be a classic." Then a sudden thought dived into my mind. Could Lesley Lynn have been in the parade after all? Could she have been in the mysterious dark limo? I couldn't imagine her missing a Littleboro parade, Thunderbird or not.

Things did change in Littleboro. And people. Some came back, like me. Wounded and limping but we crawled back.

"Where is Lesley Lynn staying?" I asked above the roar of the mixer. I was out of icing. Somehow I couldn't see her in the other completed room at Motel 3, if the other room was actually rentable.

"I didn't find that out," Ida Plum said. "Tina Marie had finished my hair." Ida Plum hung her apron on the same pantry nail my grandmother used. I had a sudden small memory flash of nostalgia. "Reba was there," Ida Plum said. "Sitting on the floor, painting her nails some god-awful color I can't even describe. Tina Marie had given her outdated nail polish to keep her entertained."

So Ossie hadn't hauled her in. "How did she seem?"

"Like Reba usually seems," Ida Plum said. "In her own world. Why?"

"No reason," I said. "No reason at all." Except that I did feel good knowing Ossie didn't have his mind set on arresting Reba, locking her up for killing the Swaringen fellow. And now we knew Allison had killed Butch, it was up to Ossie to find out the how and take care of the rest of the business of bringing a killer to justice. Which was Allison. Why did I feel so sorry for her? Love never makes sense. Ask anybody, that's what Ida Plum would say. Cupid's arrows go in many directions.

Chapter Thirty-nine

I was out of powdered sugar, not an uncommon occurrence in this house. I couldn't count the times Mama Alice had sent me to M.&G.'s for a box or three of XXXX sugar. I sometimes thought it was like magic dust. She wore it. The kitchen wore it. You could swipe your finger across kitchen counters or canisters and taste sweetness.

So it turned out that I got filled in on the rest of the story at M.&G.'s Grocery. Here I was over in the baking aisle with Mrs. Pastor Pittman, the Barbie blond stick of a preacher's wife. She tried to hide a box of cake mix, lemon supreme, behind her back but not before I saw it. She wore a lime-green dress with matching shoes. Every time I'd ever seen her, she was in a dress and her shoes always matched. Did she not own a pantsuit or jeans? Were preachers' wives not allowed to wear such things? I thought they must lead a life under a magnifying glass. Yikes.

"You heard about our Lesley Lynn Leaford?" She patted her perfect blond shell of a pageboy. Not a hair out of place.

"Yes," I said. "It sounds wonderful."

"She's staying with us. I keep our guest room always at the ready. You never know." She laughed a little glass chime of a laugh. "Pastor did the services for her father," Mrs. Pittman went on.

I tried to think of Mrs. Pittman's first name. Lynda? Lorie? Lucy? Lydia? Barbie, I decided. Of course. Barbie Pittman.

"She always kept her membership here, paid her pledges. Even after they moved."

Did preachers' wives know everything? Maybe she was the mysterious Pearl Buttons. Mama Alice had kept me posted on some of the local news while I was away, but how could Lesley Lynn Leaford's return have been missed by Pearl Buttons and her binoculars?

"Where had they moved to?"

"North, up north." She laughed. "Stockbridge, Massachusetts. Can you imagine? For her treatments. Some facility there. We had a grand time."

"We? At the facility?" I loaded my shopping cart with yellow boxes of powdered sugar.

"No, no, no." She waved the hand that wasn't hiding the box of cake mix. "The Red Lion Inn. That's where we stayed when Pastor did the services in the cemetery down the street. She paid for us to fly up."

She called her husband "Pastor"? Didn't he have a real people name? Oh my, I thought. "Oh my" seemed to be my words for the day.

"We went to the Norman Rockwell Museum and all that stuff," Mrs. Pittman continued. "It was such fun." Who knew Pastor Pittman was such an art lover? "We rented a car, did Walden Pond, Orchard House . . . he grew up loving *Little Women* as much as I did." She sighed. "Nobody reads it anymore."

I thought, Well, I did, but I liked Nancy Drew better. She had more spunk and wasn't always moaning about Marmee and sick little sisters.

"But Emily's coming back."

Emily? What Emily? She must have seen my puzzled look.

"Why, Emily Dickinson, of course. Her work has always been read, but now she's really popular. We whizzed on over to Amherst. Broke my heart."

"What?" I asked. "What broke your heart?" Who knew Mrs. Pittman was such a reader of poetry? So much I didn't know. Some people kept lovely secrets or maybe I had just never taken the time and energy to get to know them.

"Her grave, of course. It's behind a shopping center." Barbie Pittman looked pained, her perfect lipsticked mouth turned down. "A sort of strip mall. Ugh." She drew up her shoulders.

"What was all this Stockbridge business about?" I asked.

"Daddy Leaford, of course. It seems he grew up there, even posed once for Norman Rockwell. Remember that prom scene *Saturday Evening Post* cover painting? The boy and girl on a date at a soda fountain? The soda jerk was her father. He always said Littleboro reminded him of Stockbridge."

Now I had to laugh. Littleboro, North Carolina, as the flip side of Stockbridge, Massachusetts. How many people never in their lives knew there was an underbelly, another side to everything? She gave me a little three-finger wave and moved toward the checkout line. Guess she had to smuggle her box of cake mix home before somebody else saw her little secret. Did "Pastor" even know she used a mix? What else didn't he know?

Chapter Forty

Back at the Dixie Dew I iced three layers, four more to go. Ida Plum brought in sheets from the clothesline and started at the ironer. This house was filled with good home smells: baking and ironing.

Then I heard the sound of sawing and hammering from the backyard, peeked out and saw Scott with his helper, Randy, hard at work on the gazebo. Could he have it up, painted and ready for Ossie's wedding? I was betting on it, if he had to keep working on it by shining his truck's headlights into the backyard at night, or rig up some sort of outdoor light with an extension cord plugged into the back porch light. Weddings and funerals go on as scheduled most of the time and the world stops for a bit. Pauses, reflects, takes a deep breath.

The Raleigh *News & Observer,* which we counted on for our "real" news, had a half-page obituary of Debbie Booth with a cute, perky photograph of her looking as if she was alive and a listing of all her awards for food writing, her best selling cookbooks. It did not list cause of death, something I was still waiting to learn. No calls from Ossie about the finger-printing. Maybe living in Littleboro had slowed down his New Jersey angst or he was so busy basking in his marital status-to-be he'd put his big-city crime busters on the back burner. He had said I'd hear from him, but so far I hadn't. Too much wedding on his mind, maybe? I hoped.

Mama Alice had owned two of the original big old Kitch-enAid mixers on stands and I had both going. The queen of mixers, these "girls" kept on beating and mixing. Pound cakes, layer cakes, meringues, buttercream frosting, royal icing. They knew butter and sugar and flour and rose to every occasion, doing Mama Alice proud.

I piped trellises in royal icing, arbors and garden gates. Oh that I could ever have the real things in my back garden! But I piped icing and dreamed. I hadn't done royal icing in a long time, not since my teens, with Mama Alice looking over my shoulder. Yet now it felt a bit like she still stood behind me, saying, "That's it. Curve it a bit more. Curley-q she goes."

I had ordered a little bridal couple for the top, but Juanita wanted real roses, fresh roses, along with the icing ones. I guess Juanita just couldn't get enough roses to suit her. I wondered if Ossie would be the type to ever bring her roses on not-so-special occasions after they were married? Somehow I couldn't picture Mr. DelGardo with a bouquet of anything in his hand. Gun, yes. Handcuffs. But not flowers.

White roses I'd have to get delivered from Raleigh if Debbie Booth's fans hadn't bought them out from every florist in town. I bet the day of her service there would even be some enterprising vendors selling boxes of Kleenex and embroidered memorial handkerchiefs to the line of fans waiting to get into Edenton Street Methodist Church.

And I couldn't be there. I had this damn wedding to put on or pull off or whatever the occasion called for. Not that I'd be missed, but I had sent in a donation to the Southern Food Ways Alliance Debbie wrote about so much. That left some roses for other fans to buy.

Ida Plum kept the ironer going, piling up a stack of freshly ironed sheets beside her. Scott and Randy hammered away. The gazebo had a shape, skeleton though it was, and I hugged both guys, Scott the longest. He smelled like cut lumber and had sawdust in his hair. I tousled it. He caught my arm and pulled me in for another hug. "You just love to get close to real work, don't you?" he teased.

"What?" I said. "Baking, icing, decorating in a hot kitchen isn't work? At least out here you got a breeze."

I made them a snack, even whipped up oatmeal cookies. And beer, of course, a local ale Mr. Gaddy stocked in the back of his drugstore. Honey Locust.

"You're a honey," Scott said. "The girl of my dreams." He winked. "And heart." Like he could read my mind and chagrin about last night and this morning with Miles Fortune.

I had been so busy I'd forgotten about Miles and now I remembered, could guess he'd been down filming the remains of the courthouse. Perfect image for his "theme." The South in Ruins. For all I knew he could be a firebug, been the one to start it. He'd sure shown up fast and Johnny-on-the-spot to start filming it.

And here he was staying in *my* house that was two hundred years old, without a sprinkler system, built of pine boards dry as paper. Not that I didn't already have enough to worry about.

Chapter Forty-one

Ida Plum made the cheese straws and when they came from the oven we roasted Honey Hot Nuts. Then she grated vegetables for the little tea sandwiches and I made pimento cheese. No reception could be held in Littleboro without pimento cheese and some sort of pickle. Baby gherkins, you made your own or bought some at the Farmer's Market, but you had to have a sour to cut the sweets. John Blue down at the diner even had a pimento cheeseburger on his menu. It was sloppy to eat, you had to use a knife and fork, but it was really good.

After the pimento cheese, Ida Plum got two mixers with pound cake batter going full-speed for cake squares just in case the wedding cake wasn't enough. I had stored the wedding cake layers in the basement freezer and when I put in the cheese straws, I noticed behind me on the wall shelves and shelves of canned vegetables. Beets, corn, tomatoes, lots of green beans. Every pantry in Littleboro probably looked like this. Mama Alice had a backyard garden and all the summers of my childhood I had weeded, watered, picked vegetables and "got them ready for the canner." When was any of this canned? It had been years since Mama Alice had much of a garden and done canning. "It's cheaper to buy stuff now than to grow it," she'd say, "and a whole lot less work."

After she got the two freezers (in catering you had to do as much as you could ahead of any event) she froze vegetables. Except green beans, which seemed to grow better and more prolifically than anything else in Littleboro, hence our lovely Mayor Moss with her idea for the Green Bean Festival, bless her little not-from-around-here heart. Homegrown green beans were, for some universally recognized reason, not as good frozen, so every self-respecting Littleboro family canned theirs. At the end of a summer a lot of Littleborian women recited, "I put up a hundred and thirteen jars of beans this summer." Or "I did a dozen canners of green beans."

I couldn't help thinking about how different basements were from root cellars. I had a bad memory of root cellars: dark, musty smelling, dirt floors. Mama Alice's basement had a cement floor that was painted a clean-looking gray and the walls, too, were painted. A hardworking commercial washer and oversized drier we used in bad weather stood along one wall and along another was the water heater and furnace. And sure, it had shelves of canned goods, its own whole wall of them.

I picked a jar from the shelf and wiped dust off it. Probably not safe to eat. Home canned vegetables do not have expiration or "best used by" dates on them. There was always the danger of botulism if they were not properly canned.

I'd heard Mama Alice lecture on this deadly stuff as she put jars in the pressure canner, set it on the stove and set the timer. I'd listened to the pressure relief valve "jiggle" in that hot-as-hell summer kitchen many afternoons and vowed I'd never touch another green bean. A vow I didn't have any trouble keeping when I lived "up north." Evidently Maine soil is better suited to potatoes. I love potatoes. Mama Alice sometimes cooked scraped new potatoes atop green beans. I ate the potatoes, left the green beans alone.

As I stood there holding that jar of green beans I remembered all those jars in the booth at the Green Bean Festival and Mrs. Butch Rigsbee presiding over smoothies and brownies and God knows what-all green stuff. Who had tasted it? If there was botulism there, there was enough to do in the whole town, or half of it at least.

But where was the infamous Mrs. Rigsbee now? I didn't realize I'd said this out loud when I came into the kitchen still holding the jar of Mama Alice's canned green beans until Scott said, "Didn't anybody tell you about Ossie's latest civic irritation?"

Scott had come in for a couple more "cold ones" for him and Randy, then stood holding them as he closed the refrigerator with his backside. "Some woman shot up the fairgrounds. Started with the green tin man, then all the balloons one by one. That got Ossie running down there. He must have thought the whole town was under siege." Scott laughed.

This woman had to be Mrs. Butch Rigsbee. None other.

"That's awful," I said, pretending I knew nothing. Sometimes I have found that way gets more information dropped in your lap. "What's with that woman anyway? I mean, she checks in here for an hour, then shows up working for Mayor Moss and drops a hot corn stick in Debbie Booth's lap, then has this booth at the festival."

"Ossie said she said she hated the town of Littleboro and everybody in it."

"Why?" I asked hoping he didn't see my tongue in my cheek. "What did Littleboro ever do to her? This crazy woman."

"She said her husband was cheating with some woman who lived in Littleboro who had all the money from his business dealings and she was target practicing so she'd be ready when she found the right woman. But what she wanted more than her husband was her share of his business."

I thought, Oh, Reba, what have you gotten yourself into now? And me right along with you. I must have had a strange expression on my face because Ida Plum stopped what she was doing and asked, "What? What's all this business about somebody shooting at the fairgrounds who sounds really crazy? Is this the same woman who checked in here and only stayed an hour, then asked for her money back?"

"One and the same," I said, and went back to my faithful KitchenAid and the topic about which Ida Plum and I had been in deep discussion before Scott came in: Verna's plea to come home. Ida Plum had stopped by to see Verna this morning and said Verna was threatening to fly the coop from that "henhouse." Said Verna told her all those women recited their alphabet all day long. Arthritis, Bursitis, Constipation, Dyspepsia, Gout, Hemorrhoids, the whole list. They were making her sick.

Ida Plum scraped a mixer bowl and handed the beaters to Scott, who nodded his thanks and pulled out a chair. "Cake batter and beer," he said. "Yum. The rest of the world doesn't know what it's missing."

"There is no way any self-respecting human can live in that house," I said. "It's not even fit for . . . rabbits." I looked down at Robert Redford helping himself to Sherman's cat chow. Was he even supposed to be eating that instead of his own rabbit kibble? What if he got sick and it was my fault for letting him eat something he was not supposed to?

"How bad is it?" Scott handed me the licked-clean beaters.

"Snake den," Ida Plum said. "Rat's nest." She scrunched her shoulders. "You wouldn't believe it."

"Think I should take a look at her house after I take Randy his refreshment." Scott held up Randy's beer. "Maybe I should take another beer, since he worked while I caught up with my two best girlfriends." He got another from the refrigerator, asked, "Do you know why Southern girls don't sleep around?"

I groaned.

He went on to the punch line. "They'd have to write too many thank-you notes."

I laughed. Ida Plum laughed in spite of herself.

Scott grabbed her by her apron strings, twirled her around

and headed toward the door. "Stay as sweet as you are." He blew her a kiss.

"Smart aleck," she said, and laughed.

Later, when Scott and Randy knocked off for the day, I saw Scott pull his truck into Verna's driveway. The house was unlocked and I knew Scott would know if anything in there was worth anything . . . if he could see it. It wasn't long before I heard him leave. Well, I thought, he probably said to himself the same thing I had said to myself: bring in the bulldozers, bring on the dumpster bins, let the unhoarding begin. With Verna's permission of course. But I dreaded even approaching the subject with her. Would it be "kill the messenger" and she'd never speak to me again? I could live with that. Forgive me, Mama Alice, for causing a rift between neighbors.

Chapter Forty-two

I knew I had to be the one to take this on, so after supper I put Robert Redford in Sherman's crate and drove us to The Oaks, where Verna was doing "rehab" from her fall. I hadn't been to The Oaks since Mama Alice died. Ida Plum liked to say if she broke something—leg, hip, whatever—we were not to take her there. "Just shoot me," she'd say. "That's what they do to horses, only don't throw me in a ditch. Give me a royal send-off and serve moonshine and MoonPies."

When I got to Verna's room and she saw me with Robert Redford, she let out a little scream of pure joy. Robert Redford jumped from my arms straight into her lap and she started hugging him for all he was worth, laughing and crying, "My sweet boy. My own sweet boy."

I was sorry it had taken me so long to think of doing this, how much it would mean to her. After she calmed down and Robert Redford curled up in her lap, I brought up the dreaded subject of her hoard house.

"And Scott says he can handle it. Take whatever you want to sell to the consignment shop."

To my surprise, Verna laughed and said, "Why honey, I been watching that TV show and I'm not one of them people. I know I got a mess. It's just that I got so confused about what you could recycle and what you couldn't, I just let it pile up. Accumulate. And accumulate 'til it got the best of me."

I said again that Scott was willing to haul off some of the stuff and take recycling to the recycling center.

She said, "Tell him to haul off anything he wants. I'd like to start over, do to that house what all you've done to the Dixie Dew. I've put it off too long."

"What about all those shoes?" I asked. Curiosity had gotten the best of me. I had to ask.

"Oh, those," Verna said. "My sister Ella bought out the old Good Morton's store when it went out of business years and years ago, had them all dumped in that bedroom. There's a bed still in there somewhere. Ella." Verna looked pensive for a minute. "Named for Cinderella. And I guess she always had a weakness for shoes."

I had never known Verna had a sister. A much older sister? I'd lived next door all my growing-up years and as far as I knew Verna was the only person who lived in that house. Was Verna making this up or was the body of Ella still on that bed after years and years under all those shoes? Like Miss Emily in Faulkner's spooky story I'd read in my high school

English class. I didn't like Faulkner's picture of the South then or now, but I didn't have time to think about it. I'd do it to-morrow.

I took the rabbit, hugged Verna, and left. What I had dreaded had actually been a piece of cake, which made me think of Reba and wonder if she'd been bunking over at Verna's and that maybe I should warn her that revitalization was about to begin. On second thought, I couldn't imagine Reba under a roof very long. It was just that I hadn't seen her around lately.

"Actually," Scott said the next morning when he came in for coffee, "I stopped by to see Verna yesterday right after I looked around her house and suggested that before she went home I could go in and do some organizing for her. You should have seen her. She clapped her hands together, said she'd love that. That she knew it must look like she was hoarding stuff, but the truth was, she just hadn't had the energy to keep up with things. She said stuff piles on top of stuff and there was nothing in that house worth anything but her and Robert Redford, and they weren't worth much these days."

So Scott had been by before me and had already primed Verna. So much for all my persuasive powers. Scott seemed really distant at times. He knew stuff he didn't tell me. Stuff I should have known. How much did he know about Bruce and Ossie and "police business"?

"There's some really good old furniture behind all that accumulation, and once the junky stuff is out of there, after some paint-up, fix-up, it will be a grand old house."

"Did you go upstairs?" I asked, remembering Crazy Reba sitting upright in that canopy bed eating her wedding cake.

"Upstairs is clean and clear." Scott sipped his coffee. "Evidently stuff didn't make it upstairs, just puddled at the bottom. Collected. Piled up. Accumulated in avalanche proportions. Nothing bad, just stuff."

"So you clean it out enough to make it livable and Verna comes home? Then what?"

"Next step is to get down to details with her about doing what I did, and am doing, to the Dixie Dew to her house." He picked up Robert Redford. "And you can go home, buddy." Sherman rubbed his ankles. "Not you, cat. This is where you live." Robert Redford nibbled Scott's ear.

I was going to miss him. The rabbit, I meant. Maybe Scott, too. Where exactly were we in our relationship? Sunnye Deye was singing her heart out on a million commercials and maybe her way back into his heart. She was glamorous and I was Miss Plain Proprietor of the Dixie Dew Bed-and-Breakfast, a poor proprietor at that. I bet she, like Lesley Lynn Leaford, was worth a fortune. I only had debts and some sweet memories between the sheets. We rarely talked beyond tomorrow. We hardly talked at all. Could I settle with being a little bit of Scott's life? He could go out of my life as quickly and easily as he'd come into it. I knew I had to find time to go to *The Mess* office and do some microfilm reading. I just didn't know when I would.

I looked out the kitchen window. The gazebo was half-finished, and at least it had a roof. The copper roof gleamed in the sunlight. Juanita was going to love it. Her garden wedding. In my mind I could see Ossie in his white hat and snakeskin boots, Juanita on his arm, marching down my flagstone path and up the steps to the gazebo. It was a warm picture and I didn't have many of those "warm pictures" starring Ossie in my mind. Mama Alice would be proud of me for thinking "good thoughts." I was actually thinking more along the lines that with a couple more weddings I could afford to hire Scott and company to take on the Dixie Dew living-room walls, ceiling, moldings, wainscoting and floors. So far I'd only redone the most necessary of Dixie Dew rooms like the entrance hall, dining room and bedrooms, and we'd made some cosmetic touches to the bathrooms and created an office space in the pantry off the kitchen. I'd planned the office for later, but Scott had done that as a surprise, and I loved it. Computers and cookbooks. My life. And it wasn't a bad life if I could just keep people from coming to the Dixie Dew and dying or making threats on my life.

Chapter Forty-three

Ida Plum left early, mysteriously early. In fact she often left later, never early, usually saying—like she had when she first came to work at the Dixie Dew—that she had nothing and nobody waiting on her at home. Not even a cat or dog to be fed. But today I got the feeling she had learned more at Juanita's than she wanted to tell me. More about the weird woman shooting up the fairgrounds. I bet Ida Plum went by Juanita's to tell everyone there how that same woman had come to the Dixie Dew and checked in for an hour, washed her face and left. Putting in her two cents' worth to make a good story. And everybody would have loved it. A funny bit to add to Littleboro folklore.

I could just imagine the woman in the next chair getting a

haircut or perm saying out of the corner of her mouth, "Well, at least this one left alive." I knew those kinds of remarks went around Littleboro all the time, just not to my face.

"Friday, thank goodness it's Friday," Ida Plum had said before she left. "If I ever live through another week like this one, I'll move to California, dried okra or not."

"Thanks tons," I said. "You'd desert me and leave Littleboro in its finest moment? Or should I say moments? Its days of glory?" Were Littleboro's "moments" or "days of glory" when its courthouse caught fire and burned? Was that the first thing anyone would think of when you said you lived in Littleboro or were from the town of Littleboro? Up north, my hometown had been a joke and I had laughed with everybody. Now I felt ashamed. I should have defended Littleboro, the South, my heritage. I had to come crawling back home to see its worth.

Ida Plum hadn't answered, just kept going, out the door, up the walk. From the droop of her shoulders I could tell she was as tired as I felt, and the week wasn't over yet. We still had Miss Green Bean to crown.

Earlier Scott had picked up Ossie's groom's cake to drop off in Southern Pines at the fancy smancy hoity-toity restaurant chosen for the rehearsal dinner. Scott was staying for the dinner. After all, he had been invited. He was part of the wedding party, Ossie's best man. I was simply a working girl, but better working than not. I wouldn't have known what to do with my life if I hadn't been working. I'd even taught summer school and kiddie camps when I lived in Maine. One must support oneself and I felt blessed to be able to do so.

That was also the first time I'd heard Scott mention he was to be Ossie's best man.

"Why you?" I'd asked him when he told me. "Why not Bruce? That's his sidekick."

"Why not me?" Scott shot back. "I know my way around nuptials. Played music for a few in my life."

I wanted to ask if he'd also been in one, but didn't think this was the time. He brushed my shoulder as he walked by, winked and left.

So he and Ossie had gotten to be buddies behind my back. Where did Scott's loyalties lie? I thought he felt the same way about Ossie DelGardo as I did: a transplanted Yankee know-it-all. Did I have a backstabber and traitor in my life? Not to mention occasionally in my bed? Not a happy thought.

Google. That's what would tell me Scott Smith's marital status. So I Googled. What I got was a web page and list of professional appearances with a group called When Cousins Marry.

Wow. They'd played all over the place: Tokyo, lots of London gigs, Nashville many, many times of course, played from Scotland to Switzerland, Canada. I had a celebrity in my life. Hmmm. Wonder if Sunnye Deye had been on those tours? I looked over the photos and didn't see a girl singer. Just a younger Scott with longer hair either cuddling a bass guitar or behind the keyboard. I thought bass players must know just how to hold a woman. Nowhere did it say anything personal. No information on marital status. No information on day jobs, what Scott did when the group wasn't on tour. Did they play clubs? Did he do construction work so he could be out of doors in California and hear the music of hammers and saws? And why, most of all, was he back in Littleboro?

I cleaned the kitchen, watched out the window as the gazebo began to take shape.

I thought about how much I loved the long days of summer, the mild evenings that seemed to go on forever, blending into night. I remembered catching lightning bugs, letting them go, watching stars sprinkle the sky, trying to figure out the constellations. I remembered sitting on the front porch with Mama Alice and Verna while they broke the tops and bottoms from the green beans to pull out the tough strings and how the beans *plink, plink*ed when tossed into gray enamel pans at their feet. How they canned them. Some of those damn green beans were still in the jars in Verna's cellar and Mama Alice's basement gathering dust. They had outlived my grandmother. Maybe green beans were eternal.

Chapter Forty-four

After I'd showered and dressed in shorts and a T-shirt, at seven o'clock I started to walk over to Littleboro High where the crowning of Miss Green Bean would take place. I walked over as I had done when I had classes there: Mrs. Mott Saunders for English, Miss Owana Odie for algebra, Miss Jessie Schell for physical ed. I could almost hear Miss Schell's whistle in my ear as I walked. She was tough and blew an earsplitting whistle on a lanyard around her neck.

Biology. All those dead things pickled in jars on shelves along the walls. Miss Lipe, who in class once cried over a hummingbird that had frozen before it could migrate. John Michael Jones had brought it in. She was tough, too, but that day in class she let the tears loose and we all just sat there

looking at each other. We'd never seen a teacher cry before.
So many memories, things I had not thought about in so
long.

As I neared the high school it looked as if every light in
the building was ablaze. Lit up like a starship, like it could
blast off like a rocket to another planet. Otherwise it hadn't
changed a brick. Solid. It looked solid and scholarly. I bet my
old locker was there, its rusty door still half-bent.

The auditorium was the same as when Malinda and I had
graduated high school here. She, valedictorian; Lesley Lynn
Leaford, salutatorian. Me? Just someone in the audience ap-
plauding them. I looked around for Principal Dan Cashwell.
He was probably retired, as was every teacher I ever had, or
over at The Oaks with Verna, but I bet Cashwell's footsteps
still rang in the hallways. He didn't put up with sass or back-
sass and everybody knew it.

In the auditorium Mayor Moss, in a green satin gown that
matched the gathered bunches of the same fabric draped on
lattice behind her, had center stage and command of the evening. On each side of the stage were stacked baskets of green
beans. Plastic? Unless Miz Mayor had insisted on fresh and
organically grown. Who knew? All I knew was there were a
lot of green beans in a lot of baskets on the stage. Mayor Moss
handled the microphone as if she'd been born with one in her
hand. Behind the footlights, as mistress of ceremonies, she
announced each contestant, daughter of so-and-so, her age,
grade in school, hobbies and talents.

Talents? You had to be talented to be Miss Green Bean?
Like what? Sing, dance, recite an ode to the green bean?
Scott had said once early in the green bean week that he

could sing a parody: "My love is like a green, green bean that's newly strung in June." Ida Plum had put her hand over his mouth and said, "Some can sing, some can't. You can't. Stick to your keyboard, music man."

The contestants were introduced one by one as they came out to display their talent: Sally Jo, Ashley Ann, Morgan Lee and more, decked out in every shade of green nature ever made. Puke green, pond scum green, dead grass green, deep black forest green, white grape green, mint parsley, sage, rosemary and cactus green. It was fifty shades of green. In shops somewhere some mamas had raided everything green. I bet there wasn't a scrap of any kind of green fabric left in Littleboro's Calico Cottage or in Southern Pines.

And talents? Sally Jo danced with green silk scarves. Ashley Ann sang a parody of Kermit the Frog's song, but this version was about how easy it was to be green. Morgan Lee swirled and jumped with some green hula hoops. After that I lost count of the green talents.

When Lesley Lynn Leaford was announced I sat up and took notice. Here she was not only back in town but in the competition. I wondered why? What was it all about?

She came onstage in a silver gown that seemed molded to her hourglass figure. She was the only contestant not dressed in green. Was this to make her stand out, to make the judges notice her?

Then she put the microphone to her lips and started to sing the song Peggy Lee made famous, "Is That All There Is?" A wonderful rendition that sounded for all the world like Peggy Lee. Who knew Lesley Lynn could sing like that? I couldn't remember her even being in some high school play or the pitiful Littleboro chorus. She must have taken voice lessons somewhere on her sojourn.

In the middle of the song about a third of the way through her performance the words kept repeating and repeating until it stopped completely, leaving poor Lesley Lynn mouthing words and only silence coming out. Aha, a glitch in the CD. Maybe a scratch and all we got was "there is, there is" over and over.

Someone in the audience shouted, "Lip synch, lip synch."

Poor Lesley Lynn threw down her microphone and ran off the stage.

"Oops," Mayor Moss said. "We seem to have a sound system problem. But moving right along. Our last contestant is by invitation and not eligible for the contest but she is our crowning glory for all the days of the year. A glowing example of creative thinking. Miss Original Repurpose, Reuse, Redo."

The spotlight swung around in an arc, too high up, then down on Ida Plum. She stood center stage in a floor-length emerald-green velvet dress and hooded cape. I couldn't believe it. Except for her white hair she could have been right out of a Pre-Raphaelite painting. She twirled and the audience roared.

The mayor continued, "Wearing her living-room drapes in a color called Fried Green Tomato Velvet, Ms. Plum's self-designed ensemble is an example of repurposing fabrics, recycling. Her talent is just that: making something new out of something disposable, something that would have been thrown away. She completes our event . . . except for announcing the winner of Miss Green Bean."

Ida Plum had saved the green velvet drapes from Mama Alice's dining room. I thought I had tossed those drapes out when we repaired, remade and remodeled the dining room. I hung lace curtains that let in sun and light to grow pots of Boston ferns like nobody's business.

Ida Plum waved at me, pointed her finger directly at me. Lookahere, she seemed to be saying. See what you can do with throwaway but still good stuff. Repurpose. Recycle. And it's not even plastic.

There were hoots and laughter, then applause from the audience. The stage curtains closed and everyone waited. Some whisperings guessed the winner. Morgan Lee? Sally Jo?

The air sparked with electricity. I could feel the excitement. I wondered what Miss Green Bean would actually win besides a tiara, the one I'd actually seen elegantly displayed on black velvet and glowing under a light in the window of Bennett's Jewelry in downtown Littleboro. It sparkled with slivers of jade (probably plastic) baby green beans that glowed like the real thing. I was impressed. Bennett's had been in business over a hundred years. It was where you went to order your high school ring. Where was mine now? Hadn't thought of it in years. Girls went to Bennett's to pick out china and silver patterns when they got engaged. They "registered." That made the engagement official, and listed in Pearl Buttons's column in *The Mess*, which made it even more official.

But Miss Green Bean, what was she going to get besides the tiara? Fame? Not fortune. Hadn't heard any sums of money mentioned, not even a scholarship or two. A trip to Atlantic City? Las Vegas?

"Drumroll, please." Miz Mayor held up her hand and everyone waited.

The drumroll didn't roll but sounded more scattered, a bit faint.

"Drumroll," Mayor Moss said again, sounding a little exasperated.

The drummer did it again. And again a bit louder, but still not much of a fanfare.

Finally the curtains opened and there stood a woman in silver, so silver it was white. She had her back to the audience and slowly, slowly turned to face us. The audience gasped. The hourglass figure, the only contestant who had not been in green: Lesley Lynn Leaford in the flesh, but less of it than I remembered. She was stunning. Miz Mayor laid the gleaming tiara lightly on Lesley Lynn's white-blond hair, then handed her a sheaf of okra stalks. The crowd hooted with laughter.

Ida Plum came from backstage, snatched the okra spears, bowed to the audience and said, "These were supposed to be mine." The audience laughed again.

Miz Mayor regained her composure, bowed and said, "Meet our Miss Green Bean." She gave Lesley Lynn a bouquet of green bean vines that sported baby beans and was wound with a bright green ribbon. It really wasn't tacky, just kinda cute.

Lesley Lynn, in her silver slinky way and dress, stepped off the stage and started walking though the audience. She carried her bouquet, waved, waved and smiled a smile wide as a moon. Anybody who didn't know would think this was just another crowning of just another beauty queen of something. And it was. Until someone in the audience shouted,

"Hey, was this thing rigged? She didn't even sing. Just lip-synched. That's cheating."

Another voice piped up, "Yeah and she's not even wearing green."

Then others in the crowd called "Fake, fake, fake" and "Uncrown her" and "Who judged this blankety-blank thing?" Several people stood and started to leave.

A couple of renegade boys hopped up on the stage, grabbed the baskets of green beans, threw them by handfuls into the audience where people caught them and threw them back at Lesley Lynn, who held both hands up to shield herself. "Help," she yelled. "Those things hurt." She hiked her dress up to her crotch and ran up the aisle. I heard the auditorium doors, then the front doors of the school, slam behind her. That was some fast exit.

The boys onstage continued to toss beans until they'd emptied the baskets into the audience.

"They aren't even real," said a large man in a red-striped shirt. "They're plastic."

"You can't cook 'em, you can't eat 'em. All you can do is throw 'em," a tall woman in a denim dress said. She sounded disgusted at the whole idea and handed her beans to the person beside her. "Here," she said. "You do with them what you want to."

A skinny boy in droopy cammo pants stood up and threw beans into the crowd. I could see his crack as he jumped up and down, throwing beans.

"Food fight," someone called to him. Then someone else shouted, "Food fight!" The air was suddenly green with small projectiles.

Where was the mayor? Onstage I saw she had quickly tried to wrap herself in as much of the maroon velvet stage curtains as she could pull close to give herself some protection. No green bean missiles were going to touch our gal.

I dodged green beans, pulled some from my hair and ran up the steps onto the stage now greenly littered with beans. They crunched under my feet.

"Are you okay?" I asked the shivering and shaking Miz Mayor.

She nodded her head yes, wrapped herself tighter. "I never thought anything like this could happen in Littleboro. It's so peaceful. So quiet."

"Only on the outside," I said pulling her toward the rear exit doors. Behind me the melee was in full swing of beans, beans, beans everywhere. It had turned into a game and among the laughter were shouts of "I gotcha" and "Bet you can't bean me."

If Ossie had been in town he would have been in the middle of it, calling for order, etc. But Ossie was in Southern Pines being toasted and roasted. He might have even been hoisted to the shoulders of some of the men in the audience and hauled outside to be dumped on the ground and assisted to his police car. Would he have teargassed the citizens of Littleboro? Did he even own tear gas? Anything for riot control? One would think Littleboro would be the last place on earth one would ever be needing such. Not in this quiet, sleepy, backwoods burg.

Originally I had headed backstage to look for Ida Plum but I ran into the mayor first. I wanted to find Ida Plum for my ride home. I did not relish walking alone in the dark streets of Littleboro tonight. When I was growing up, Mama Alice kept her *Gone With the Wind* lamp burning in the hall outside my childhood bedroom. I slept with my door open so I could call out when I had a bad dream. I had them often as a child and even now sometimes as an adult. I put little night-lights in all the guest bedrooms at the Dixie Dew, not only for safety's sake, but for others, like me, who just needed a little bit of light to get through the dark.

Ida Plum was nowhere in sight.

"I'm walking," I told Miz Mayor at the stage door, "or I would offer you a ride home."

She had pulled part of the stage curtain loose from the ceiling and whatever held it, then rewrapped it around herself. She looked like a fuzzy maroon mummy wearing green shoes. "Mr. Moss or our driver—someone—is here with the car," she said, and disappeared through the backstage door and down the steps. I heard car doors open and close, the soft purring of a very expensive motor start up, pull away, then get fainter as its taillights disappeared in the night.

"Wait," I had started to call after Mayor Moss as she went out to the back parking lot. I wanted to ask if I could snag a ride home in her fancy smancy Rolls, but too late. The car was gone. I'm not the type to ride in a Rolls-Royce anyway. And it's hard for me to ask for anything. Mama Alice raised me to make do or do without. I pride myself on being a do-it-myself person. Only in desperation do I send out a cry for help, and I have been in a few desperate situations where I had to cry. But I reminded myself the walk to the Dixie Dew was only a few blocks, it wasn't raining, and after all, this *was* Littleboro.

Maybe I could still catch Ida Plum. I started to ramble through hanging dusty drapes and thick curtains that were probably the originals when the Littleboro High auditorium was built back in the dark ages. No Ida Plum. No one backstage at all. Just pieces of old sets, flats and props. All the mothers who earlier had helped daughters get dressed must have packed their makeup kits, hair dryers, curling irons and steamers and hauled off home. The place reeked of silence. And it was spooky.

I called, "Ida Plum. Ida. Where are you?"

I pulled out my cell phone, punched it on. Nothing. The screen stayed dark. I tried again. The battery must be dead. Dead, dead, dead. I put it back in my pocket.

"Ida Plum," I called again.

Surely she couldn't have gotten out of her "curtains" costume so fast. I heard only my own footsteps in the dark and semi-dark. God, this place was spooky. I pushed aside a mass of rotten curtains half-hanging from the ceiling and called again. "I. P. Duckett? Where are you?"

No answer. I saw something or someone on the floor beside a tall stack of chairs. It looked like something rolled up in a rug. Something big and bulky enough to be a body. A dead body. "Please, please, please don't let it be Ida Plum," I said as I stood there. Please, please no. She had no enemies. Who would want to hurt her? Had she been so close to me that someone would do something to her to get at me? Me, who had done nothing.

I reached down and tried to turn the rolled-up something over. It wouldn't budge. Then I tried again to roll it over and one end of the rug flapped loose, lay open. I unrolled it a bit more to make sure there was no body, nowhere. It was just a rug rolled up and pushed aside. Nothing and nobody in it. I scolded myself for letting my imagination even suspect such a thing. Whew. The dark and the quiet were getting to me. And the spooks.

Ida Plum was nowhere around. Maybe she had gone home in her "curtains." Gone home the same way she had come, in her own car. When the melee started she'd probably gotten the hell out of there like any sensible person would do. Not like me, hanging around a deserted backstage, poking around where anything could happen. Not someone alone after everyone else had left. A prime target for danger. For anything.

I took the back way out from the stage to a deserted parking lot. People sure could get out of places fast when something was over. I thought of all those plastic green beans littering the auditorium floor and seats and probably even in the light fixtures. A night to remember. Was Pearl Buttons in the audience? Would she capture this event for the environs, the historians of Littleboro? The night of the Littleboro riot and great green bean fight.

Our poor Mayor Moss. She had planned such a unique event, a night to make history. And it sure had. Plus she lost her cool. For the first time I'd seen beneath her sleek exterior, all her polish and poise. Would she pick up her husband, her turtle and leave Littleboro in her Rolls just when she had begun to make her mark? And would Littleboro be better off? Or worse? We certainly had lacked for innovation and forward thinking in the past and look where that had gotten us. Same old, same old. Staid, stuck in the boonies of the past.

"Progressive" was not a word in many Littleborians' vocabularies. But was that a bad thing?

I took a deep breath, told myself I was all grown up and this was Littleboro, and I bravely headed toward home. I had walked these five blocks home from school a million miles and too many times to count. In the daylight though. To and from. First Littleboro Elementary, grades one through seven, then Littleboro High, grades eight to twelve, where I met Malinda. Our lockers were side by side. Mine was rusted and caved in and the door wouldn't close all the way. Malinda painted hers purple. I did mine in wild pink. In those first years of integration the school officials didn't care what we did as long as we didn't create a disturbance. They must have heard and read reports from other school systems and held their breaths. There were few black students in Littleboro and they were mostly like Malinda, smart and friendly. I never saw her without a smile, a ready laugh. I was lucky to be her best friend, sorry we had those empty lost years when we hadn't kept in touch.

Now, even in the half dark, getting darker fast, my feet still knew all the cracks in the sidewalks even if I couldn't see them, knew the places raised by tree roots growing underneath. I walked past the gym, the football field, past the tennis courts and wondered who used them now that Father Roderick was dead. I had a momentary shiver remembering how I had been the one to find his body. Poor man. So young, so darn good-looking in his tennis garb, such a bright future ahead in the Catholic Church.

I had always felt afraid walking these streets home, though I had not done it at night very much and I couldn't remember ever walking it alone. After football games there was a lot of noise, cars roaring and popping down the streets, people still celebrating a win or just because it was Friday night and they were seventeen and had a car with Daddy's gas in it.

Now there was only quiet. Too much quiet and too many shadows. I didn't remember it being so dark, so few street-lights. Shadows from the willow oaks, always slow to leaf out, seemed large and dark and full of danger. I remembered the scene in the movie *To Kill a Mockingbird*, where Jem and Scout are walking home from a school event and Scout gets attacked by Bob Ewell but rescued by Boo Radley, who was played by a young Robert Duvall. Oh where was my Boo Radley Duvall when I needed him?

How many Bob Ewells were out there in the night? Not to mention Mrs. Butch Rigsbee. I had heard she'd been given a citation and paid a fine for shooting balloons at the fair-grounds. She'd claimed target practice but word was Ossie charged her with destroying property and disturbing the peace. Why had he not arrested her and put her in jail? What would it take to make this man do his job? It seemed to me he just sloughed it off, shrugged and looked the other way, when he could have been serious and done his bit to keep Littleboro clean and quiet.

Chapter Forty-five

Few lights burned in any of the houses I passed, mostly from upstairs windows where someone lay reading in bed, but most probably watched TV. The good God-fearing people in Littleboro tended to go to bed early. Once in a while I'd hear a dog bark or howl, though there was no moon to howl at. Most dogs I saw outside these days were being walked on leashes, probably better for their own good and ours as well. "No moon" made me think of honeymoon and poor Reba. She'd never be a June bride and never have a honeymoon, or a groom.

When I was twelve I'd had a paper route, delivering *The Mess* Wednesday afternoons after school to these same houses, these streets. I had some frights being chased by dogs, especially one white German shepherd who loved to wait around the side of the house where he lived until I walked past. He'd come charging out, sharp teeth at the ready, chomping his chomps and a growl down his throat that made my heart drop to my shoes.

I made myself not run. Do not run. Do not show fright. Stay steady. Keep walking. Keep your hands close to your body. That's what I told myself now.

I remembered when that white German shepherd got close enough that I felt his hot, wild breath on the back of my legs, he would slink back and sit down on the sidewalk. When I glanced over my shoulder, he seemed to be laughing. I know that dog laughed. Heh heh, scared you, didn't I? Then he'd scratch awhile, lick his lower parts at length, and sprawl out on the sidewalk and go to sleep.

Even with so little light from the streetlights, I saw my shadow. It looked so alone and vulnerable, a clear target if there ever was one.

I began to recite from memory the Robert Louis Stevenson poem beginning "I have a little shadow that goes . . ." Mama Alice had taught me to read from *A Child's Garden of Verses*. She read the poems so often to me she thought I'd probably memorized them so she pointed her fingers to words at random places on the page. I read them. "Lord," she said to Mama, "this child can read." After that there was no stopping me. I read every book in the children's section of the Littleboro Library and started on the adult section, which meant I had to sneak past Hazel Grogan, the librarian. If I tried to check out a book she didn't think suitable for my age, she'd withhold her inked date stamper high above the book and ask, "Did your mother approve your reading this?" Only after I lied would she reluctantly stamp the due date and hand it to me, shaking her head as if to say, "What is this world coming to."

After I finished reciting "The Land of Counterpane" and "The Swing," I started on Bible verses: "Yea, though I walk through the valley of the shadow of death . . ." Maybe I should have said those first?

Quiet hung over the neighborhood like fog. I heard my own footsteps, sounding hollow and afraid. I kept walking. Two streets to go. No traffic. I smelled gardenias, heavy, brown-tinged and sweet. I always hated the smell, same with magnolia blossoms. Too sweet, like too much vanilla or rotting fruit. Or overripe bananas?

I kept walking. Then I thought I heard a rustle in the shrubbery, saw something move. Oh damn, I thought, is this the house where that white German shepherd lived? He's got to be dead by now. Some people though, when one dog died, they just replaced it with another of the same kind, same color, hoping for the same personality. I hoped the German shepherd was not among the replacements.

I kept walking. Something white slunk from the bushes. Smaller than a dog, moving very quietly. Had to be a cat. A white cat. One of Sherman's friends? Did Sherman prowl this far? I'll bet he did. "Here kitty," I called to the white cat and it came over, let me rub it, arched, purred under my fingers, made me feel better for a few minutes. Then the cat turned and went down the street the way I had come.

That's when I saw the parked car I hadn't noticed before. I had walked past that car and never thought a thing about it. Now I looked back, saw its low lights on, heard the motor running. Waiting for someone? A date? Movie? Not this time of night. It was nine thirty and Littleboro's only movie theater had closed years ago. For a while afterwards some church held services in the theater and I thought, why not? Good job, reuse existing space. They used the old movie marquees for cute sayings like SEVEN DAYS WITHOUT PRAYER MAKES ONE WEAK or WITHOUT THE BREAD OF LIFE, YOU ARE TOAST.

Whenever I looked back the car kept coming closer, moving very quietly, very slowly behind me. Spooky. The car stayed with me. What the hell?

Chapter Forty-six

To get to the Dixie Dew I would have to cross the street but if I crossed, the car could speed up, run me down. *Wham, whap,* I'd be flat on the ground in seconds and the car long gone, roaring up the street with no witnesses, no one the wiser. Hit-and-run, plain and simple. Would Ossie even investigate? I somehow couldn't see him going door-to-door asking for witnesses. I'd probably not even make the front page of *The Mess,* just a line or two at the bottom of the obituary page.

I could knock on the door of one of these houses, ring a bell, ask for asylum, but would anyone answer, much less let me in this late at night? It wasn't really late and this was Littleboro, but no one I knew lived in these houses. Their kids had grown up, gone away to college, joined the military, discovered the world and never come back. No jobs here, no reasons to return. The parents? They'd died, sold or left most of these houses to move to a retirement community. They rented them out or left them vacant. A lot of the houses looked vacant, but I couldn't tell at night. I couldn't see if there were cars in the driveways, bicycles on the lawns or furniture on the porches. It was so damn dark.

I kept walking. The car kept following. One more block and I'd be on Main Street at the Dixie Dew. Then I saw someone standing on the sidewalk in front of me. A man. A man holding out something in front of him that glinted in the streetlight. Metal? A gun? He stood in front of me, the menacing car still following behind. I heard the low growl of its motor.

I felt trapped tight now. If I kept walking I'd run into the man in the dark on the sidewalk in front of me. He could be working in tandem with the black car following me. If I tried to cross the street, the car could speed up and run me down, leave me mangled and bleeding on the street.

The man kept coming closer. Whatever he had in his hand was at his side now. He stopped beside a tree, waited, still holding the thing that glinted in his hand. He lowered it. I heard a metal *click* and a whirring sound like fishing line being reeled in. It looked like a dog leash, one of those string things you control with a trigger to lengthen it or make it shorter, but I didn't see a dog.

He stopped, waited there on the walk. I walked nearer, relieved. A dog walker would be friendly, safe, kind, take me in, let me use his phone or drive me home. All the above or any of the above. I'd take any of the above, with pleasure and appreciation.

"Dogs," the man said as I got closer.

I recognized the voice. Pastor Pittman, dressed in striped pajamas and red felt slippers.

"Yes," I said, "dogs." Then I saw the dog that walked him, a blond cocker spaniel who trotted out from a big boxwood beside Pastor Pittman.

"Honey," he said.

Me? I wanted to ask. Was he making a pass at me? Honey? I wanted to answer yes. Hug me. Hold me. Make me feel safe. Call me anything. Just thank you for showing up when I needed somebody.

"Excuse me?" I asked.

"The dog," he said. "That's her name."

"Nice name, Honey," I said and reached down to pet her. Cockers waggle all over and melt when you touch them. "Nice dog." Oh, nice, nice dog. Thank you for being here.

The car behind me in the street suddenly brightened its lights, sped toward us and roared past. I felt a rush of cool air.

"Kids," Pastor Pittman said and shook his head.

"Kids, I'm sure," I agreed and crossed the street toward home. "Nice night."

I started running toward the Dixie Dew. Running as if my life depended on it, which it very well may have. Whoever was in that car was not making nice with me. They were following me, out to do me harm, but why? Hadn't stolen anything or cooked up anything. I was so ordinary, so law abiding, so careful in my little life, my everyday days. I hadn't rigged the Miss Green Bean contest or thrown any beans in the food fight.

I ran like the Devil himself was after me. Ran, ran, ran as fast as I could. My breath got shorter and my heart felt hard in my chest. When was the last time I'd run? Walking didn't cause the frantic, fast breathing I felt now in my chest.

Chapter Forty-seven

When I saw the porch light of the Dixie Dew—my own porch light—one last spurt of energy got me to the steps, where I almost collapsed. I stopped for a second to catch my breath a little, then ran inside, locked the door behind me and stood with my back against it. Still breathing hard, I closed my eyes. I was home. I was safe. I was alive. I let out a long, slow, relieved breath. Whew. Thank you, Jesus.

I heard a noise and opened my eyes to see, halfway up the stairs, two very small, white feet. Real? or did Dixie Dew have a ghost? Who stood on the stairs in the Dixie Dew? Who? Miles Fortune was the only guest and he either wore custom-made running shoes or very elegant Italian loafers. And he had big, male feet!

These little white feet belonged to a child or someone small, someone in a long white dress. A ghost? We didn't have a ghost at the Dixie Dew. Not unless Miss Lavinia, the first guest who'd died in my B and B, had come back to haunt me. Debbie Booth was too newly dead to be a ghost yet.

"Go away," I said, and waved my hand. "Go on. Get out. Get you gone." That sounded pretty good. Commanding. Definite. "Git."

"Beth?" squeaked out a tiny voice. "It's me. Lesley Lynn Leaford?"

"What are you doing?" I demanded.

She let out a small sort of strangled sound and I saw another person on the stairs behind her, holding her left arm around Lesley Lynn's throat and waving a gun with the other.

"Awurk," I said. "Who are *you*?" I must have sounded like a very confused owl.

The person holding the gun pushed poor Lesley Lynn down a few steps and I saw the flyaway, crazy blond hair, the tattoos on the arm holding the gun. Mrs. Butch Rigsbee. Lesley Lynn gurgled.

"Who are you and what are you doing here?" I finally blurted.

The woman laughed. "What do you think? You hussy."

"Not me." I put up both hands.

"You were in his motel room. I saw you go in. You answered his phone. I saw you go out, hiding behind that preacher man." She was screaming now. The spit from her words glistened on poor Lesley Lynn's left cheek. Lesley Lynn squeezed her eyes closed.

"I wasn't seeing your husband. I don't even know your husband. Never saw him before in my life. Honest."

Lesley Lynn waved a frantic arm.

"Let her loose," I said to Mrs. Rigsbee. "She doesn't have anything to do with this."

"Please," Lesley Lynn said, grabbing at the muscled arm around her throat.

"Let her go!" I said again.

"Okeydokey. Here she comes!"

The woman turned Lesley Lynn loose and she slid down the stairs, *bumpety, bumpety, bump,* landing at my feet. She stood and shook herself, like she could shake off this whole nightmare.

"What did she have to do with anything?" I asked as I reached for Lesley Lynn.

"Why, nothing," the woman said and waved her gun. "I had to have somebody hostage. I had to have somebody between me and this 'who's on first, doesn't know shit from shinola' law enforcement in this town. They sure didn't seem concerned when I talked to them earlier this week. Nothing. Acted like a cheating husband was just another cheating husband. Podunk. This town is Podunk. I'm holding this so-called beauty queen and marching her down to that little bitty hole of a police station until I get somebody in this town serious about finding my husband."

Nobody had told her that her husband was dead. That Bruce and Ossie had even identified the killer. They had probably been trying to contact her where she lived and didn't know she was here in Littleboro. Of course if they had listened to me in the first place, I could have helped them find her. Ossie thought from the get-go I had made up the whole thing about her threatening me.

"So that was you in the car? The one following me." I put my arm around poor Lesley Lynn, who was shivering like Sherman does when he comes in soaking wet. I looked down to see if she was licking herself. No, just shivering. Poor thing. One minute she's onstage in the spotlight getting her crown of glory and the next being kidnapped by a crazy woman. What a roller coaster of a night.

Lesley Lynn wavered and rocked against me. I put both arms around her. Both of us rocked.

"Stand still," Mrs. Rigsbee said. "So I can shoot you."

Lesley Lynn still rocked. I put up my hand, as if that would do any good, as if it could stop a bullet. Used to work in the *Wonder Woman* comic books. Or was it *Superman*? I read more *Wonder Woman* than *Superman* when I was growing up.

"Don't you dare."

"I mean it," Mrs. Rigsbee said, and came down a few steps closer.

I thought about her shooting the balloons at the fairgrounds. Practicing. Maybe she's not such a good shot.

"Don't do it!" I screamed.

Chapter Forty-eight

About that time the gun went off with a loud *pop*. Mama Alice's big hall light fixture came down on me and Lesley Lynn in a lot of hard chunks and knocks and clatter. I instinctively put up my arms to try to shield us as the little glass hangy-downs rained around. Some of them hit my head and probably Lesley Lynn's, too. Glass fell in tinkles at our feet, all those hanging doolollies Mama Alice used to put me on a ladder once a year with a bucket of soapy water to clean, were now broken shards of glass. It looked like somebody had dumped a barrel of cracked ice on us. All that glitter. Glass and more glass.

With a dull thud followed by some bumps and thumps, Mrs. Rigsbee rolled down to land at the foot of the stairs. She lay still, glass on top and all around her. And us. For a moment the loud bang and crashing thumps still rang in my ears, then it was quiet. A strange sort of eerie quiet seemed to surround us.

At the top of the stairs stood Miles Fortune, holding Mama Alice's *Gone With the Wind* lamp. "I hit her with it," he said with a laugh. "And it didn't even break." He put the lamp back on the small hall table that stood on the landing. Mama Alice loved that lamp with its round white globes, the pink and green painted flowers.

Mrs. Rigsbee lay in a tangled heap at our feet. Miles came down the stairs.

"Is she dead?" I asked.

He lifted her limp wrist and bent to check the pulse in her neck, which I noticed had a tattoo of a match in flame on it. Weird. But so was this whole thing.

"I didn't hit her hard enough to kill her, I don't think," he said.

By this time Lesley Lynn had let go of me and stood looking down at the body on the floor. She wrapped both arms around herself like she was freezing cold. Both of us just looked at the body at our feet, a very large, lumpy, not moving body at the foot of the stairs. By some miracle nobody was bleeding.

Miles Fortune pulled his cell phone from his pocket, a phone whose battery wasn't dead like mine, and called 911. I heard him tell them no one was hurt. I looked at Lesley Lynn, who nodded she was all right. I echoed her nod as Miles talked. "We don't need medics," he said, "just the local law people."

By this time Mrs. Rigsbee had come to, sat up and asked for a slug of "something to cut this hellfire headache."

I groaned. At least the ambulance and the EMTs wouldn't come, but where was Ossie when I really, really needed him? At a bachelor party, probably paying some lap dancer or pole dancer or whatever guys thought was wild and funny. And getting looped, or snookered or whatever they called it. I hoped he'd get stopped on the way home. Pulled over, maybe ticketed for DUI by the highway patrol. Or did professional courtesy come into play more often than any of us ordinary citizens thought? Scott was with Ossie. Maybe as best man he'd be the designated driver. "Best man"! Just the two words reminded me how Reba got confused and started this whole mess.

Miles and I helped Mrs. Rigsbee to the living room where she sat on the couch, bent at the waist, head down and holding it. "When I find whoever hit me, he's gonna be a dead SOB," she muttered.

Miles and I exchanged looks that said don't say a word. Say nothing.

I handed Mrs. Rigsbee a small cordial glass of Mama Alice's blackberry wine. "Sip it slowly," I said. I even gave her a cocktail napkin, which she promptly unfolded and used to mop her face.

"Air," she said. "I need air."

Fifteen minutes later Bruce Bechner rang the doorbell. I let him in, showed him into the living room.

"This woman"—I pointed to Mrs. Butch—"kidnapped Lesley Lynn, tried to shoot me, shot down my grandmother's chandelier and I think you need to arrest her."

Mrs. Butch stood and took a few steps toward Bruce. She had both hands on her hips and walked hard, like she was ready to stomp a hole in my floor. (I knew it wouldn't take much.)

"My husband is missing. He was last seen in this piddly Podunk town and somebody, somewhere better find him for me or—"

"Let's go down to the station." Bruce took her arm, smiled at her sweetly and started to lead her from the room. "I've got a fresh pot of coffee brewing. We'll sit down and have a nice little chat. Then we'll talk about your good husband."

"He wasn't good!" she screamed as they left. "He was a no-good, rotten, lying, thieving snake. He turned on me. Turned rotten after I married him. More rotten every year."

She was still spluttering as they went into the night. Poor Bruce, I thought. You're going to need that pot of coffee.

Only then, when the door closed behind them, did I relax and introduce Lesley Lynn to Miles, who extended his hand. She accepted it with hers, which was still shaking. He patted her hand.

"She's our newly crowned Miss Green Bean," I said.

"And I missed getting her crowning on film. What was I thinking? The grand event of a lifetime." He laughed and went into the dining room. "Ladies," he said as he crossed the hall, "I think we all need and deserve a little bit of libation, if Miss Beth doesn't mind."

"Please," I answered.

He returned with two cordial glasses and the decanter of blackberry wine, poured one each for me and Lesley Lynn.

"This is the stuff for civilization, for shock to delicate systems."

I offered a toast to Miss Green Bean and Lesley Lynn smiled. Weakly.

Then Miles produced a shot glass and a dusty bottle of Scotch I thought I recognized. "This"—he held up the bottle—"is my stuff. The kind of stuff with guts. I gotta restore mine." He poured himself a slug, downed it, poured another. "In the back of the corner cupboard," he said as if he had read my quizzical look. "That's where I found it. Good stuff." Shaking his head side to side as though he'd come upon scenes like this all the time in L.A. where somebody was making a movie on every corner, he said, "I don't know what all this business was about, but things are better sorted out in the daylight."

I took Lesley Lynn upstairs, ran her a hot bath in Mama Alice's big old footed tub, poured in the bath salts, and told her to climb in and soak. That's my remedy for a bad day and this had been a bad day and a bad night. Then I brought her some of my flannel pajamas (good old L.L.Bean), a robe and slippers, turned down the bed where Miss Lavinia had slept her last sleep and told Lesley Lynn good night and I'd see her in the morning.

Downstairs Miles had swept up the glass. "Somehow hanging up there, that fixture didn't look like it had this much glass in it." He emptied the last of it in the metal trash bin, the big one with the Norman Rockwell *Saturday Evening Post* Thanksgiving cover stamped on it, the grandmother smiling as she served a huge turkey on a platter to her adoring family.

What a lot of sweet rot we all tried to live up to every Thanksgiving. The trash bin tinkled as he carried it to the kitchen, then he said good night and headed up the stairs.

I looked up the number for the Presbyterian manse in the well-worn Carelock County phone book and called from my dependable landline telephone. Barbie Pittman answered. I told her Lesley Lynn was spending the night here at Dixie Dew. She thanked me, said she wouldn't have worried. Would have just assumed Lesley Lynn was staying with her aunt.

"Her aunt?"

"Yes. Her aunt Calista."

Wow, I thought. There was only one person with that name in Littleboro: our mayor, Miz Honorable Moss. The whole world must be related, and it is a very small world.

I followed my own advice for a good soak in a tub with bath salts, lavender oil and anything else therapeutic I could pour in. I needed it. Afterwards I put on my favorite flannel pajamas and robe and padded in my slippers to check the house for the night.

Sherman was curled in his bed by the back door, Robert Redford beside him. I yawned, so tired I felt limp and my bones were loose. I checked the back and front door locks and fell into bed. Tomorrow *had* to be a better day.

When I was just about asleep I jerked awake and sat upright in bed. What had happened to Mrs. Rigsbee's gun? Where was it? Had Bruce taken it? Had he even asked about it? I think he just wanted to get her calmed down and down to the station. Maybe there he could handcuff her to a chair since we didn't have a jail or even a courthouse anymore.

Where would he hold her? Probably run her over to Moore County jail. In the middle of the night? I bet she'd scream and cuss the whole way there. But what had happened to the gun? I couldn't remember. I was too tired at the moment to remember anything clearly. I went back to sleep.

Chapter Forty-nine

The next morning when I went in the kitchen to start the coffee, there stood Scott holding the gun. Pointed right at me!

"Whoa," I said, holding up both hands and starting to back out.

"What's this doing in the wastebasket with all that glass? All those little dead hangy-down things?" he asked.

When Miles Fortune had swept up the glass he probably hadn't noticed Mrs. Rigsbee's little silver handgun, the kind you could stash in a pocket or a purse, and he'd dumped it all in the wastebasket. There had been a *lot* of glass dangles in a heap and scattered, plus the hall was dark without the overhead light.

I nearly fainted. "It's loaded," I said.

He took the bullets out and laid them in a saucer on the table, then handed me the gun.

"What do I do with it?"

He grinned. "Put it under your pillow, my love."

I was in no mood for his humor. I put the gun and bullets in my kitchen junk drawer and started the coffee. Then I sat down and told Scott the whole thing.

"So where's Lesley Lynn now?" he asked.

The first thing I had done when I woke was go upstairs to take Lesley Lynn some clothes: a pair of my jeans, a T-shirt and some flip-flops, just some stuff to get her decent enough to go back to the Pittmans. I figured she must still have her own underwear and wearing it two days in a row wouldn't kill her. She wasn't in the bedroom where I'd left her. The door was open, but the bed was empty.

I stood in the doorway. Disbelieving was the only word that came to mind to describe how I felt. Shock was another, and then some others, none of which I said out loud. Where the hell was she? Had she left and I hadn't heard her? Had I slept like a rock?

The door to Miles Fortune's bedroom was closed. I lightly knocked on the door. When I didn't hear any movement from inside, I very carefully turned the knob. It wasn't locked. I eased the door open very slowly, peeked my head around and saw Lesley Lynn curled next to Miles Fortune in his bed.

"Shh," he said with a little smile. He held up a finger. "She got scared in the night and came in here."

I nodded and gently closed the door. Yeah, I thought. I just bet she did.

"Is she still asleep?" Scott asked. "Up there?"

"I guess," I said, thinking this bed-hopping was a first time for my B and B and I was willing to bet it wouldn't be the last. I only hoped it wasn't going to happen too often or I'd have to change the advertising to "Doing It at the Dixie Dew."

"Buckets," said Ida Plum when she came in, taking off her purple raincoat, hanging it on the rack. "It's raining buckets and not supposed to stop all day."

Ossie's wedding day. How appropriate, I thought. The skies are crying because this whole thing is a big mistake. Then a second thought: it's Juanita's wedding day, too, and maybe the third time is the charm. And maybe I was just in a gloomy mood, when what was called for was Panic with a capital P.

"I can try to get a tent," I told Ida Plum, but at the last minute every rental place in Southern Pines was probably already booked.

"Ground's already saturated," Ida Plum said. "All those high heels would sink up to their ankles. Not to mention muddy trouser legs, and anybody, especially the bride in a very expensive long dress that cost her half a down payment on a car or house, would ruin their clothes. Of course the bridesmaid's gown would be ruined, too."

"I say move it," Scott said. He took off his wet jacket, ran his hand across his wet head and reached for the coffeepot.

"Where to?" Some church? Somehow I couldn't see Ossie in his white hat walking down the aisle of First Presbyterian Church even if Pastor Pittman was doing the service. Ossie would probably be packing some firearm even then, though he didn't strike me as the type of hard-nosed cop who eats, sleeps and breathes the job.

"I'd say somewhere indoors." Scott looked at an empty muffin warmer basket. "Our Mr. Fortune up and gone?" he asked.

"In and out," I said. "He just left with Lesley Lynn." I'd seen them leave as Ida Plum was brushing the rain off her coat with a tea towel. Miles had guided Lesley Lynn gently down the stairs and out the door. I wished he *was* gone, although he was a paying guest and I seemed to be suffering a dearth of those lately. At least I thought he was a paying guest. We had his credit card number and Ida Plum said it was one of those gold or platinum cards. He had saved my life. Maybe I owed him a free room for that. Or more. How did one ever repay someone for saving your life? I didn't know.

"I'd say you got space in the living room and front hall. You got the dining room already set up for doing receptions. I say move the furniture to the walls, stand some flowers around and go with it. Necessity is the godmother of making do with what you got. You got indoor space," Scott said.

But the living room was not renovated. Walls had peeling wallpaper so old it had lost all color and looked like ancient newsprint. If the pattern had once been huge roses or violets or checks or stripes no one could guess it now. The fireplace mantel was rotten on one side and the mirror over it so old the silvering on the back crackled. Nobody could see anything in it. And the floors! Rugs had dry rot and places so bare you could see the weave of the backing. "Threadbare" was the word. I stood looking at the word made flesh.

"So we roll up the rugs and I toss them in Verna's overflowing dumpster. Get the Betts Brothers to bring in as many white flowers as they can get their hands on and nobody will notice," Scott said.

"What about chairs?" I asked.

"What were you going to do outside?"

"Well, stand, I guess. A wedding ceremony doesn't usually last that long and Juanita said she's keeping this one simple."

"So everybody stands for the ten minutes it takes Pittman to read some words and the bride and groom to mumble 'I something, something, something.' Soon as the cake is cut and all the food inhaled in the dining room, you clear the table, we take out the leaves and ta da, let the dancing begin."

"I don't see a thing wrong with that." Ida Plum stood in the doorway to the kitchen. "Except where do they put all the raincoats and umbrellas? Is there by any chance among all that stuff at Verna's something such as any sort of coat-rack?"

"I'll look," Scott said.

When Ida Plum saw the wastebasket full of glass I told her about last night. She poured herself a second cup of coffee, almost downed it in one gulp, and said, "You gonna bother Ossie with all this on his wedding day?"

"No," I said. "Besides, Bruce was here. He can tell him if he wants to. Mrs. Rigsbee is under arrest and since we have no jail anymore, he probably carted her over to Pinehurst. Or Vass. If Vass even has a jail. Either way, she shouldn't be a problem."

"Probably Pinehurst," Scott said. "And today, at least today, I've got an inside job. No gazebos." He pronounced it "gaze bows" and winked at me as he left by the front door, minus umbrella. Mr. Macho, taking on the elements with only a windbreaker and nothing on his head.

Miles Fortune had worn a well-seasoned London Fog trench coat plus some type of Sherlock Holmes hat and opened his "brolly" as he escorted Lesley Lynn out into the downpour. Still a mystery man who came and slept, ate and left, taking Lesley Lynn with him. Was he taking her to her aunt Calista's house? Or L.A.? After all she was a beauty queen. And I still had a niggling suspicion he might have had something to do with the courthouse burning. Was he the kind of documentary maker who'd set a fire just so he could film it? Burn down our town icon and hotfoot it out to wherever he came from in the first place? I confess when I cleaned his room I sniffed extra hard for any evidence he'd been closer to the fire than just a bystander, anything that would confirm my suspicions. So far, nothing.

According to Malinda, who dropped by on her way to work, word was the fire chief had no idea what started the fire that reduced our beautiful courthouse to a blackened Confederate soldier and some empty standing brick walls.

"But," I said, "sit down and let me tell you my latest. Bigger news. I found Butch Rigsbee."

I handed her a mug of coffee, indicated a stool at the kitchen island.

"I'm en route." She took the coffee. "Just stopping in to hear the latest. Spill and don't leave anything out."

I told her all, including the details of Allison's confession, how I found the body, the Old Spice and everything.

"I didn't know they still made the stuff," Malinda said.

"That must have been the giant-sized bottle. Imagine embalming with Old Spice."

"Where did he take Allison?" Ida Plum asked. "Police station? Then where? We have no jail," she said again and clucked her tongue at all this latest Littleboro news.

"The wedding?" Malinda put down her coffee mug, shrugged into her raincoat. "What's going to happen with that?"

"According to Scott," Ida Plum said, "we're taking it inside. Juanita's garden wedding is going to be dry."

"I hope you don't mean sans alcohol." She laughed. "Weddings are the only time I get champagne. There *is* going to be champagne, isn't there?"

"Prosecco," I said. "That's what the groom wants. And I've ordered some local brews. Scott suggested those."

"Including some green bean wine?" Ida Plum said.

"Is there really such a thing as green bean wine?" Malinda raised an eyebrow. "Don't save me any." She looked as if she'd never put anything green to her lips again in her life. And I wouldn't blame her.

"Absolutely," I said, and shuddered a little. Not on this earth would I ever put a touch of green bean wine to my lips. Ugh. Scott may have been joking. Surely nobody had made a wine out of beans. But then stranger things happened. Look at vodka, made from potatoes! But at least it wasn't green unless they added a tint.

Malinda stood in the half-open doorway, gave us a two-finger goodbye wave and was gone.

In Littleboro, when you hear the same rumor with most

of the same details then you figure you're getting close to the truth. With the Allison story, everyone would know the truth and it was so awful it probably wouldn't need to be embellished. I was sure at least some extra details would travel in the area of what really happened though. Put enough versions together and you're in the ballpark of the truth.

I put an emergency call in to the Betts Brothers for any white flowers they could get their hands on, preferably fresh. The plan had been to use both plastic and silk and mix in a little fresh in pots for the outdoor deal. My grandmother would have been horrified at the idea of plastic flowers, but Bobby Betts said they did it all the time and so far nobody was the wiser, especially for the outdoor weddings. "Fresh just melts," he said on the phone.

"Plastic," I said. I was half-horrified.

"These days even some bridal bouquets are plastic," he said.

I remembered how Reba had stuck her plastic bouquet in a vase of water in the motel room. Poor Reba.

Now I was all the way horrified. Where was the sentiment? The romance of roses and lily of the valley? Orchids? I'd seen Mama Alice cater weddings where the bridal bouquet was one huge white orchid that had been flown in from some exotic island halfway around the world.

"Whatever," I said. "See you about three this afternoon?" I had final decorating touches, a couple more swags around the top for the wedding cake and a couple mixers full of buttercream icing to make for the cake squares. Thank goodness I wasn't doing meringue. Not in this weather.

Chapter Fifty

By the time the Betts Brothers van drove up in front of the Dixie Dew, I was covered in buttercream, but the five-tiered cake was a work of art, all scrolls and swags and icing roses. I had not lost my touch. "Yay!" I shouted when I finished and set it on the middle of the dining-room table. Sure Juanita had said seven tiers, but with enough Prosecco she'd be beyond counting, and of course, I'd lower the price. Today I just couldn't handle another two layers.

At four o'clock the sky was still pouring buckets. It had not stopped, paused, or slacked a mite all day. Rain fell in silver sheets off the porch roof.

After the Betts Brothers did their do and left, Ida Plum and I stood in the hall, looked into the living room and told ourselves the whole thing was a bower of white. With the candles lit, the effect would be breathtaking. At least we hoped it would.

When the white stretch limo stopped in front of the Dixie Dew, Ida Plum and I totally expected Juanita and her "party" to step out, holding umbrellas of course. The rain had not slacked all day.

We went to the front porch to get close-up looks as the bride arrived.

Instead we saw a little twig of a girl scoot up, hand out, ready to ring the doorbell. She scooted to a stop on the top step, announced, "Miss Deye will be alighting momentarily. Her hair and makeup people are not finished." Then the pixie person in a black smock asked, "Where are the photographers, the newspaper reporters? Inside? Is someone from *People* magazine here yet?" Her perky little acorn of a face with half-black hair, half-green, she, or he, looked as if it had never seen a calorie outside a head of lettuce.

"Photographers?" Ida Plum and I looked at each other. "Reporters?"

"They plan to arrive later," I lied. Something that was getting to be a habit. Had I been hanging around Allison too much and it was rubbing off on me? "But please come in out of the rain."

"Yes," Ida Plum said. "Get in out of the wet."

The elfin of a girl whirled around and sprinted through the puddles back to the limo, slammed shut the car door.

Ida Plum and I stood on the front porch to see who (or what) would pop out of that limo next.

We waited, noted the engine kept running and running the whole time and there seemed to be movement going on inside, but no one came out.

We waited some more, looked at each other, shrugged. "Didn't she say momentarily? How long exactly is momentarily?" Around here in Littleboro, a person might say, "I'll be with you directly," which meant sometime in the near future, after I'm done doing what I'm doing right now. Momentarily was a big-city word.

Ida Plum looked at her watch.

I heard Sherman in the hall scratching to be let out, so I opened the screen door. He darted out, followed by Robert Redford fast on his heels. Those two were inseparable.

I looked at my watch, almost turned to go back to my cake icing, my scrolls, swags and roses, except I knew I'd wait as long as it took to see the famous Miss Deye, this return of the native, our local daughter made good giving her grand entrance and to be there to watch her milk her "moment" for all it was worth. Photographers! Reporters! Had she forgotten this was Littleboro?

At the same time I dreaded it. Who was I to even be in the same "moment" with a woman who had been the toast of L.A.? Her singing voice on scores of commercials, everything from shampoos to car rentals to vacation cruises. Her voice talent had gone around the world. I almost felt like ducking out, going back and hiding behind my icing bowl in the Dixie Dew kitchen. What if Scott, seeing her again, decided he wanted his life back with her? What was life in Littleboro compared to the bright lights and glam of L.A.?

All that fame and money? All the glitter and glory? What did I have to offer? Work and a warm bed. A sincere heart, an honest relationship.

Finally, the door to the limo opened and two people, "pixie" plus another of almost the same ilk, emerged holding the biggest umbrellas I'd ever seen, and also they held some sort of canvas cover that made a canopy to keep Sunnye dry.

Mama Alice would have said, "Does she think she's sugar and a little bit of rain is going to melt her?"

Then, in a flurry of fabrics, feathers and feet, Sunnye Deye got out of the car, stood and shook herself like some giant plumed kiwi-colored bird. Even her hair, what there was of it, was kiwi green. Glowing green.

Well, I thought, she got in tune with the theme of the week, if a bit ill timed. And this was a new shade of green. One we hadn't seen this week.

When Sunnye came onto the porch, she flung open her feathered cape and I saw that she had *found* all the weight Lesley Lynn Leaford had lost. A few hundred pounds of it. Sunnye Deye had become a big woman. She shook herself again, wrapped the feathered cape closer, held it in front with long, green-painted nails that matched her cape and hair. "I may have lost my voice," she croaked, "but they love me, love me every ounce and pound in Prague. They say my skin reflects light and I do have plenty of it." She laughed showing little sharp, pointed teeth, wiggled her wide hips. "I do *art* films." She teetered a bit on her high, high heels.

Ida Plum and I looked at each other. What did she mean by "art films"? Did she mean porno films? Nude? Was this

our beauty queen who had been scheduled to lead the parade and crown our Miss Green Bean? Did Mayor Moss
know about all this?

"Where's the parade?" she suddenly screamed and waved
both hands in the air. "I want my parade."

"Honey," Ida Plum said, "that was two days ago. It's all
over. Everything is over. The parade's done gone."

"Where's my Scottie Pie?" Sunnye then tuned up to a
whimper. "He's supposed to be here. I need my Scottie Pie."
She sounded as if she intended to increase her volume and
start wailing louder any minute.

Did she mean Scott? Was he her Scottie Pie? I couldn't
believe it. I giggled and Ida Plum poked an elbow in my ribs,
said, "Hush."

I heard the screen door open and close behind me. Scott
had come from Verna's. He must have seen the limo and knew
what was going on, what to expect. He stood very close to
my side, put his hand on my shoulder.

"Scottie Pie," Sunnye screamed and came toward us. She
lurched and almost fell forward. Those heels were not meant
to balance all those pounds of Sunnye.

Scott leaned close and whispered, "She's full of it."

Did he mean bullshit or alcohol? Or ego? Or all three?

"Sunnye." He let go my hand and went to her. "You missed
it. You missed everything."

Her entourage waited in the rain, the two elfin people plus
the driver in a starched black suit and cap.

"Oh," I said. And oh, I suddenly saw why Scott returned
to Littleboro. Fame and fortune had not been kind to Cedora
Harris. Or maybe that lifestyle had been too much for him.

Too unreal. What we had the most of in Littleboro was Reality spelled with a capital R. And work. A way to earn our living, a purpose.

As Scott started to hand Sunnye over to her "staff" who had waited in the rain with their canopy and umbrellas, Robert Redford hopped toward the front steps, stopped and gazed up at Sunnye with his big, pink eyes.

Sunnye screamed, grabbed Scott, almost pulled him over. "Don't let it get me. Keep it away." She started shaking, jerked away from Scott, ran, rocking on her heels, waving both hands in the air, ran, ran, ran toward her limo. She splashed through puddles and rain that poured down in sheets, dampening her feathers.

Her driver opened the door with Sunnye screaming, "They bite. Rabbits have big teeth. They bite. Get me out of here."

Her two elfin people ran behind her, jumped in and slammed the door. They roared away.

Scott gave a little two-fingered dismissive wave (or salute?) as they left. "I guess that was that." He turned toward me, said, "I had forgotten she's afraid of rabbits." He reached down and patted Robert Redford on the head. "Thanks, ole buddy."

He gave me a hug that lasted a little longer than usual, whispered, "I've got your gazebo walls already constructed. They're nice and dry in my shop. If the rain slacks, I can put them up in no time." I guess that meant he was sticking around, by me and for me, and most of all, he would stay in Littleboro. My heart felt light enough to sing.

I finished the cake, set it in the middle of the dining-room table. Ida Plum and I whizzed around getting the kitchen cleared and clean, all the sticky wiped off, bowls and beaters, counters and cabinets and the floor mapped to a shine.

We barely had time to shower and change into presentable people ready to celebrate. And I had a feeling I had more than a wedding and some profitable Dixie Dew business to celebrate. Everything, but the rain, was going in my favor if just for a little bit.

Ida Plum changed into something dressy and purple as a muscadine grape. "Perfect," I said. "That's your best color." I remembered how she stood on the porch of the Dixie Dew one morning before I was even ready to open as a bed and breakfast and offered to help. She had helped. Been my good right arm, best friend, guide in a thousand ways and times.

I put on my polished cotton dress of pink and green that almost matched the fabric I used for tablecloths for my Pink Pineapple Tea and Thee room. I liked to think I was a sort of walking billboard.

At five thirty the bride alighted from her "carriage," which was actually a black stretch limo, and the first thing I saw was Juanita in black. "My Lord," I said to Ida Plum as we peered out the dining-room windows, "is she wearing a black wedding dress?"

"I think it's just a cape," Ida Plum said. "Look at her hair."

"My Lord," I said again. Juanita looked like she had a huge pile of cotton candy on her head. Her three-tier hair was pink and orange. "If it matches her dress, you be sure to reach over and put your hand over my mouth so I don't giggle too loud."

"Agreed," said Ida Plum, who went out to meet Juanita on the porch to take her wrap.

And yes, when revealed, Juanita's hair did indeed match her strapless, pink-orange swirl of a dress. She quickly pulled up the long dress train and held it in front of her. Behind her came Tina Marie, who worked with her at Kurl Up and Dye. She was wearing a black, strapless, clinging sort of long dress. She carried a Pekingese puppy under her arm.

"PooPoo doesn't like getting wet," she crooned, her lips in the dog's face so close he licked her nose with a tiny pink ribbon tongue.

Ida Plum poked me in the ribs, reached down and grabbed my hand and put it over her mouth. "PooPoo? PooPoo?" She nearly bent in the middle laughing. I cupped my hand tighter, so tight I felt her breath's warm, wet sputter.

"Okay," I pulled myself together. "We got to get this show on the road." That sent her into spasms of giggles so hard she dashed toward the kitchen.

Half of Littleboro started to arrive: Mr. Gaddy with the Mrs. on his arm. He held an umbrella over her. Then Birdie Snowden from The Calico Cottage came. She held a wadded-up, big, lace-trimmed handkerchief. "I always cry at weddings," she said. "It pays to be prepared."

Then people I didn't know, who probably worked at the courthouse and knew Ossie, showed up and almost every woman of any age in Littleboro who went to Juanita's beauty shop on a regular basis came in sprayed and lacquered to a sheen with poofs and beehives that would withstand a tornado. Even Clyde Edgemont from Clyde's Used Cars sidled in at the last minute and Eikenberry squeezed in near the door. Both the living room and hall were packed with people. Standing room only. Packed like sardines.

Next came Ossie—in the police car, of course, with Bruce driving. Didn't the man own a personal vehicle? Was the car part of his perks? And as I asked myself that I wondered where was the man's personal residence? Did he even have one or had he been sharing Juanita's "nest" the whole time he'd been in Littleboro? None of my business, which meant I needed to get to the business at hand, so I opened and held the door for Ossie and Bruce. This time Ossie walked in like an invited guest, a guest of honor, which he was. He bowed at the waist and handed me his big white hat, which I hung on my hall tree. He brushed rain from the shoulders of his very elegant black suit. Rented from some swanky place in Pinehurst I bet. Didn't look like the kind of suit he'd own.

"You aren't supposed to see the bride before the wedding," I said quietly, almost in a whisper.

He smiled. Ossie had a very nice smile, one I hadn't seen before, and a gentleness in his eyes. He ran his hands through his hair, thick, wavy hair that matched his thick, dark eyebrows, which in the past had made me feel scared and threatened. He looked a little like a middle-aged Dean Martin, who I always thought was just plain handsome.

I led him into the living room where he immediately went to stand by the fireplace, like the whole thing had been rehearsed, which of course, it had not. He posed, hands on top of each other at his waist. Just like a picture. Now all we needed was the bride, the best man, the maid of honor, a preacher, and some music.

Scott had set up his electric piano keyboard at the front of the dining room and began playing some sweet old songs like "Let Me Call You Sweetheart," something I didn't recognize, then "I Have Always Loved You" and "My Eyes Adore You." I often forgot Scott was at heart a musician. He seemed to do so many practical things, like carpentry and roofing and painting and Sheetrock so well. A Renaissance man, a man for all seasons, reasons, yet not a pretentious bone in his body. I had to remind myself of that. A good old boy who was actually *good*. Good as his word, good as his work, good as his heart. Then the music changed to *Clair de lune, Pachelbel's Canon* and finally to *Lohengrin*.

Scott, in a white dinner jacket, pink cummerbund and pink bow tie, motioned Randy to take his place at the keyboard and came up beside me. After all, he was in this party and Ossie's best man. I was still bothered by Scott being Ossie's best man. When had this happened? Why wasn't it Bruce Bechner, who had been Ossie's sidekick since Ossie came to town? I peeked in the dining room. Randy, who was Scott's aide-de-camp, was also a musician and had taken Scott's place at the keyboard. All musicians know other musicians. Musicians love company. And audiences.

Tina Marie walked up to stand opposite Ossie and Scott. She held PooPoo under one arm. Then everyone waited.

There was some whispering among the wedding party, then I heard the front door bang open and Pastor Pittman poured in, wet as a drowned rat. "Sorry, sorry, sorry," he said. He shoved his umbrella in the stand, slicked back his hair and rammed his finger in his ear like he was trying to get water out.

He rushed to stand before the mantel. He dripped a wet trail all the way but it actually made a sort of aisle. I thought, Legal, I guess, but not a solemn ceremony if it's done by a soaking wet minister who keeps trying to ream water out his ear.

There was quiet, a bit of rustling among the crowd, and then Randy, instead of *Here Comes the Bride,* played "Oh What a Night," and Juanita sashayed in and up to the mantel, twisting and shaking everything she had: boobs, butt, arms lifted aloft and her bouquet like a pink spotlight in her hand. The crowd laughed, really laughed. Juanita and Tina Marie laughed loudest of all. "Surprise!" she shouted and ran up to Ossie, who grinned ear to ear and shook his head. He seemed to be saying to himself, What a lady. And she's all mine.

Tina Marie took Juanita's bouquet of huge, bright-pink stargazer lilies and held it along with her own smaller one: two giant lilies instead of three. PooPoo squirmed under her arm. The pink flowers matched their hair. Both of them were so radiant nobody would notice my shabby walls and peeling ceiling. I only hoped the dog wouldn't get down or start barking.

Pastor Pittman wiped water from his Bible and began the ceremony. I'm sure he knew all of it by heart and had the Bible for backup. When he asked for the ring everything stopped. Ossie looked at Juanita, who turned around just in time to see little Elvis in a white suit come flying in, the two wedding rings tied to a satin pillow, flopping. "Here," he said to Juanita, "take it," and threw the pillow at her. Then he ran back to Malinda at the back of the room. She picked him up, kissed the top of his head, and I heard her say, "You did a good job, sweetie. You were just perfect."

More mumbles, rings exchanged, then Pastor Pittman's pronouncement. What began as cute little puckerings of a kiss between the bride and groom became an all-out deep, lingering looooong kiss that had the crowd swooning.

"I didn't know Ossie had it in him," Ida Plum said at my elbow, then she wiped her eyes with her apron tail. "Allergy," she said. "The lilies."

"Ha," I said, "lilies, my foot. You're as tenderhearted as the rest of us."

Tina Marie handed Juanita the dog. Ossie took Juanita by the arm and they strode through the crowd amid hugs and handshakes. Hugs for Juanita, handshakes for Ossie, who Ida Plum said looked "right happy."

I thought, Right happy . . . for now. The Pekingese had a triumphant grin that seemed to be saying, We're fine now, one happy little family, but just you wait. I could feel real sympathy for Ossie coming in second to a Pekingese named PooPoo. Lord help him.

I started pouring punch. Randy popped Prosecco corks. Sandwiches disappeared, cheese straws inhaled. The pickles and mints vanished. The cake was cut with Juanita feeding Ossie the first bite, then toasts of Prosecco, clinking glasses all around, while I cut more cake and laid the slices on plates. Thank goodness I still had all my grandmother's catering supplies. The little glass punch cups and plates sure saved having to buy and use those awful plastic things.

"Do over, we gotta do it all again." Somebody rushed in, cut through the crowd. Miles Fortune, this time minus Lesley Lynn on his arm. I had forgotten about him. Or a wedding photographer. Had Juanita even hired one? Was I supposed to? Okay, so Miles Fortune to the rescue for the third time.

I turned the uncut side of the cake around. Juanita and Ossie posed, fed each other cake, toasted with champagne glasses and smiled practiced smiles while Miles clicked and pressed the flash. Then he said, "Now back in the living room. Wedding party, please." He waved his hand like a director.

I picked up empty cups and plates all over the place and carried them to the kitchen, where Ida Plum loaded the dishwasher.

Sandwich platters were empty, the bottom of the punch bowl had only dregs left and the kitchen was stacked with empty Prosecco bottles for recycling. I was tired. One wedding under my belt. Despite the downpour, it had gone off pretty good. Who could help that the preacher was late and wet? Elvis had hung back on his mother's skirts until she had to push him to run up with the rings. It was a sweet, sweet wedding.

Randy started playing some dance music on the keyboard and I watched couples pair off: Birdie Snowden with Pastor Pittman, Malinda with Bruce Bechner. Elvis trailed them, still with his hand wound tight in Malinda's skirt. They made an odd figure on the dance floor.

Mayor Moss had cut out early after telling me it was a beautiful wedding and I had done a super job. She was dressed in turquoise linen with matching hat, shoes and purse. She looked like a drop of rain had never touched her. Crisp, fresh and totally smart, in word and dress.

"Rubber," she said when she saw me looking at her little turquoise slippers with flopping white flowers on the toes.

"Oh," I said. "Rubber. Good."

People on the porch and in the dining room danced and laughed and danced some more. Not the wild, "Hey, man" shaking, loose, fast-and-furious kind of dancing, but slow and dreamy. I was thankful for the covered porch even as the rain had slowed, slacked almost to a heavy mist. I knew more downpour was hanging up there waiting to descend.

Juanita went upstairs to change into her "going away" outfit and I couldn't wait to see it. When she stood at the top of the stairs, I gasped. She had on a pale pink, very elegantly tailored linen pantsuit. Her hair was tamed into a smooth and skillfully done, sophisticated chignon at the back of her neck. She wore pearl earrings and a long, looped strand of pearls down to her waist. Gift from the groom, I wondered, or had Juanita bought them for herself? Either way the whole effect was quite tasteful.

"Ready?" she called and held her bridal bouquet high above her head. A few of the crowd gathered at the bottom of the stairs and waited. "Ready?" she called again.

"Ready," someone called back.

"One," Juanita said. And waited. Then she said, "two, three" very fast and hurled the pink missile.

It landed in Malinda's arms and everybody laughed. Malinda looked embarrassed, flushed. Her face reddened. Elvis reached for the bouquet and she gave it to him.

"Thatta boy," somebody said. "Give Mama a head start."

Then the crowd chanted, "Garter, garter, throw the garter." All the guys gathered at the base of the stairs.

Juanita lifted her leg. Someone said, "Woohoo." She slid down her garter, then lifted it high, twirled it around and finally let it fly.

The garter landed in Ossie's hands. He actually blushed and everyone applauded.

The bride and groom, and PooPoo, left in the rain, dashing to the curb and into the limo that had brought Juanita to the Dixie Dew earlier. It was too wet to light sparklers, not that I had bought any, and nobody had confetti, for which I was eternally grateful not to have to try to pick that stuff up afterwards. Nobody threw rice anymore. Somebody had said if it was picked up and eaten by birds, it killed them, so I saved some songbirds' ugly deaths. Everyone followed the bridal couple's exit in a flurry of raincoats, umbrellas, goodbyes and good nights.

As I started to close the French doors to the dining room, something or someone moved behind me, grabbed my arm. "What? Who?"

Chapter Fifty-one

Crazy Reba had been standing behind the door. She was crying. "Best man," she said. "He was a better man."

"Who?"

"My God," she said. "I killed God's best man." Reba wore her own makeshift wedding dress and held the bridesmaid's bouquet. Tina Marie must have given it to her. And where had she found her bridal dress? I had left it with her flip-flops and cell phone in the backseat of Lady Bug. And she must have seen it, knew it was hers. Of course. Somehow I had not seen Reba in the wedding crowd. She must have been at the back of the room, blended in. She handed me the cell phone, which had died long ago.

"Reba," I said. "Honey, it wasn't your fault. You didn't kill that man, whoever he was. Don't you worry anymore. Ossie has gone away and he's not going to put you in jail again. We don't even have a jail anymore."

She hugged me. I could feel she didn't have a thing on under that length of lace. Not even a pair of Verna's long-legged bloomers.

I cut a big piece of the wedding cake and put it in a box for her. She clapped her hands as I gave it to her. "June bride," she said. "I'm a June bride." I noticed she had her big glass gob of a ring on. Good for her. At least she had a keepsake from all this misadventure.

"It's raining. Too wet for you to sleep outside. Why don't you go over to Verna's and that bed you like upstairs. Verna won't care." I helped Reba into a raincoat someone had left. With a piece of cake in hand, she meandered down the walk. I saw her turn toward the house next door and felt better knowing she was in the dry. I had started to tell her to put the piece of cake under her pillow and she'd dream of the man she was to marry, but I didn't want to confuse her. She was confused enough already.

I picked up, cleaned up, and Scott helped put the leaves back in the dining room table and move it back in place. Ida Plum did the breakfast setup and I figured Mr. Fortune might forgo his daily run and sleep in. I hoped so. Ida Plum was spending the night in one of the empty bedrooms upstairs. Three were empty since Ossie had sent Bruce over earlier in the day to take off the crime scene tape. I didn't know what it meant, but hoped it was good news. Debbie's funeral was being televised and I hadn't decided if I'd watch over at Verna's, maybe sit on that bed upstairs and eat some cake with Reba. So much better than trying to fight the crowd for parking places at the church. Tomorrow I'd decide. And tonight it didn't seem so far away.

"Did anybody say where Ossie and Juanita are going on their honeymoon?" I asked Scott as we pushed the last chair in place.

"Somebody said South of the Border," Scott said.

I laughed then he opened his arms and folded them around me for the nicest kind of celebration, as if to say, we've done a good job and a half. I felt his chin on the top of my head, his breath warm on my ear. "Mm," he said. "I love your ears. So little and pink. Like seashells." He ran his finger around the rim of my ear.

Did he have any idea what a turn-on that was? Was he being a tease?

"Come on," he said. "I want to show you something."

"What?" I asked. He took my hand and I followed him through the kitchen, the back porch and down the back stairs to the yard. The soggy yard was slick with wet grass.

"What?" I asked again, not a minute sure he knew what he was doing. "It's still raining."

He clicked a tiny light on his cell phone and led me to the gazebo, the gazebo so newly finished I smelled treated wood, paint and varnish. "Shhh," he said and reached down, rustled something in the dark. "Wait."

"It's pitch-dark," I said. "It's raining." Rain began to beat harder on the metal roof. I was going to get soaked going back to the house to go to bed. Probably to sleep alone.

"Sleeping bags," he said, and I felt something soft unroll at my feet. "Come." He pulled me so close his bow tie caught on my ear. He flicked off the tie, and I heard him toss it to the floor. He took off his jacket and shirt, unzipped and slid off his pants. "Now," he said. "Your turn. I'll wait. We've got all night."

Afterwards, I lay my head on the softest pillow I'd ever felt. Scott had even provided pillows for us. Amazing, wonderful man. Rain beat a steady, soothing rhythm on the metal roof and I thought yes, yes, this is what I came home for. Why had I waited so long?

Scott leaned so close to my ear I felt his warm breath. "I could love you the rest of my life," he said.

And I said, "Yes. Me, too."

Scott fumbled around in the sleeping bag, said, "I have something for you." Then he handed me Reba's ring. That godawful chunk of glass. He shone the cell phone on it, slipped it on my left-hand ring finger.

"Where did you get this?"

"From Reba," he said. "Traded her a giant Heath bar for it."

I laughed and kissed him soundly and then we slept.

Chapter Fifty-two

In the end, Bruce Bechner tied all the loose ends together. He said Ossie knew when they collected the stuff from that room in Motel 3, where Reba had been with her "God," that something was not fitting together right. The clothes and shoes were too big for the body, the one Reba thought she killed.

Allison from Motel 3 saw the description of the mystery man in *The Mess*. She went into the police station, told them he was their handyman, a drifter they'd hired to do some of the demolition work at the motel. He had been there when Reba and her "God" checked in.

"So Reba killed the man that she thought was God's best man."

"We don't think she knew," Bruce said. "It was botulism. The green beans. We had them analyzed."

"Green beans?" I asked.

"Reba's picnic from Kentucky Fried. Those green beans were in a Tupperware bowl."

I *knew* KFC didn't send their beans out in Tupperware.

"But where did she get the beans?" As soon as I asked the question, I knew the answer. She could have gotten them from half a dozen or a hundred basements or fruit cellars anywhere in Littleboro. Verna's? Mama Alice's?

Bruce read the answer on my face, said, "And Debbie Booth? Same thing. Botulism. Could have come from any jar, anywhere at the fairgrounds."

"But what about Mrs. Butch Rigsbee? The one making threats on my life and his? She dropped a hot corn stick on Debbie at the luncheon and was making green bean smoothies at the fairgrounds during the Green Bean Festival. And she shot up the green tin man, all the balloons. Kidnapped Lesley Lynn, shot down my hall light fixture. What about her?"

"Disturbing the peace. Destruction of property. She's out on bail. Got a warning that she was never to roll her little red wagon down the streets of Littleboro again."

"What about the dirty business?" What was that all about? Allison was just in the middle? Butch a sort of runner?

"Ossie has been on this one for a while. That's why he was sent here," Bruce said.

"Sent here? You mean he didn't come to Littleboro because he wanted to?" Maybe that explained some of his attitude.

"It's ongoing. Allison and Butch are little players in something bigger than Littleboro." He put his finger over his lips. "And you have to promise me that you don't know a thing."

"Is Mr. Moss involved?"

"I've said too much already." Bruce put both hands in his uniform pockets.

"Can you at least tell me what all else was in God's truck?"

"You want to see?" Bruce reached in his desk for a set of keys.

I followed him to the locked storeroom behind Wanda Purncell's desk. Bruce unlocked, flung open the door and I saw stacks of boxes.

"What?"

Bruce opened one box and I saw smaller boxes, all neatly labeled. "Prescription drugs. Rigsbee was hauling them from Canada to Florida. Black market."

"Oh," I said. "But they're legal, aren't they?"

"Not as in you can get all you want when you want them if you know where to get them. There'll be black market as long as there is a market," Bruce said, and shut and locked the door.

"What happened to all the money? The cash Butch Rigsbee was carrying?"

"Swaringen had it in his backpack. Ossie's got it locked up. I guess Swaringen planned to hightail it out of town after he ditched, or killed, Reba. We'll never know now, will we?"

I looked at Bruce under a new light. He'd been in Ossie's shadow so long I hadn't really ever seen him.

We bumped fists.

Back at the Dixie Dew Ida Plum swept the front porch. Next door at Verna's, Scott's truck was loaded with stuff for the recycling. "Looks like they're moving Hell and there goes the first load," Ida Plum said.

"Miles Fortune still here?" I asked, hoping against hope he had paid his bill, packed his bags and taken his itchy heels and his dimple cross-country. Or even flown across the pond to another filming. I just wasn't sure about him. Much, much too good-looking. Dimples had always been my downfall.

"Paid in full," Ida Plum said. "And I've already cleaned his room." She handed me the broom and I finished sweeping the walk.

"I know something you don't know." She stood with her arms folded across her chest, grinned wide.

"You know lots I don't know." I turned around. What I didn't know was behind her grin. "So spill."

"Our Mr. Fortune didn't go far."

I waited.

"He's bunking with Miz Mayor, Calista Moss. Lesley Lynn may be an added attraction, too." Ida Plum grinned. "He seemed real taken with her when they left. Wonder if he'll film the turtle, Nadine? Make a nice nature documentary, wouldn't it? Told me he was shooting the Moss house as the 'after' for his documentary. Going to show how all the run-down, shabby South can really be cleaned up, painted up, fixed up and look like a hundred million dollars. Which is probably what it all will cost."

"Like God with money," I said, and we both laughed and laughed.

Littleboro was all right. The real honest-to-God *God* was in His Heaven and everything on this little piece of green earth was okay. Or close to okay. At the moment.